LUXE

ASHLEY
ANTOINETTE

ST. MARTIN'S GRIFFIN

NEW YORK

LUXE. Copyright © 2015 by Ashley Antoinette. All rights reserved. Printed in the United States of America. For information, address St. Martin's Press, 175 Fifth Avenue, New York, N.Y. 10010.

www.stmartins.com

Library of Congress Cataloging-in-Publication Data

Ashley Antoinette, 1985–
   Luxe / Ashley Antoinette. — First edition.
     pages ; cm
   ISBN 978-1-250-06697-8 (trade paperback)
   ISBN 978-1-4668-7488-6 (e-book)
   I. Title.
   PS3601.S543L89 2015
   813'.6—dc23

2015019064

Our books may be purchased in bulk for promotional, educational, or business use. Please contact your local bookseller or the Macmillan Corporate and Premium Sales Department at (800) 221-7945, extension 5442, or by e-mail at MacmillanSpecial Markets@macmillan.com.

First Edition: September 2015

10 9 8 7 6 5 4 3 2

I dedicate this novel to Symullia "Gram" Neely. I am so blessed to have known and loved you for twenty-nine years. I will never forget you, and my love for you is so deep that it will burn inside of me every day that I am gifted to walk this earth. You were a spitfire, you took no nonsense, and you called it exactly the way that you saw it. It was your world, lol. If I can live with half of the strength that you exuded while you were here, I will be unstoppable. I can vividly remember you picking me up just to sneak away to Birch Run and shop for the day when I was a kid. I remember you picking me up every Sunday for Galilee. I remember you picking up all the grandkids to take us to Ponderosa. You wouldn't eat anywhere else. That was our spot, lol. You would have thought it was a five-star chophouse, but back then it was equivalent. I remember you talking Mama into letting me go out with friends when I became a teenager. I remember you talking Papa into giving me money out of his stash for homecomings and proms. You even sent me halfway around the world to Japan, simply because I asked. When I turned eighteen you gave advice, hard advice, that I wasn't ready to receive at the time, but now as a grown woman, I hear it all and I value it. That advice is like gems that I can place in my crown of womanhood. I am filled with your wisdom because you made sure that you gave it to me no matter how often I resisted. I love you. I always have.

I always will. You are my Gram, and there is not a day that will pass that I won't miss you. You will forever live in my mind and heart . . . in all of our minds and hearts. I am so happy that Quaye had a chance to know you. There is no one like you. They don't make them like you anymore.

When I envision you, I think of you and Papa in Heaven, sitting on your Susan Street Porch. Papa has a beer in his hand and you are looking over your "Numbers" book. Meanwhile, the both of you are watching over all of us. You're probably shaking your head at some of our choices, lol, but don't worry—we always keep you in mind. You did your job phenomenally. . . . we all have our "Symullia Neely Philosophy" tucked away inside our hearts. No worries, we'll pull it out when we need it. So rest easy next to Papa. It comforts me that you're reunited and a part of God's kingdom. Your pain is gone. He has a new angel on his team, and what a lovely one you are. I love you so much. Tell Papa I said hi and give him a big ol' hug from Quaye. Rest peacefully together, my guardian angels.

I can't say it enough. . . . I LOVE YOU, Grandma.

PROLOGUE

Three months, seven days, six hours, and twenty-two minutes. That's how long it had been. "One day at a time. Every day counts, every hour, every minute, every second," Bleu whispered as she sat in her car, surrounded by the darkness of night while gripping the steering wheel for dear life. There was urgency in her tone . . . panic . . . fear, because although she was completely alone, she was afraid of herself. Her heart pounded furiously. With the power of thoroughbred horses it beat, causing her shirt to rise and fall with her distressed breaths. She could feel herself weakening as the tears slid down her face. Mascara marred her flushed cheeks. Snot rested on her trembling lip. She needed help. *Three months, seven days, six hours, and twenty-three minutes.* It was how long she had been clean. She distinctly remembered the last hit she had taken like it was yesterday, and the thought of the euphoric rush it gave her caused her to become aroused. Her nipples hardened and she clenched her thighs because the possibility of feeling that type of high once more was seducing her. Her knuckles turned white as she held on to the steering wheel with a death grip. She wished that she could glue her hands to it, to stop herself from doing the inevitable.

"Please, God, please," she whispered, but she knew there was no use in praying. She had prayed for everything her entire life only to end up empty-handed and disappointed. The devil had ahold of her. It was like her soul had been compromised from the moment she had taken her first breath. That was the only explanation for her hard-lived existence. Nothing came easy, and anything good that came to her was quickly taken away. One blast. That was all it would take to end her misery. She had not thought about getting high in three long months. In fact, a huge celebratory trip had been planned to commemorate the accomplishment. She had done it. She had kicked the vicious drug habit that had taken ahold of her. She had lasted three months, seven days, six hours, and twenty-four minutes, but now it was calling her.

She reached into her bag and pulled out the package. It was eerie how the rock cocaine seemed to sparkle in the Baggie. She poured the small rocks out into her palm and marveled briefly. She licked her lips, her mouth suddenly dry as her body craved the drug. She could feel the hair rising on the back of her neck. It was like a thousand bugs were crawling up her legs, starting at her toes and making their way up her thighs to her spine. She itched, she wanted the hit so bad. With her emotions on 10, she was susceptible to sabotage. Overwhelmed by desire, she turned her purse upside down, causing all of the contents to spill over her front seat. Grabbing the water bottle from her cupholder and a ballpoint pen out of the mess, she was on a hunt for paraphernalia. She rolled down her window and poured most of the water out. She was like a surgeon as she drilled a hole into the side of the bottle. She bit the end of the pen, causing the ink vial to come out, hollowing out the shell of the pen. She had done the routine so many times she had it down to a science. Most crackheads would just hit the rock straight out of the pen, but Bleu liked to think she was above that. That desperate toke would only lead to burnt lips and fingertips and she had her looks to uphold. In the thick of it she had glass pipes, but the poor man's version would work just as well . . . she was chasing the high and it didn't matter at this point how she caught it. Her eyes searched through the mess on her passenger seat until she found a condom and a cigarette. When she had picked up the habit she told herself that nicotine was the lesser evil compared to what she could have been smoking, but in her heart of hearts she knew that a true addict always kept cigarettes handy. The ash residue from cigarettes was necessary to make a functioning crack pipe. She held the cigarette between both lips while her hands opened the condom. She threw the sticky rubber out of her window and then used the foil wrapper to top off the water bottle. She emptied the ashes onto the top of the foil and then inhaled sharply as she placed a nice-size rock on top of it all. Her eyes were as big as golf balls as she applied the flame. Her long red stiletto nails far fancier than those of any crackhead anyone had ever seen. The rings on her fingers were far too expensive to be on the hand that was hugging the makeshift pipe. This wasn't supposed to be her life; Bleu was supposed to be so much more, but as the tears slid down her face and the smoke accumulated inside the bottle, she couldn't help but think of how this tragedy had begun . . . it all started with just a little Adderall and speed. Who would have thought it would have ever gotten this bad? Three months, seven days, six hours, and twenty-five minutes were all wasted as she wrapped her lips around the hollow pen. . . .

I

One year ago

The buzz of the fan blew through the small liquor store as Bleu carried a case of beer, balancing it against her hip as she walked. The summer heat made the inside of the store feel like an oven, and her shirt stuck to her back as she worked up a small sweat. It was sweltering and even the flies were too exhausted to buzz around in the suffocating temperatures. It had been a melting summer. A heat wave had swept through the Midwest and Bleu was miserably displeased.

"Bruno, I came here to pick up my check, and you put me to work!" she grumbled as she carried the heavy boxes and placed them into the cooler.

"I got you; I got you! I'll add a couple bucks to your pay. That fucking Max called in. Saturday is my biggest night. This idiot calls off on the day the deliveries come in. I swear I don't know why I keep him around," Bruno, the store's owner, said as he pinched his fingers together while waving his hand as he chastised.

"Because he's your son," she replied with a smile as she blew her side bang out of her face to stop it from sticking to her forehead. She stepped into the beer cooler and threw her head back in relief. The sudden drop in temperature provided a temporary relief. It had been a long summer. She had just graduated from high school, and instead of celebrating her new independence with friends she was about to say good-bye to, she had spent the past few months working day and night just to afford college. Unlike her classmates, nothing was being handed to her. She had been accepted to UCLA on a partial scholarship, but she could still barely afford to attend. Bleu would be eating ham sandwiches and Oodles of Noodles just to get by, but it didn't matter. L.A. was her getaway. It was her ticket out of Flint, Michigan. Born and bred in a city of hustlers and killers, she loved her hometown, but it was a known fact that the nothingness of it all would kill her slowly if she didn't pursue her big-city dreams. She peered back at Bruno, who was signing for the beer shipment, and then placed her headphones in her ears. She slid her back down the wall and took a seat right there in the freezer, grateful for the cool air.

John Legend crooned through her iPod as she bobbed her head and lip-synced to the soulful tune as she gave herself a break.

"Fuck it. I'm not supposed to be here anyway. Thirty minutes won't hurt," she mumbled. She sat down and leaned against the freezing wall, zoning out as she counted down the days until she made her departure from Fli-city. In one week flat she would be a ghost. This was the last check she would pick up before telling everyone to kiss her ass good-bye.

She crawled over to a stack of boxes and pushed them aside until the vent behind it was exposed. Reaching inside, she pulled out an old can that contained her entire life's savings. She couldn't keep it at home. Too many people ran in and out of her father's house to ever keep all that she had earned there. The music in her ears drowned out all sound as she pulled her money out of the can. It was every dollar that she had made since her freshman year of high school. California had been her dream ever since she was a little girl and she had been saving for it as long as she could remember. As she flipped through the bills, she realized that she had saved $11,000, a dollar at a time. It wasn't much and would probably be spent on books and supplies within weeks, but she was going anyway. She was headed to L.A. with a dream that only an eighteen-year-old could believe in. There was beauty in her youth . . . she saw the world through optimistic eyes where everyone else around her saw cynicism. She was young and fearless. She was tired of the poverty-stricken streets and gunshot sounds outside her window. She could practically hear the sound of the ocean already.

BOOM! BOOM!

She sat up in alarm. The sound of gunshots chased away the sound of imaginary waves.

She snatched the earbuds out, thinking that maybe she had been mistaken. Maybe a truck's exhaust had backfired, or the loud clang of the Dumpster being emptied had interrupted her.

Frozen in fear, she breathed rapidly as her heart ached with sudden uncertainty. There was urgency inside of her sounding off, telling her to flee . . . that danger was near. Then she heard it again and this time there was no mistaking it.

BOOM!

Gunfire.

She frantically crawled to the entrance of the freezer.

"Fuck you shoot that nigga for?! How the fuck we supposed to get in the safe if he dead?!" one of the robbers asked in frustration.

Bleu's eyes watered as she saw Bruno lying on the floor, a pool of crimson spreading beneath his body as he gurgled on his own blood. His eyes were wide with fear as his fingers reached for her.

"He-hel-help," he choked out. Tears stung her eyes as she covered her mouth to stop herself from crying aloud. She shook her head as she placed her trembling fingers to her lips. He was reaching for her, begging for her to help him, but all she wanted was for him to stay quiet and not reveal her hiding spot. Bruno was dying, and as much as she wanted to help him, her feet wouldn't move. Her eyes darted to the two masked gunmen who had invaded the store.

"Fuck it, we'll just take what's in the register!" the other one shouted. He pulled off his mask as he spat, "It is hot as fuck in this bitch. Make sure you grab that security tape." The look on his face would forever be etched in her mind as he stomped over to Bruno's body and aimed his gun. Treacherous. These young boys were merciless and fear pulsed through her like a live current.

Bleu closed her eyes as she anticipated the shot.

BOOM!

She jumped, hitting the case of beer behind her, causing it to crash to the floor, announcing her presence. Her eyes widened in fear as she looked for a place to hide, but there was nothing but walls around her. She was trapped.

"Fuck was that? I told you to clear this mu'fucka out! Go back there and see!" one of the men shouted.

Terrified, she felt her hands shake violently, because she knew that she was about to die. Flint was full of Tony Montanas. She knew that the men had come with intentions of robbery but had no problems leaving with double murders on their résumés, and she was shaken. Like a deer in headlights, she watched as one of the men came into the freezer, gun drawn, finger curled around the trigger.

"Bitch, get cho' ass out here!" he barked as he spotted her. He snatched her out of her hiding spot, fisting her hair as he dragged her out into plain view.

"Please, please, please don't kill me. I swear to God I won't say anything. I swear. Please," she pleaded. "My name is Bleu. I'm only eighteen years old. I don't want to die. I . . ." She had learned that somewhere. She had not thought she had been listening when she had taken self-defense as her elective class in school, but now here she was, rattling off facts to endear herself to these wolves . . . these men who had suddenly come into her life and turned it upside down a week before she was set to start the rest of her life.

"Shut the fuck up and open the safe!" the man growled as he grabbed her by the back of the neck and pushed her toward the bulletproof glass. Her feet tripped over Bruno's big body and she stumbled, her hands sliding through a sea of blood as she tried to break her fall. She panicked as the deep burgundy liquid soaked through her clothes. Her legs were like noodles as she stood, hands stained, as tears began to flow uncontrollably.

"I don't know how to open the safe. Please. Just p-p-lease l-l-et me go," she whispered, stammering over her words as fear caused potholes to interrupt her normally smooth cadence. "I just work here . . . I don't know how to open the safe . . . I'm just a—"

BOOM!

Bleu fell to her knees. It felt like a hot iron had been placed onto her lower back and was burning its way through her insides as the bullet traveled through. *They shot me,* she thought, in a state of disbelief as she placed her hands on the floor in front of her. She gasped, struggling to inhale as she watched the world around her move in slow motion. Searing pain. That's what it was . . . undeniable, excruciating, severe pain. It was like none other that she had ever felt before, and she knew that she was dying. She tried to keep her eyes open because she knew that if they closed she might never open them again. Everything around her moved in slow motion as she tried to crawl. One hand in front of the other, slow . . . desperately searching . . . for what she didn't know. Perhaps for safety? For help? Bleu just wanted to get out of there, but the oxygen in her lungs was dwindling slowly and the room was beginning to spin. She collapsed on the ground and sipped in air slowly. *I'm dying,* she thought as she blinked slowly. She had a ground-level view of the scene as she watched the feet of the robbers as they ran around her as if she weren't taking her last breaths right before their very eyes. They rushed to the cash register. She heard them open the cash register and then empty it, and then they fled out of the store as she gurgled on her own blood.

The bell above the door jingled as they stormed out, leaving her to die. She was choking, drowning, suffocating, as she struggled just to breathe. This slow burn was torture as she bled out; the pain was so unbearable that she wished death would just take her quickly. She lay chest-down on the floor, her hand resting next to Bruno's lifeless one as she waited for the end to come. She used her last bit of energy to open her clenched fist, stretching her fingers until she felt the tips touching Bruno's hand. If she was going to die, she didn't want to do it alone. As she lay leaking on the cold floor, she realized that she was just another girl from Flint, Michigan. She hadn't done anything. She hadn't seen much. She was simply another soul of the city who had been lost too soon. She had almost made it out . . . but almost didn't count.

Beep . . . beep . . . beep.

The sounds roused Bleu from the darkest sleep she had ever succumbed to. It was as if she were walking out of a thick fog. She had been in limbo, stuck between life and death. Waking up was no easy feat.

Her eyes felt as if they were sewn closed as she tried her hardest to open them. When they finally fluttered open, she saw flashes of the world around her. Flowers and balloons surrounded her. She silently wondered who had sent them all.

Not many people paid attention to her on an ordinary day. Surely these arrangements weren't meant for her. She felt the wetness of tears slide down the sides of her cheeks as she willed her eyes to stay open. Suddenly terror filled her. Almost instantly flashbacks of the shooting ran through her mind. *BOOM!*

She would never forget the sound of that gun blasting off in her ear. She was swallowed up by the darkness in the room. The only light that peeked in shone through the vertical blinds, which had been drawn closed. The sounds and smells around her told her that she was in the hospital, and as her eyes darted around the room, they fell upon the crumpled body that was sprawled awkwardly in the chair across from her. *Noah*, she thought, immediately recognizing her sleeping friend. He had been by her side since grade school. Dealing with a drunk for a father, a disappearing mother, and friends who changed colors like traffic lights, Noah was the only constant in her life. She opened her chapped lips to call his name but immediately felt as if she were choking on her own tongue. She gasped for air as she struggled to catch her breath. The monitors she was hooked to wailed in alarm as her heart rate spiked from her panic, and a nurse came rushing into the room, waking Noah up with the commotion.

"What's happening?" he asked as he rushed to Bleu's side.

Bleu's eyes were wide with fear as her hands reached for the tube that extended from her neck.

"Bleu," the nurse spoke, getting her attention. "You can't speak until I remove the trach. The doctors had to insert one because you were unable to breathe on your own. I need you to calm down, okay?"

Bleu felt Noah grab her hand and hold on to her tightly and then a pinch to her arm caused everything to slow down.

No, no, no, I don't want to go back to sleep, she thought as she watched the nurse slide the needle out of her arm. *No, no . . .* her mental objections were in vain. Within seconds it was lights-out again.

✳ HER DREAMS ✳

"What the fuck do you do? Huh, Wayne? You lay around this bitch and smoke up all my shit, but you don't contribute shit back in this mu' fucka! I cover the rent, put food in the fridge. The fuck you got going on?"

Bleu heard the shouting. Hell, everyone heard the shouting. The thin project walls left little room for privacy, but the entire building had gotten so used to Sienna and Wayne's arguments that no one even batted an eye. As Bleu drew on the pages of the blank notebook, she blocked out the noise. This was life. When she was younger, the yelling would cause her to cry for hours. She had been terrified of the screaming. The screaming oftentimes was the precursor to hitting, and she used to be so afraid that she would pee her pants. Now she didn't even bat an eye. She was eight years old, a big girl now and too old for all those damn tears. Or at least that's what Sienna, her mother, had told her. So instead, she drew. She would zone out for hours as the incessant arguing became the motivation for her skilled pencil.

"Bitch, you don't pay shit. Section 8 keeps this roof over your head!" Bleu's father barked. The bass in his voice thundered as he spoke. He and Sienna were so loud they were practically shaking the walls. *"And the food stamps you get you sell off. You ain't even got enough food in this bitch to feed our fucking baby because your junkie ass smoke all the shit up!"* Wayne shouted.

Bleu shook her head as she sighed. Her small hand floated over the paper with grace as she drew a detailed picture of a California beach. She hadn't ever seen one in person, but the pictures that she had seen on the TV served as good enough motivation.

"Who the hell you calling a junkie, Wayne?" Sienna asked. *"If that ain't the pot calling the kettle black. You hypocrite mothafucka! As a matter of fact, get your black ass out. Get out and don't bring your ass back until you have some money in your pockets. I'm tired of taking care of a grown-ass, no-good, mothafuckin' man. You coming up in here eating, shitting, and smoking, but not helping replace shit. Kind of man are you? Fucking crackhead."* Her words were lethal and she was known for her curse outs. Her sharp tongue had just cut him down to size. Her tiny frame didn't make her much of a fighter, but her mouth did more damage than her fists ever could.

"Takes one to know one, you miserable bitch!" Wayne shouted, his pride wounded, as he grabbed his car keys and his winter jacket.

"And take your goddamn daughter with you! Don't nobody need her ass in here sitting around looking like you. Both of you mothafuckas can get the fuck out!" Sienna shouted.

Bleu's heart stopped when she heard her mother mention her. She hoped that her father took her with him. Her mother was broke, and apparently Bleu's father had smoked the last of her stash. A *sober Sienna was a mean Sienna and Bleu wanted no part of that. Whenever Sienna kicked Wayne out of the house, he would be gone for days, and in his absence random men would fill his place. Willing to do anything to satisfy the urge to get high, Sienna would often screw her way to her next fix. She was a beautiful woman, with a tight ass and firm breasts. Despite the fact that she sucked on a glass dick daily, she still prided herself on her looks. It was all Sienna had ever had. "There was no way I was letting you suck the life out of my titties, little girl. I'd let you starve before I was left with saggy little flapjacks. These are moneymakers," she would often brag. Bleu never knew if it was meant as a joke, but somewhere deep inside of her she knew it was the truth. Her bedroom door opened and her father walked in. He was tall and slender. His used-to-be-handsome features had diminished. Years of drug use had taken a toll on Wayne.*

Wayne Montclair. He had been a big deal in the city once upon a time. So had her mother. A known hustler with a pretty little down chick on his arm. Sienna and Wayne had been Flint's very own Bonnie and Clyde until they both became a bit too dependent on the product. They became lost in the trenches of addiction and had lost all credibility in the streets. They became the customers to the very same corner boys they used to supply. Bleu knew what he was—his crackhead tendencies were too hard to hide—but in her mind she had made up a completely different story of who he was. A banker. A shop worker. Sometimes she imagined he was a lawyer. Anything was better than reality. Crack cocaine had sucked the life right out of him . . . her mother too, and with each hit they took they robbed Bleu of more and more of her childhood. Her little eyes had witnessed far more than they should have.

"Hey, baby girl, grab your shoes. Roll with Daddy for a while. Your mama tripping," he said as he peeked his head through Bleu's cracked door.

She scrambled as the sound of Teena Marie filled the apartment. Bleu knew what that meant. Her mother was preparing herself for company, and Bleu didn't want to be there to witness the transaction. Sex for dope. The sound of her mother's moans always made Bleu's stomach turn and she hurriedly pulled on her old gym shoes to make sure she wasn't left behind.

Her mother stood back, sipping beer from a 40-ounce brown bottle as she sneered in disgust. "And don't bring your broke-ass back without no money or no smoke!" she shot.

As Bleu was hustled out of the apartment, she avoided eye contact with her mother. As soon as Bleu and Wayne stepped into the hall, the putrid smell of piss and weed hit her. She hated her life. She wasn't one of the lucky kids who came from a loving home and ate three meals a day. She had to survive. Everything that she had was used, old, and worn . . . sometimes stolen. She went to sleep with a low growl in her stomach more often than not. She was living in the struggle and there was no way out.

"Where we going?" she asked as she followed her father down the staircase and out the front door.

"We're just going out for a spin. Give the old dragon a chance to cool off," he said. "Miserable-ass bitch." Bleu knew the last part wasn't meant for her to hear and she pretended she hadn't as she climbed into the passenger seat of his car. The chill inside the '85 Regal was worse than the winter hawk outside and she bundled her puffy coat tightly around her. The zipper had broken two winters ago, so she pulled the sides together to stay warm.

"It'll warm up," Wayne said as he slid in beside her and rubbed his hands together vigorously.

"It's okay; I'm not that cold," she responded, knowing that the heat in the beat-up car didn't work. She only said it to soothe her father's bruised ego.

"I'm sorry, baby girl," he said. She looked up at him and could have sworn she saw tears in his eyes. He was apologizing for more than the busted heat. Her life was not supposed to be this way. She deserved better. There had been plans for better, but life had gotten in the way. A lot of bad choices had led to this. Young love gone sour had made her a bitter reminder of what Wayne and Sienna used to share. Bleu symbolized the only beautiful thing that they had ever created together. Every other part of their love had been ruined by their addiction.

He put the car into gear and began to pull away from the projects when she saw her best friend, Noah, racing her way. "What up, Mr. M, slow this bucket down," the precocious twelve-year-old said as he tried to keep up with the car as it moved at a slow crawl out of the lot.

Wayne hit his brakes and looked over at the boy.

"Where you going?" Noah asked.

"Just riding," Bleu replied.

"Yo, Mr. M, you happen to be going by the school? I've got football practice, but its' too cold to be out here walking," Noah said.

"Hop in," Wayne said.

Bleu opened her door and leaned up her seat as Noah squeezed into the back.

"Good looking out," he responded.

"I've got one stop to make before I swing you by the school," Wayne said.

"Cool," Noah replied. He was four years Bleu's senior, but he had the wisdom that only the streets could put in him. The precocious boy was full of wit and more protective over Bleu than her own father was. She and Noah were two peas in a pod. They spent hours talking and dreaming about what life would be like when they were finally old enough to make it on their own. She would become a world-renowned artist and he a football star. They had it all mapped out in their heads . . . all they had to do was make it to the finish line, but with them coming up in a city like Flint, the odds were against them.

Wayne pulled over, stopping in front of a bank as he mumbled to himself. "Damned bitch got me jumping through hoops in my own damn house." He turned to Bleu. "I'll be right back, baby girl. Keep the car running so that heat can kick in."

She knew he was saving face in front of Noah. Both Wayne and Bleu knew that the raggedy car wasn't producing anything extra. Heat was a luxury; they were lucky that the ignition had even turned over. She nodded and watched as he exited the car in haste, stuffing his hands in the pockets of his coat as he disappeared inside.

"You straight? I heard the yelling," Noah said when he and Bleu were finally alone.

"Yeah, I'm straight," she replied. "After a while you get used to it."

"You know you can stay the night in my room . . . anytime you want. Just climb up the fire escape," Noah said. "I'll make sure I leave the window unlocked."

"I'm okay," she reiterated, slightly embarrassed. Her situation wasn't a secret. If her bummy clothes didn't give it away, the fact that Sienna had been caught on her knees sucking dick for rocks more than a few times did. Bleu's father even had been seen breaking into abandoned houses just to steal the copper pipes. Things were bad, and while the other kids on the block teased her to no end, Noah was always nice. He made her feel normal and accepted. He had let his fists fly plenty of times on her behalf. Noah was the one person in her life she could depend on, and for that she was grateful.

"Don't be proud, B," he said. "If you need me, just come up."

Bleu nodded, but before she could reply the sound of an alarm blared through the air as her father came running outside at full speed, a gun in one hand and a pillowcase full of money in the other.

"Oh shit!" Noah exclaimed as Wayne jumped into the car, tossing the pillowcase in the back.

"Daddy! What did you do?" Bleu yelled in alarm as she looked at the frightened look on his sweaty face. He threw the car into reverse and recklessly backed out, running over the curb and sideswiping the car beside him as he accelerated.

"Agh! Daddy!" she exclaimed. "What are you doing?"

"Everything's okay, baby girl. Everything is going to be just fine," he said, but she saw the terror in his widened eyes. They told a different story from the one his mouth was shouting.

"Oh shit, B, look!" Noah called out. She turned to look and found him holding banded stacks of money up in both hands, but she was quickly distracted by the flashing lights that were fast approaching.

"Daddy, stop! Stop the car!"

Police sirens wailed as Wayne flew through the streets.

"Just put your seat belt on, Bleu," he coached as he gripped the steering wheel with both hands. "Hold on tight."

He was in over his head. He hadn't thought things through. All he knew was that his back was against the wall. He was strung out and in need of his next high. On top of that Sienna had chewed him apart with her words, making him feel like less than a man for not being able to provide.

"Do something!" Sienna had told him. "Do any fucking thing except what you been doing!"

She had pushed him, and in a desperate move he had made the biggest mistake of his life. Drugs made people do irrational things. He had realized it almost as soon as he had brandished the gun inside the bank. The look of pure fear displayed in the bank teller's eyes had filled Wayne with regret. He was just a man, living wrong, addicted to the devil himself. Robbery wasn't Wayne's game, but it was too late to take it back. So he had stuck up the joint as remorse filled him.

Wayne pushed his old car to the max, but the beat-up old thing was no match for the Hemi engines of the police cruisers. They were right on his tail. He was driving so fast that the view outside of the windows was one big blur.

"Daddy, please stop!" Bleu screamed as she held on to the door handle tightly.

"I'm sorry, baby girl. I can't," he whispered. He saw the upcoming highway entry and waited until the last possible second to turn sharply onto it, throwing the police cars behind him off slightly. The car took flight, jumping the curb at full speed and landing violently.

"Wooo! Hooo!" Wayne shouted, victorious. By the time the police turned around and merged back into the chase he would be long gone.

Bleu's tears clouded her vision as she turned to look at a shaken Noah.

He reached his hand between the seat and the passenger door, and she held on to him tightly.

"I did it, baby girl. Fuck your mama gon' have to say about all that money in that bag? Let's hear her run her mouth now!" Wayne shouted with a laugh, but he was stunned to silence when he saw the police barricade up ahead. The entire expressway was blocked off, and as Wayne slowed with the pace of traffic he gritted his teeth in frustration.

Bleu knew exactly how this chase would end. So did Noah. The silence that filled the car was eerie as Wayne twisted his clenched fists around the tattered leather steering wheel.

"Daddy?" Bleu called, voice shaking as tears now streamed down her face. The police were now out of their cars, on foot, walking through the lanes of slowed cars with their weapons drawn. Wayne threw his car in park and then frantically grabbed his gun. He looked at Bleu and then at Noah. "You take care of her, lil' man," Wayne said.

He opened up the car door as the cops swarmed around him cautiously.

"Let me see your hands!"

"Daddy?" Bleu called. Wayne looked down at her, cowering in the passenger seat, trembling, and his heart broke. He was supposed to be a better man. "I don't want you to die." Even at eight years old she knew what would happen if he got out of that car gun in hand.

Wayne blinked away tears as he nodded while looking at her whimsically. "You deserve more, mama. Be more," he said. He tossed the 9mm onto the seat of the car and then put both of his hands up in the air.

"On your knees! Now!"

Bleu watched as her father assumed the position, apparently giving up. A sense of relief flooded her but didn't last long. The police hadn't noticed the extra gun that Wayne had tucked securely against his back. He just couldn't go out without a fight. His addiction was too full-blown to shake cold turkey, and if they threw him in jail he knew that it would be torture as he was weaned off of it. He wasn't ready to face that reality, because with it came all the devilish things he had done all for the sake of the high. In one swift movement Wayne pulled out the gun. The police didn't hesitate to fire.

BOOM! BOOM! BOOM!

Over and over again she heard the shots as they rang out into the air. "No!" she screamed as she tried to climb toward him, but the feeling of Noah pulling her back prevented her from moving.

She watched in horror as bullets riddled her father, jerking him left, then right, shattering the windshield and barely missing her as Noah held her down. The firing seemed to last forever, and when it finally ceased she bolted across the seats and out of the driver's side. The sight of him brought her to her knees. Blood soaked through her jeans as she screamed, "Daddy! Wake up! Please get up!" She looked around in slow motion as the police stood around her. Even Noah stood, speechless, as they all watched a little girl mourn the death of her father. Her face twisted in agony as she tried to pull his heavy body up from the cement. His eyes were wide open but lifeless. The coldest chill traveled down her spine as the realization hit her. She was holding on to a dead body, looking into eyes that no longer had a soul behind them, trying to listen to a heart that no longer beat. It terrified her, but she couldn't bring herself to let go. Wayne hadn't been perfect, but he was the only father she had, and her heart was heavy with sadness. She refused to move, latching on to him because she knew that it would be the last time she would ever touch him. Every time the officers tried to pry her away she would kick and scream until they gave up. They stood all around her, just looking. Her mother wouldn't come. They had no way of contacting her. She didn't have a phone. Wayne, even in his most feigned-out state, had loved Bleu, and although she hated what he did, she could never hate who he was. Her daddy.

Finally, after an hour, the police chief arrived. Her refusal to move was garnering media attention and the story had flipped to possible police brutality. The elderly graying white man burst through the crowd.

"What the fuck? This has turned into a complete circus," he muttered.

"She won't move. Anyone goes near her and she goes crazy," one of the officers on-site informed him.

"Get her out of here. Take her back to the station until we can get in contact with the mother. We've got some questions to ask her about the robbery. The boy too. Do this one by the book and get these fucking cameras out of here. And confiscate cell phones. The last thing I need is for this to go viral. The mayor will have my ass," the man bitched.

Noah knelt beside Bleu. "Come on, B. You got to let go of him," he said.

His words were unconvincing, but she knew that he was right. Reluctantly she got to her feet. Her tears had dried on her face, but her soul still cried. She was in shock, stunned into silence as she found her footing and stood. As she looked around her at all the people, it seemed unreal.

The lady she watched on the news was there. She knew her face because it was the one of the few channels they got in their cable-less household. Between the police and the citizens who had been stopped on the highway during the chase, it felt like the entire city looked at Bleu sympathetically as she walked side by side with Noah toward an awaiting squad car. She felt Noah's fingers intertwine with her own, but she was too distraught to squeeze back. Still, he never let go. Little did she know he never would.

Bleu said nothing, partly because she couldn't answer the officers' questions, but mostly because even at eight years old she understood that the police were not on her side. As she sat in seclusion in the small room, she stared off into space. She hadn't spoken one word since the police had brought her and Noah in. The police had separated her and Noah, treating them as if they had committed the crime themselves. She was terrified. What had the police done to her father? Where was Noah? How long were they going to keep her here? She just wanted to go home. There was no clock in the small room. In fact, besides the table that she was sitting at, it was all white walls. She had no idea how long she had been there. Minutes felt like hours, and she grew increasingly anxious the longer they made her wait.

She rested her head atop her folded arms as she stuck her butt out in the chair while scraping the crust off of the table with her fingernail. She had cried so much that her tears had left salty residue behind. Nobody seemed to care that she had just seen her father gunned down. Her hollow stomach was sick, partly from hunger, mostly from grief. The police were trying to reach her mother, but Sienna wasn't the type of woman who could be tracked down. If she didn't want to be found, she wouldn't be. She was probably out on a crack binge, sucking dicks for a fix, and until the police located her, Bleu wasn't going anywhere. Bleu didn't even know if she wanted to go home. Everything would be different now that her father was gone. It would just be her and Sienna, an inevitable recipe for disaster. She was her mother's greatest mistake. Wayne wouldn't be around to take the brunt of Sienna's bitterness over her failed life; Bleu undoubtedly would become the new victim. She dreaded it like the plague. She feared it because the extent of Sienna's resentment would be revealed. Bleu was a motherless child. It didn't always take death to create a maternal disconnect. Bleu lived right under the same roof as her mother and had never felt anything other than indifference from the woman who had birthed her. With her father dead she was doomed. The worst was yet to come.

When the door opened, more men in black uniforms with shiny badges entered, but this time they were followed by a familiar face.

"Oh, baby," Ms. Monica, Noah's mother, whispered as she looked at Bleu with tears in her eyes. She was covered in dried blood; it was on her face, her hands, soaked into her clothes. She was a disaster and Ms. Monica's heart broke at first sight.

"You all should be ashamed of yourselves," she said as she walked over to Bleu, large leather Coach purse hanging from her shoulders. "Come on, Bleu. I'm gonna take you home, baby," she said.

Bleu took Ms. Monica's hand and followed her out of the room. Noah was waiting in the hall and jumped to his feet, hustling to Bleu's side as soon as he saw her.

"You all right?" he asked, concerned. They had both witnessed something that eyes that young should never see, but such is life in a city like Flint. Kids never truly got the chance to be young. There

were too many uphill battles along the way to adulthood, which aged them before their time.

She nodded, but he could tell that she was lying. They didn't speak as Ms. Monica led them to the car. Bleu was traumatized into introversion, and Noah just didn't know what to say to make it better, so he opted for saying nothing at all.

"Bleu, why the hell you with Ms. Monica? Is that blood? Where the hell is your daddy?" Sienna asked as she peeked out of the cracked door of her apartment.

"Sienna, we need to talk," Ms. Monica said as she stood behind Bleu and Noah, her hands protectively placed on each of their shoulders.

"Talk for what? What this damned girl done did now?" Sienna asked. "Didn't you leave here with Wayne's ass? Where the hell he at?"

Sienna's eyes were bloodshot red and dilated, her hair all over her head, and she let her satin robe fall open slightly, revealing herself unabashedly.

The smell of crack invaded Bleu's nose. She didn't know if Noah or his mother could smell it, but she had been around it enough to know exactly what it smelled like. Her mother's sweaty skin and disheveled appearance was a dead giveaway that she was high. She was vulgar as she flashed her personals, not even feeling the draft between her legs as she stood there. Bleu was filled with an embarrassment so great that she wanted to cry.

"Sienna. Pull yourself together. Something has happened," Ms. Monica stated with disdain in her voice. Bleu heard the cynical tone that Ms. Monica used. She was judging Bleu's mother. Everyone *judged her. Sienna made it easy for people to talk shit because her shit was never together. She was a disgrace of a mother . . . a disgrace of a woman . . . a waste of perfectly good air. In that moment Bleu hated her. Sienna stood, high as a kite, probably fresh off the block, and she was oblivious to the fact that their lives had been changed forever. Bleu doubted if the news would even affect her.*

"Excuse me?" Sienna countered.

"Wayne was killed, Sienna," Ms. Monica revealed.

The news hit Sienna like a ton of bricks as devastation destroyed the smug expression on her face. The revelation had blown her high, grounding her, as it felt like a fist was squeezing her chest. Bleu could never understand the unusual bond that Sienna and Wayne shared. They had grown up together, gotten money together, and fallen from grace together. Their fights were bad, and they had gotten trapped in the clutches of addiction, but through it all they had done so together. Wayne had been a life companion . . . one who forgave her indiscretions because he had had a few of his own. They had a closet full of skeletons that they had filled together. The only reason why she and Wayne ever fought was because of their history. He reminded her of how good life used to be, before she had ever taken her first hit. He knew how amazing she once was, and it reminded her of how worthless she was now. They had once been a young couple with dreams, but life had turned them into two people linked by a love for a common drug. Crackheads. It was all they would ever be. There was no rewriting their fate. Tears accumulated in her eyes.

"How?" she asked.

"They said he tried to rob a bank. The police shot him. The kids were in the car," Ms. Monica replied.

"Get in the house," Sienna said to Bleu.

Bleu timidly stepped forward, but Ms. Monica pulled her back.

"Sienna, so help me I will call CPS on you. Get your act together and leave that shit alone. You take care of this little girl," Ms. Monica threatened.

Sienna was pulsing with hostility and anger as Wayne's death haunted her. She needed a release and the rocks she had in her pocket were more than enough to compensate, but Ms. Monica wanted to put herself in the line of fire. "Stay out of my business. What I do with my child is none of your concern. Don't turn your nose up at me, Ms. Holier than Thou. You ain't no saint. You ever bring CPS to my door and I'll bust your little food stamp scam right on up," Sienna threatened. She pointed her finger inside the apartment. "Now, Bleu, get your little ass in this muthafuckin' house."

Bleu rushed inside, running to her room, overwhelmed, afraid, angry, hungry, worried . . . she felt so many things. She hated her life. Why had she been given such a miserable existence? She would never understand. Where was her white picket fence? Her loving mom? Her hardworking dad? Bleu had been dealt a bad hand . . . a hand that made it impossible for her to win. She heard the sound of Teena Marie as her mother turned up the speakers full blast. There would be no hugs of reassurance for Bleu, no time spent together to process this loss. Bleu had never felt so alone. Her father had just died, but Bleu knew that it wouldn't be long before the next man came to take his place. She wouldn't be surprised if her mother called one of the dope boys over so that she could smoke her own pain away. Bleu walked over to her window and lifted it and snuck out onto the fire escape. She climbed up the two stories and tapped on Noah's window, catching his attention. He rushed over to let her in.

"What's up, B? You okay?" he asked, concerned as he helped her inside.

Ms. Monica knocked on the door, and Noah placed his finger over his lips, signaling Bleu to be quiet. He hurriedly pushed her toward the closet, hiding her before he ran to the door. He opened it. "What's up, Ma?"

"Boy, you ain't slick. Don't 'what's up, Ma'?' me," Ms. Monica said. "Bleu, you can come on out, baby. You ain't got to hide. You're welcome here anytime." Bleu climbed out of the closet, embarrassed, as she kept her head lowered.

Ms. Monica walked over to her once she saw that Bleu was still dressed in the bloody clothes. Her heart ached for Bleu. She bent down and said, "I'm sorry about your daddy, baby. He made some bad choices . . . so did your mama, but you don't have to. You can be better than them. Just because they were caught up and addicted doesn't mean you have to grow up and be that way too. Okay?"

Bleu nodded.

"Now go on in the bathroom and take a hot bath. I'll have some clothes for you when you get out, and there's dinner on the stove. Y'all come down and fix some plates when you're ready and keep this door open," Ms. Monica preached.

Bleu was grateful for Noah and Ms. Monica. They were the closest thing to normal in her life . . . the only people who truly cared.

2

"Hey, hey, B, wake up for me," Noah said when he saw the signs of movement as she stirred in her sleep. She came out of her restless sleep, grateful that reality had interrupted the memories of her past. Noah sat anxiously at her side. She could tell he was forcing the smile that was on his face in an attempt to hide his concern. The smile on his face didn't match the look of despair in his eyes. She could see the worry written all over him. Bleu lazily fluttered her eyes open and gave Noah a weak smile. He was a sight for sore eyes, but she could see the sadness in him as he stared at her over the long lashes that guarded his light brown eyes. His dark skin was reminiscent of night and wrapped over his ballplayer's frame like Saran Wrap. He was usually so strong . . . so confident, and on her weakest days he always held her down. One smile from him was like charging a battery in her back because she knew that he smiled for no one else. She owned it. Bleu was the only person he gifted it to, but as he sat before her, rubbing his hands over his fresh fade, she saw nothing but worry and grief. It shrank him so much that it looked as though his broad shoulders were weighed down by emotion alone. He rushed to her bedside and she placed a weak hand on his cheek as he gripped her hand and kissed the inside of her wrist.

"You're all right, B. You're going to be good. I promise you."

She cleared her throat, preparing herself to respond. She winced in pain as she brought her hand up to her bandaged throat.

"You had a breathing and feeding tube in. There were tubes everywhere, B. It'll hurt to talk for a while. You don't have to say anything. Just rest. I'm here," Noah said as he reached out and grabbed her hand.

She held on to him for dear life, intertwining her fingers with his as she took a deep breath and closed her eyes. Tears snuck out of her eyes. Everything hurt. It hurt like nothing she had ever felt before. Her entire frame was sore, stiff, and it felt as if her insides were hollow. She held out her hand, motioning to all of the flowers.

"I know, right?" Noah said. "You get shot and all of a sudden you're the most popular girl in town."

She smirked.

"It's from the teachers and some of the people we graduated with. The shooting was on the news; the police are making it a big deal. Straight-A student and valedictorian gunned down in her own neighborhood. It's all over the place. You were touch-and-go for a while there. A lot of people were worried," he told her. "I've been here every day."

"He hasn't left . . . in fact, he refused to leave. Day and night he has been here for two weeks."

Bleu and Noah looked up as the head nurse walked in. He lowered his head and blushed slightly as he shook his head dismissively. "Nah, you know I had to make sure you were okay. That's all."

"You are a very lucky young girl," the nurse said. "Had you arrived even a few minutes later, you wouldn't have made it."

"When will she be able to talk?" Noah asked.

"You can speak now. It will hurt, but we actually encourage you to begin speaking so we can make sure that the trach we put in didn't damage your vocal cords. Just take it easy. The doctor will be in to make his rounds. In the meantime just hit your button if you need anything. My name is Nurse Rhoda," she said before making her departure.

When Bleu and Noah were alone she finally spoke. "So where is my mama? Did she even bother to come?" Bleu asked, grimacing. Every word that left her mouth felt like razor blades slicing her throat.

"We don't got to talk, just rest," Noah said, switching the subject.

Bleu snaked her head and widened her eyes. She didn't need to repeat the question in order for Noah to know she was demanding answers. Even shot up and injured, she was a spoiled brat. During their ten-year friendship he had always catered to her. There wasn't much he wouldn't do for his best friend and she knew it.

"She's been around, B. She was here for the first few days. She was worried and crying, but you know how she is. She could only stay so long before—"

Bleu turned her head away from Noah as tears clouded her vision. She knew the end of his sentence. He didn't even have to speak the words. Her mother had been addicted to crack cocaine Bleu's entire life. She was surprised that Sienna had even shown up at all. *She left me here to chase her next high,* Bleu thought in despair. "Your pops came by too," Noah said.

"He's not my pops," Bleu shot back, referring to Larry, the man her mother had married a month after Bleu's father had died. The thought of Larry made her cringe. He had moved into her and Sienna's apartment and made himself at home too quickly. When he had first come around Bleu had thought he was okay. He kept food in their refrigerator. He had a stable job and Sienna seemed to be happy. Of course she was, because instead of tricking for her next high with multiple men she only had to suck one dick for it now. Larry kept her high, supporting her habit, because when Sienna was high she was easy to persuade. He was a wolf in sheep's clothing and the night that he had snuck into Bleu's bedroom was the night when his true colors had been revealed. He had raped her while her mother was passed out in her room and afterward he had cried like a baby while begging Bleu not to tell anyone. He had told her that if she did CPS would take her, and the last thing she wanted was to be separated from Noah. So she remained quiet and kept the ugly secret. Larry had never touched her again and they hadn't spoken of it, but she had never forgotten. She hated him, but with her mother strung out and in the streets more than ever, he was all that Bleu had. In some sick way she had come to depend on him.

"I know, B. I'm just telling you that he was here and he was worried. A couple of your classmates came through too," Noah said. "My mom has been up here every day to bring me food and check on you. She knew I wasn't leaving until you opened your eyes. I couldn't miss that. I knew you would want to see more than doctors and nurses when you finally came to."

"I got shot and my mama didn't even wait around to see if I was going to wake up. She couldn't stop smoking long enough to make sure I was still alive." Bleu laughed to stop herself from crying as she shook her head. She didn't know why her life had to be so hard. She had been cursed with the most rotten set of parents and a sick son of a bitch for a stepfather. They were half the reason why she was determined to get the hell out of Flint. It was a city that would suck the soul right out of you, and she refused to be trapped there.

"I'm sure she's worried, B," Noah said. "She's down bad, but her heart is here with you. That has to count for something, right?"

Bleu turned her head away and didn't respond, because they both knew that the actions of her mama didn't count for shit. Bleu wanted to be angry, but the feeling that resounded loudly within her was disappointment. It ached so badly that the sorrow drowned her. Instead of waking up seeing relief in the eyes of her own mother, Bleu awoke feeling abandoned. It was something that she should have been used to by now. She had learned long ago that expecting the least out of Sienna was a way to save herself from disappointment. Her heart hurt, but she said nothing, tucking her feelings away so that they didn't make her weak.

"I know it ain't UCLA, but you can stay here as long as you need to, a'ight, B?" Noah said as he carried her box of belongings into the one-bedroom apartment. It wasn't much, but it was his, and anything that he had she was welcome to.

"Thank you. I swear I won't be here long. As soon as I'm able to I'm going to head west. I just need a place to rest my head for a while," she said as she limped into the apartment. It had taken everything in her to get up the stairs, but she silently welcomed the pain. It reminded her that she was alive. "They deferred my scholarship until second semester, so I have until January to get myself together. I don't have any money, Noah. I don't want to be a burden," she whispered.

He set down her things and turned to look at her. "You're good, B. You don't need nothing. If you had money I wouldn't take it. I got you. On everything you're good. I've got a little bit of something moving on the block. Money isn't an issue," he said.

"You what?" she asked, heartbreak lacing her tone as she stared at him in shock. "Noah, what are you doing? I thought we talked about college, about getting away from the bullshit."

"Everybody don't got a way out, Bleu," he responded desolately. "I'm not like you. I'm not good at the book thing. I graduated four years ago, B. That school shit is over for me. I'll let you do the college thing while I take over these streets."

"But we had plans; we talked about college for hours . . . I thought you were just waiting for me to finish high school—"

He cut her off before she could get worked up. "You talked, Bleu. I listened to your dreams. Your plans. That was never in the cards for me, so let's drop it. That school shit. That's your thing. Don't worry about me. You just worry about getting better."

She fell silent, because there was no point in arguing with Noah. Once his mind was set that was it. Her heart was broken for him, however. She told herself that she would make it happen for the both of them . . . go off to school, get on, and come back for him. He was her best friend and had gotten her through so many hard days. There was no way she was leaving him behind to get sucked in by the game. There were only two ways out: prison or death. She feared those destinies and knew that he deserved more than the bad hand he would eventually receive.

"Come on, B. Let's get you in bed and order some food. You been on that liquid shit for weeks. You need to get your weight up. You looking like skin and bones," he said.

"Ha." She smirked as she climbed into his bed.

"Only reason you're not on the couch is because you're fucked up," he said with a wink.

"You better stick a pillow between us and get on the other side. Ain't no telling what kind of miles that couch got on it," she said jokingly. She winced and she gritted her teeth as a sudden shock of pain erupted through her. Laughter was like an internal earthquake and Noah immediately noticed her discomfort. He grabbed the prescription bottle out of his pocket and poured two painkillers out into the palm of his hand. He passed them to her and then disappeared for a few minutes before coming back with water. She swallowed them and then leaned back against the mountain of pillows as an awkward silence filled the room.

"Nah, take the bed. I'll crash on the couch. I'll be out most nights anyway. Just rest. I've got to make a few runs. I'll try not to be long. If you need me, text me," he said.

She nodded and then watched him depart. When she heard the front door close, she exhaled. It was the first time since waking up that she had been alone, and it gave her too much time to think. She was trapped in a world that she was supposed to be three thousand miles away from.

3

Noah flipped his hood over his head to shield himself from the falling rain as he stepped outside. Stuffing his hands deep in the pockets of his hoodie, he made his way to his car. He needed some air. Bleu had made plans for his life that he had never intended to fulfill. He wasn't a schoolboy. All he knew was the struggle, and he had plans to hustle his way to the top. They each had dreams, but they were drastically different. He had his sights set on taking over the streets and with Bleu recovering in his home he had to take care of her. She was another mouth to feed and his nickel-and-dime hand-over-fist sells weren't enough for the both of them. If she was going to depend on him while she recovered, he didn't want her to want for anything. She was his best friend. He would give her the world, but first he had to get it.

Their bond had been cemented by a decade of telling each other everything. A part of him was happy that she was now forced to stick around a little longer. He loved her more than anyone else in his life. The older they got, the more beautiful she became, and the more his feelings crossed the fine line that led to something more. He would never speak of it, however. The life that Bleu imagined in her head left no room for dope boys or street kingdoms. She wanted the white picket fence. That was the reason why she wanted to run so far away from the hood. He didn't blame her. She had lived the hard-knock way. As soon as she had announced her plans to go away to college, Larry had rented out her bedroom. He wouldn't even give it back to her after she was shot. She still had to get out, which was the reason why Noah had opened up his small, humble abode to her. He would hold her down as long as she was willing to stick around, but he knew that his moments with her were short-lived. His hope was to make enough money so that she would choose to stay home, in Flint, with him, where she belonged. He wasn't naïve, though. Bleu was the type of girl who deserved a big-city life. If he held her back she would grow resentful, so he would just have to settle with the time they had left. As soon as she was better, he would have to kiss the only girl he had ever loved good-bye. The thought alone caused a dull ache to spread through his chest. Hopping in his '85 Cutlass, he started the raggedy car and pulled away from Black Wall Street, the infamous projects that he called home.

Noah walked into the smoky trap house; instantly the smell of weed invaded his nose, lifting him slightly as he took a seat at the table next to Keon. Keon, a local kingpin in the making, dabbled in heroin. While the rest of the city was making it snow with cocaine, Keon had carved out his own little niche and was getting money while building a small empire for himself. Noah wanted in and had been getting hit with small amounts on consignment. He needed product, however. Keon had him on some small-change shit. Noah was ready for a come-up and Keon could smell the thirst coming off the young wolf from a mile away.

"What up, bro?" Keon asked as he focused on filling the vials in front of him. He trusted no one and still bottled up his own product himself. He didn't need the cook-up spots or the naked women with doctors' masks. He was his own factory. He had it under control. It may have taken him longer to get the job done, but he knew he wouldn't steal from himself. "Hit this," he said as he extended a Kush-filled blunt.

"What up, K?" Noah greeted as he shook his head and waved his hand, declining. He pulled a small knot out of his pocket and put it on the table. "I know it ain't much, but I want in. Don't play me with this little nigga shit. That's five thousand dollars. I need to flip it ten times over. I'm not trying to be a worker, my nigga. I don't want no consignment and I'm not trying to move your work. I'll get my own spot so I'm not taking your custos, but I'm ready to build my own," Noah stated.

"Nigga you in high school what you know about building your own?" Keon said mockingly. Noah knew he was young, but he was also hungry and had the tenacity of a man twice his age.

"I pump more of this shit for you than you do for yourself, bro. You either bring me all the way in or I'm out," Noah proposed with a straight face. Keon, known for his gunplay, was silent as he absorbed the young buck's words. Noah knew that his ultimatum could create hostility and the small .45 that he gripped in his lap ensured that he had the advantage in case Keon wanted to pop off. Noah had never used it, but he wasn't afraid to and would body Keon without a second thought if he felt threatened. There was a tense silence between them, and Noah held his breath until he saw the corners of Keon's mouth melt away into a smirk.

"You young niggas want it all," he said with a bit of displeasure. "A'ight, we can work something out, but if you want in you going to have to put up half of the buy-in. This little five thousand dollars ain't going to do it," Keon said as he tossed the small knot back to Noah. "You trying to come sit at my table you gon' at least have to put up twenty. If you trying to make some paper, I've got a job for you. A little something fell across my lap. I'll pass it to you and take a small fee off the top."

"What's the move?" Noah inquired. He was interested. It was only a matter of time before he had to get his hands dirty. He would never survive in a game this treacherous if he didn't. He needed to make a name for himself . . . to earn his place. He needed to put in work to gain respect. Nothing would be given; it was all earned through blood. Even the most papered-up hustler could be clowned if he hadn't earned his stripes. The time was now and Noah wasn't turning down any opportunity to cement himself in the game.

"My little niggas knocked over a liquor store a few weeks ago. The bitch who work there got popped, but she still breathing. They need that problem taken care of and they're willing to pay big money to whoever makes it happen, you feel me? They got an address and everything. She's a witness and they need her to disappear," Keon stated.

Noah's breath caught in his throat as his stomach went hollow at the mention of the job. He kept a poker face as he replied, "How much?" He needed to know the price that was placed on Bleu's head.

"Twenty thousand dollars," Keon said. "If you in it with me, that's ten racks each. I was gonna do it dolo, but another pair of eyes is never a bad idea. I'm in that bitch tonight if you with it," Keon said. Noah wasn't a fool. He knew that the bag must have been double that. Keon was taking his fee off the top for simply plugging the job.

"Murder ain't my game," Noah replied.

"Yeah, well, somebody gonna make that bread. It may as well be us," Keon replied.

Noah's temperature rose as he thought of the danger Bleu was in. Bleu's stepfather knew that she had moved in with Noah, and he knew that her parents would give her up without a second thought. Noah was trapped between a rock and a hard place as he thought of the bounty. Keon was known for his ruthlessness, and if Noah had to choose between riding for him and protecting Bleu it was a no-brainer.

BOOM! BOOM!

Noah put two bullets in Keon's belly. Keon fell back out of the cheap chair as he looked up in astonishment while gripping his bleeding torso.

"You shot me?" he gasped in disbelief as Noah stood

abruptly. He never knew how badly he would shake when he pulled the trigger. He was just as fear filled as Keon as they both realized the weight behind Noah's actions. "You mutha-fucka!" Keon growled as he reached to his waistline to draw his pistol.

BOOM! BOOM! BOOM!

Noah hit Keon with three more shots, one landing in the middle of his forehead, laying him to rest permanently. Noah's eyes shot frantically around the room as he put his hands to the sides of his head in distress. The contents of his stomach erupted as he rushed to the kitchen sink.

"Arghhh!" he spewed as he breathed frantically while gripping the sides of the sink. "Fuck! Fuck!"

The smell of feces filled the air from Keon having released his bowels when the last breath left his body. The smell was disgusting and Noah wiped his mouth with his hand, feeling the walls closing in on him. It was the reaction that most had after catching their first body. An extreme queasiness filled his gut as he tried to counter the urge to vomit with deep breaths. Murder would get easier with experience, but today he was an amateur and fear urged him on as he grabbed the bleach from beneath the kitchen sink. He poured it down the drain, cleaning out his own vomit, and attempted to wipe down the things he had touched in the house before making his departure.

Rushing from room to room, he searched through the entire house until he stumbled upon two shoe boxes, tucked away in the top of a closet. Popping the tops, he realized what he had found. A half a brick of heroin sat neatly inside one of them, and the other was boxful of money. His heart raced and his eyes widened as he realized he had found Keon's stash. Noah scooped up both boxes and took one last look at Keon before stepping over his body and walking calmly out of the house. In case any prying eyes were watching, he didn't want to be the nigga rushing from the scene of the crime. He was grateful for the dark of night as he flipped his hood over his head and made his way to his car. He pulled off with mixed emotions. He was remorseful, feeling like scum for pulling the trigger, but he knew that when he weighed Keon against Bleu she would always win. Riding for her was a no-brainer. It was a sin Noah had committed on her behalf in order to keep her safe, but he knew that Keon's death wouldn't stop the bounty. Another shooter would simply step up to the plate. Noah couldn't gun down an entire city; instead he would have to keep Bleu hidden until he could get her on her way to Cali. It was the only way to keep her safe. Now their good-bye was inevitable, but he would rather care for her her from afar and know that she was safe than selfishly put her at risk. Love was a bitch and so was karma; he only hoped this murder wouldn't come back on him in the worst way.

4

The incessant banging on the door woke Bleu out of her sleep, but as she opened her eyes it felt as if she were living in a dreamworld. The medication that she was on did little to numb her pain. The wound that had been left behind was so gruesome that she was afraid to look down at it. Despite the fact that it didn't work, she was still grateful for the medication because it made her sleep. As long as she was unconscious, she couldn't feel the pain, but someone was interrupting that, dragging her into a wakeful state and forcing her to feel. She rolled over onto her side and put her weight on her elbows as she breathed deeply, gritting her teeth before she pushed herself up off the bed. The room seemed to tilt, making her feel unsteady on her feet.

KNOCK! KNOCK! KNOCK!

"Wait a minute!" she shouted in frustration as she placed her hands along the wall. She was floating. After doubling her prescription she was kite high. It felt like she was walking on clouds as her feet sank into the plush carpet. By the time she made it to the front door of the apartment she was panting and had worked up a slight sweat. It was as if she had just run a marathon. Her body needed rest. She was overdoing it, trying to force herself to get better before she actually was. If money hadn't been a factor she would still be recovering in the secure wings of a hospital. She looked out of the peephole and frowned in confusion.

"Larry?" she asked. She stepped back and shook her head, thinking that perhaps she was higher than she thought.

"Bleu, it's me. Open the door," he said.

She stood on her tiptoes and peered through the peephole again, confused. He hadn't called her that since the night he had raped her, and hearing it now instantly brought tears to her eyes. She then turned her head and looked across the room to the clock. *It's close to midnight; what is he doing here?* she thought.

She opened the door slightly, giving him just enough room to see her eyes.

"Larry? What are you—"

Before the question could leave her mouth Larry fell, as a silenced bullet crashed through his temple. She felt a forceful push as someone rammed his shoulder against the door. She jumped back as the door's security lock at the top stopped the door from opening completely. She backpedaled slightly, tripping over her own feet as she cursed herself for taking a double dose of medicine. She was incapacitated physically and mentally. As she stumbled to make her way back into Noah's bedroom, the chain gave way to the force on the other side. Pure panic invaded her as she saw the goon rush into the house. She tried to run, but her legs were so heavy that she clumsily fell to the floor, rocking her entire world when she made impact.

She roared as agony took over her body. Bleu scrambled to stand but knew that she had no wins in her current state.

"Keep your ass down there, bitch!" the intruder barked as he leveled her with a sharp kick to the abdomen.

She yelled out, completely broken, as her entire body quaked in torment. She had barely survived the gunshot wound. This attack would surely kill her. The pain alone would send her to her maker. It was like an earthquake, splitting her in two as the pain radiated through her entire body. She was too vulnerable to defend herself. She couldn't run or fight back and she curled into a fetal ball, trying to shield herself from the blows.

The man towered over her and flipped her over onto her back, causing their eyes to meet. "Any last words, bitch, before I send you to your maker?"

She nodded, frantic, as tears built in her eyes. She opened her mouth and replied, "You'll beat me there."

A look of confusion crossed the goon's face.

The bullet that Noah sent through the back of his skull ended him, and his body dropped to the floor. Deadweight. If Noah had shown up even a minute later . . . the thought alone made him shudder.

"B," Noah whispered as he rushed to pick Bleu up from the floor. She crumbled like the fragile girl she was, her tears free-flowing as he cradled her in his arms. He picked her up with urgency and rushed her to his room.

"Lock the door, Bleu. Don't come out until I tell you to, you understand?" he asked.

The look in his eye scared her, but she nodded her head in obedience. "Larry . . . he shot him . . . he's . . . he's . . . dead," she cried out of shock more than sympathy. She had wished death on him for years and, finally, someone had come to serve Larry's karma.

"Fuck Larry. He brought that nigga here, Bleu. Don't cry for him," Noah said before disappearing down the hall and closing the door behind him.

Overwhelmed, Noah sent his fist through the wall, damn near breaking his knuckles, and pulled it back. He placed the palms of his hands against the wall and breathed heavily as he bowed his head. He had started his day as a young hustler just trying to make a dollar and had ended it with two bodies on his street résumé. He knew that murder and money went hand in hand. He had to be ready for this, but it didn't make it easier. He was selling his soul to protect one girl, but she was worth it. Noah shook his bleeding hand as he pulled out his cell phone with the other. He was about to make a call that he had said he never would. Drastic times called for drastic measures, however.

Khadafi Langston was Noah's father. He had never seen the man or even spoken to him before, but Noah's mother ensured that Noah knew his father's name. Noah had looked up the number almost a year ago and had never used it. His father had never been in Noah's life; he didn't even know if the man knew he had a son. The affair with Noah's mother had been a one-night stand, a casual fling, but the birth of Noah Langston was the result. As chance would have it, hustling was in his blood. Khadafi was the biggest kingpin Flint, Michigan, had ever seen, and Noah was about to call him for the first time. Noah wasn't dumb. He knew that he couldn't get rid of the two bodies that were lying in the middle of his living room. That required resources . . . a professional, and there was only one man Noah could reach out to. Just as he was about to press dial, police sirens rang out in the distance.

"Noah!" Bleu called in distress as she suddenly snatched open the bedroom door. "The police are coming up," she said, frightened.

Noah never got to make his call, as his brain went into overdrive. He rushed to Bleu and cradled her face while staring her in the eyes. "We have to get our story straight and we don't have a lot of time to do it."

"He came to the door with Larry. . . . He . . . he . . . he killed him and then muscled his way inside the door. I th-thought I was g-g-oing to die," she stuttered.

"I came in and surprised him from behind as he held you at gunpoint. We tussled and I knocked the gun out of his hand, but he had another gun in his waistline. He pulled it on me and then you scrambled for the first gun and shot him in the back of the head. You feared for your life and you thought he was going to kill me. You understand? He brought both of these guns here. These belong to him. A'ight?"

She nodded her head in panic as she went over the details

in her head. Noah hoped that she had it down, because one of those guns had two bodies on it and he could go away for life if anyone connected the dots of what had really occurred that night. He picked up the gun and placed it in Bleu's hands and told her to pull the trigger.

"You need residue on your hands," he explained quickly as she shook uncontrollably.

"I'm scared," Bleu admitted as tears fell.

"I know . . . I know, B. I got you," he whispered.

At that moment four armed police officers infiltrated the apartment, guns drawn, aiming from Bleu to Noah, trying to assess the situation at first glance.

"Show me your hands! Put the gun down!" they yelled.

Bleu lifted her hands and let the gun fall to the floor with a clang.

"Get on your knees!"

Noah got on his knees with his hands planted firmly behind his head. He had seen the routine enough times to know how to not get shot. "She can't get on the ground. She's been shot. She's the victim in that store robbery that happened about a month ago!" Noah yelled.

"Please, I was just released from the hospital today," she whispered.

She trembled like prey as a female officer approached her. "Place your wrists in front of you, dear. We don't know what happened here, but we still have to cuff you. I'll be gentle," the woman said.

"I . . . I shot him," Bleu whispered. "I thought he was going to kill me."

The female officer lowered her voice, whispering, "Sweetheart, I don't know what happened here, but you don't say one word without a lawyer, okay?"

Bleu nodded her head as she was escorted out into the night. Every resident who lived in Black Wall Street seemed to be out as the police walked her to the squad car. Life moved in slow motion as she met the eyes of the neighbors. It felt like she was taking the long walk of shame, and as the officers stuffed her in the back of police car, she saw the officers escorting Noah out. It hit her. He had saved her life. If it were not for him, she would be the one the coroner would be tagging. She stared at Noah through the window with tear-filled eyes and mouthed, *I love you.* A simple nod was his only reply as the car started and pulled away.

5

"I'm looking at five years, Bleu," Noah said as he gripped the phone and stared at Bleu through the thick glass that separated them.

Her heart broke when she heard the news, and pools of emotion immediately gathered beneath her lashes. "But how? I told them what happened. They let me go! Why are you still in here?" she asked desperately.

"I had a brick of heroin on me that night. They don't even want to pin the bodies on me. They're concerned about the dope. If I fight it I could get life, Bleu. I can do a quick five and be out. I'm going to take the plea," Noah replied, trying to sound as if this entire plan were okay.

"Noah," Bleu whispered, heartbroken, as she placed her hand against the glass. "I'll wait for you. What you did for me, the way you look at me . . . I finally see it. I love you and I'm going to wait for you, no matter how long it takes," she promised.

Noah grimaced as he sniffed loudly, trying to contain his emotions. He had wanted to hear her say this for years. He had been in love with this one girl since it was innocent enough to be just a crush. She mattered most to him, and as he stared into her beauty, he was mesmerized. She wasn't overly sexy, but she was just his type. Brown skin, shoulder-length hair that fell in messy curls around her face, hips wide, waist slim, and a smile uniquely hers. A small gap rested between her two front teeth, just big enough to notice. Bleu hated it, but like a mole was to a model, it was more a gift than a curse. Her body more dangerous than the curves of a racer's path, he had enjoyed watching her walk away from him so many times before. Today, however, he dreaded it, because he knew that it would be the last time. He just stared at her, gripping the phone as he tried to paint a picture of her beautiful face in his head. He knew that he couldn't keep her. There was still a bounty on her head. She was like a walking money bag. Anyone with a thirst for some quick cash would try to off her. With Noah locked up, she would have no protection. She would be a sheep among wolves. Every gun in the city would be at her head until she was dead. She couldn't stick around and wait for him, but he knew if he told her the truth . . . if he told her that he loved her more than the air in his lungs . . . that he saw his future in her . . . that besides money she was the only thing that occupied his thoughts . . . if he told her these truths, she would stay regardless. He had to lie to get rid of her.

"Don't wait for me," he responded.

She frowned in confusion. "What? What are you saying to me, Noah?"

"I'm in here because of you. You brought that heat to my crib and now I'm doing a bid behind it. You Hollywood, right? That was your dream? You're off to sunny California, and I'll be rotting away behind concrete and steel bars. You've overstayed your welcome, B. I should have never taken on your burdens. Maybe you should just catch that bus to the West Coast," he said without flinching, showing no emotion.

She blinked in confusion as her mouth fell open, flabbergasted by his rejection.

He saw her feelings fold as a hint of heartbreak reflected in her eyes, and it ate away at him that he had caused it.

"Noah—"

"Just go, Bleu! Damn!" he interrupted. "High school is over. It's time we went our separate ways." He got to his feet and slammed the phone down. He didn't even turn around to give her one last glance before he disappeared out of her sight.

Bleu stood abruptly, pushing out of the chair with so much force that it fell to the floor. Everyone turned to look at her, and she rushed out of the room, embarrassed and in despair.

By the time Bleu made her way back to Noah's apartment, she had made up her mind. She was leaving town. *Fuck this cruddy-ass city,* she thought as she tore down the police tape and pushed open the door. She stopped and her heart skipped a beat when she saw the blood-stained floor where her stepfather and the man who had attacked her had fallen. The smell of death lingered in the air. She was almost afraid to walk inside. Taking a deep breath, she willed herself forward. *I can't stay here*, she thought. She would lose her life if she stayed in Flint. It was the city where the good died young, and she felt the ruthlessness firsthand. She wouldn't even stay to put her stepfather in the ground. Noah was the only person who could have talked her into remaining, and he had made it clear he wasn't interested. Bleu made her way to the bedroom and gathered her things. She didn't have much to her name. She would leave most of it behind, except for a suitcase full of clothes. Struggling and in need of rest, she managed to drag her bag out of Noah's room. He didn't want her there. He blamed her for everything that had happened, but what hurt most was that he hadn't returned her sentiments.

She had never known a pain so great. Every part of her hurt. Her heart was broken, her spirit crushed, and her body healing from a shooting that should have killed her. Bleu's pain overwhelmed her as she pulled her suitcase all the way outside. She didn't stop until she was standing in front of the bus stop. The next bus didn't come for another twenty minutes, more than enough time to change her mind, but she knew that this was it. This had been the plan all along, and when her ride finally arrived, she stepped onto the bus without looking back. She had no love for a city that had no love for her. *Los Angeles, California, here I come.*

6

The bus ride was a blur. After countless transfers, days of traveling, and slipping in and out of consciousness from the pain pills she had taken, Bleu had finally arrived. La-la land . . . the place where dreams came true. This was it and as she stepped out of the Greyhound station with her bag in hand she looked around in amazement. She had done it. She was here. After years of imagining what it would be like, she was standing in the middle of the city . . . inhaling the smog-filled air.

Now what? she thought. She had no plan. She had missed the first half of the first semester. She couldn't just drop into her classes. She was too far behind. She had hopped on a bus and traveled across the country with no real clue of what she would do once she arrived, but after everything that had happened to her, she had no regrets.

She looked left, then right, slightly overwhelmed by the magnitude of her new surroundings. She didn't have any money. She couldn't get a room. She would have to spend her first night on the streets.

"Hey, you need a ride?"

She looked down the block to the cabbie who was sitting on the hood of his car. A cigarette dangled between his fingers as he blew smoke into the air. Knowing that her pockets were on E, she shook her head to decline. "No, I'll walk, thanks. But can you tell me where UCLA is?"

"You're walking to UCLA? From here? At this time of night?" the cabbie asked.

Bleu nodded. She was fully aware of her peculiar destination. It was 1:00 a.m., but she just had to see it, up close and personal. She had researched it and looked at pictures a thousand times, but she wanted to plant her feet on campus. She deserved to.

"Can you just point me in the right direction?" she asked. "I don't mind walking."

The Hispanic gentleman smashed his cigarette into the curb and then tossed the butt before ruffling his fingers through his jet-black hair. "Come on; I'm going that way anyway. I'll give you a lift," he offered.

Bleu didn't move. She was young, but she was from the murder capital. If he thought she looked like easy bait, he was mistaken. "I'm good," she said, declining his offer.

"Hey, it's on the house. I'm not trying to get you," he replied. He could sense her skepticism and he held out a finger. "Hey, look at this." He went into his glove compartment and pulled out his state license. "You're a smart cookie," the cabbie stated. He held it out for her. "That there is my state permit.

I'm licensed to drive this here piece of shit. This is a big city. You're smart to worry, but if you see one of these you're safe to get inside. Okay?"

After inspecting it thoroughly, she removed her cell phone and took a picture of the man's face.

"I'm sending your picture to my parents," she lied. "If you kill me, at least the police will know who to look for."

The cabbie held out his hands in amusement, then clapped them together and said, "Good idea! Now let's get you to UCLA."

She climbed into the back of the cab and watched as the driver climbed into the front.

"I'm Eddie, by the way," he introduced himself.

"Bleu," she replied as she stared out of her window. The city was so alive. There were lights everywhere, and people were out walking and talking as if it were the middle of the day.

"So what's your story, Bleu? You a runaway?" Eddie asked.

She furrowed her brow but didn't answer as she continued to stare out of the window.

"No offense. I've been driving cabs for ten years. A lot of young girls with one suitcase have come out of that bus station. This city is like a magnet for girls with stars in their eyes. What do you do? Act? Sing? Or dance?"

"I'm a student. I was accepted to UCLA," she answered somewhat boastfully. She wasn't the average birdbrain with a talent that would probably never blossom into a career. She was smart; she had aced every test she had taken since grade school. Her brains had been her ticket out, not some pipe dream.

"Oh, well, you're a little late, aren't you? Classes started a while back," Eddie stated as he shifted his eyes from the rear-view mirror to the road.

"Yeah, well, I got held up," she responded vaguely.

She crossed her arms as they made the trek across town. When he finally pulled onto Sunset Boulevard she peered out of her window in amazement.

"This is it," Eddie said. "That's Royce Hall."

She sat, slightly intimidated, as she stared at the empty campus. It was massive. It appeared to be larger than her entire hometown at first glance.

"You going to get out?" Eddie asked with a chuckle.

She turned to him and said, "Thanks for the lift."

"No problem. Good luck," Eddie replied. "Hey, if you're ever in the mood for some good Mexican food, my wife owns a restaurant." He handed Bleu a folded menu and gave her a wink. "It's good eating."

She smiled and answered, "I'll have to come by then. Thank you for the free ride. Have a good night." She stepped out of the cab, lugging her suitcase behind her, and she made her way down the red-brick path. Royce Hall was beautiful. Surrounded by a lawn the size of a football field, with a beautiful fountain, it was larger than any building she had ever seen in Flint. It had character, and she could only imagine the type of genius minds that had been lucky enough to ever grace its halls. "I made it," she whispered. She took a deep breath and walked over to one of the large trees before setting her things down.

Even if she had the money to sleep in a five-star hotel, she would still prefer this very spot. She took a seat in the grass, leaned her back against the large tree, and looked around. She was in love. She belonged here. This massive institution with its green grass and beautiful architecture would be her new home, at least for the next four years, and it felt right. Bleu had always been a big-city girl trapped in the surroundings of her humble upbringing. UCLA. Los Angeles. This was where she belonged. As Bleu closed her eyes, she fell asleep completely comfortable under the night sky. She had no idea what this city had in store for her, however. The change of pace and scenery had seduced her upon first sight, but she had stepped into a whole new world. Wealth and status ruled this city. While she was used to dealing with hoodlums and hustlers, she had never encountered the privileged and pretentious. This was an entirely different league and she would need more than street smarts in order to play in this game.

7

"Hey!"

Bleu felt a nudge as someone kicked the bottom of her shoe, awakening her from her sleep. She frowned as she placed her hand above her eyes to shield them from the sun while staring up into the face of the security guard before her. "You're not supposed to be sleeping here. Unless you want to be arrested for loitering, I'd advise you to get up and get moving."

Bleu slowly stood on her feet, grimacing slightly as she fought through the discomfort of her healing wounds. "I'm a student; relax!" she shot back as she grabbed her suitcase. The sun had barely risen above the clouds, and the sky was a shade of amber that caused her to stop and admire the view. "Sunny California" was an accurate description. It wasn't even 6:00 a.m. and already the heat was starting to settle in. The campus was practically deserted at this hour. A few lone souls wandered to prep for early classes, but nothing else moved. It was peaceful and Bleu couldn't wait to get started on this journey. Walking around campus was like being in a city within a city. It was huge . . . too big, in fact. She had been to a few college parties back in high school, but this campus seemed to dwarf any that she had ever stepped foot on. After an hour of walking, going to the wrong building, and asking various students for help, she finally located the admissions office. She didn't know what she would say or do, but she had to give it a shot. She was now more eager than ever. She had to attend. She didn't care if she had to make the painful trek around campus while recovering or if she had to stay up all night every night to catch up; she just wanted to be here. Besides, she had nowhere else to go. Everything took effort. Going up the steps, pulling her bag behind her . . . it was all a task, and by the time she stepped into the air-conditioned building she was out of sorts. Sweaty and flustered, she blew out a sharp breath as she found the office that she had been searching for.

"How can I help you?" the woman behind the counter asked.

Exhausted, Bleu set her bag at her feet and leaned into the counter. "My name is Bleu Montclair. I need to speak to my admissions counselor." She reached into her cheap handbag and pulled out her acceptance letter. She opened it, hands shaking, as she could feel herself growing weak, her breathing labored.

"Are you all right?" the woman asked in concern.

"No, no, not really," Bleu responded, out of breath as the pain in her chest intensified. "I was accepted here and then I got shot, so I couldn't come right away, but I'm here now. I rode a bus for hours to get here. I just want my shot. I'll do anything to start classes. I'll catch up on the work. I'll take extra classes . . . get a tutor . . . just please, I have to start."

The blond woman was moved to tears as she came from behind her station. Desperation hung in the air like humidity, making it thick as sympathy weighed down her chest. The woman placed a hand on Bleu's back and guided her to the seating area. "Sit here, honey. I'll get one of the admissions counselors for you. I'm sure someone will be able to help you," she said.

She hurried away and Bleu frantically rummaged through her purse until she located the medicine bottle. She was overexerting herself and she knew it, but she hadn't come this far to turn back now. She took out one of the pain pills and popped it into her mouth, swallowing it without water. She needed the ache in the middle of her chest to go away. It wasn't the physical pain that overwhelmed her. It was the mental chains that shackled her to her past, making her think that she would never make it out of the hood. She felt bound to a city that had no love for her, and if UCLA turned her away she would be stuck there forever.

"Ms. Montclair?"

Bleu looked up and into the dark eyes of a middle-aged woman with olive skin and kind eyes. Her blond hair was sparse, barely hiding her aging scalp from the world, and her clothes two sizes too big for her frail body. This old bat was the gatekeeper to higher learning, and Bleu only hoped that she would let her in. "I'm Cindy Staton. I wasn't expecting you until next semester. I was so sorry to hear about what happened to you," she said. Her smile was polite, but confusion was revealed in her gaze. Bleu understood. She had dropped in, unexpected, injured, and asking for a chance. "Please let's go into my office so I can see how we can work this out."

Bleu stood and followed her into a comfortable office. They sat before Ms. Staton continued. "How are you?"

"I'm alive," Bleu replied as she lowered her head in angst. "I would really just like to start school."

She could see the skepticism in the lady's face as she shook her head. "You've missed so much."

"I know. I know. I'm willing to do the work to catch up. I swear I can do this. I just have nowhere else to go. I took a chance on coming out here. I can do this. I will, no matter how hard it is," Bleu assured her.

The counselor was silent for almost a minute as Bleu sat impatiently awaiting an answer. Against Ms. Staton's better judgment, she nodded her head. "Okay. Okay. I'll admit you. Let's get you registered and then send you over to Student Housing to iron out your living arrangements."

"Yes, yes!" Bleu exclaimed. Her smile couldn't be contained. "Thank you so much." After so many things had gone wrong in her life, finally something was going right.

"Who the hell are you?"

Bleu froze when she opened the door to her dorm room and saw the group of girls sitting on both beds.

"Who are *you*?" Bleu shot back to the girl before her. She was pretty, exotic, with slanted eyes that gave away some Asian in her heritage but brown skin that exposed her true flavor. She was petite, with style for days. Her jet-black hair fell in layers down her back. The group of girls were dressed impeccably. Shoes with red bottoms adorned their feet while Chanel and Louis V handbags dangled from their arms. Bleu walked completely into the room, dropping her suitcase at the end of the bed that was unmade.

"Umm, what are you doing?" the girl asked.

"I'm your roommate and I'm making myself comfortable," Bleu replied. She waved her hand at the two girls who were seated on her bed. "Excuse me," she said as she tried to maneuver around the girls.

One of the girls sucked her teeth and didn't budge as she turned her attention back to Bleu's roommate. Bleu sighed. She had tried the decent approach. She was exhausted and her tolerance for bullshit was at an all-time low. She didn't have time for a battle of wills with these spoiled little rich girls.

"Excuse me," Bleu said.

It was as if she were speaking to herself. They dismissed her without even looking at her, making her temperature rise. "Move your ass off my bed," Bleu said, losing patience for this high-fashion mob of mean girls.

The girl moved as Bleu's roommate snickered as she leaned over her vanity to apply her lipstick. Her makeup was done to precision, and when she was satisfied with her look, she popped her lips and blew herself a kiss. "What are you? Some kind of gangster? Where are you from, Detroit or something?" the girl asked, causing the others to cackle condescendingly.

"Where are *you* from?" Bleu shot back.

"Beverly Hills," she said curtly with a smirk. "Don't touch my shit, okay?"

A knock at the door interrupted the war of words as the door opened. A light-skinned dude with a curly Mohawk and a skater boy swag stepped inside. He was attractive but a little too clean-cut for Bleu's tastes.

"Hey, baby, we're almost ready," the girl said.

"Come on. You're going to make me late. You know that's bad business," the guy complained. He looked at Bleu and nodded his head. "Who is this?"

"This is nobody," the girl responded.

Bleu ignored the snarky remark as she popped open her suitcase. She hadn't anticipated not getting along with her roommate, but this siddity broad in front of her was making it clear that she was the head bitch in charge. Clearly they weren't going to be friends.

"Chill out, China," the guy said.

"I don't have to chill," she replied.

"I'm Bree," the guy said as he turned to Bleu.

He extended his hand. She reluctantly shook it as she replied, "I'm Bleu."

China sighed loudly as she rudely added, "And I'm bored." She headed for the door. "When you're done with this little conversation, I'll be in the car." She headed out as Bleu frowned.

"Yeah, this isn't going to work," Bleu scoffed as she turned to finish unpacking her things.

"Give her some time. She's queen bee around here. She's

not used to the competition of another pretty face. She'll warm up to you. She's like that with everybody," Bree said. Bleu didn't respond as she continued to remove clothes from her suitcase.

"You're not from around here, right?" Bree asked as he looked her up and down. Suddenly she was uncomfortable in her skin. Back home she was the pretty girl on the block, the one all the boys wanted but had been unable to attain, but here she just seemed out of place. If all the girls were like China and her friends, Bleu would stick out like a sore thumb, and not in a good way.

"Is it that obvious?" she said with a smile. She turned and flopped down on her bed.

"Don't worry about it. It's a good thing," Bree replied as he backpedaled out of the room.

Bleu leaned back onto the bare bed. She had nothing, no sheets, no comforter . . . all she had was one suitcase full of clothes, and even those threads would only last her about two weeks. She had to come up with a plan to get money if she was going to survive, and fast. She was so overwhelmed. There was so much changing in her world, and the one person she had to talk to had made it clear that he didn't want her. Suddenly she stood and rushed over to China's desk. Bleu didn't care if Noah didn't want to hear from her; she was going to contact him anyway. She located a notebook and snatched a piece of paper from inside. She nabbed a pen and then retreated to her bed to pen her letter. She didn't even know where to send it, but an Internet search would help her locate him. He was her person . . . her best friend. He was all she had in the world. She was going to write to him until he responded, and even if he didn't, writing her emotions on paper would help her make sense of her new surroundings. Despite the fact that she had only been there for a few hours, she could already tell that she was out of place. Noah was the only thing familiar in her world, and even if he never responded her letters to him would get her through.

8

Left. Right. Right cross. Uppercut.

Noah said the combination in his head repetitively as his fists assaulted the heavy bag. Each time his fists hit, he grunted as he worked himself to exhaustion. Five years. He had caught a raw deal and the aggression that he had pent up would eat him alive if he didn't hit something. It hadn't even been a week and already being locked up was driving him insane. Sweat dripped down his muscular frame as his hands moved with the swiftness of Ali. It wasn't until Noah heard the loud buzzer sound off, letting him know that rec time was over, that he stopped. He hated everything about prison life. The way they were watched every minute of every day, the way their cells were tossed upside down without warning for inspection, the way they had to report for count numerous times a day. They were herded like sheep . . . better yet, like slaves. These five years would take a toll on him. He knew that he would not emerge the same. He would mature faster than any nigga on the outside because inside the wall it was survival of the fittest. There was politics to it all. He had already been approached by the Ocks, but he wasn't interested. He didn't want to affiliate himself with the Muslim religion just to establish protection. He respected what they stood for, but Islam wasn't his belief, so he declined, leaving him naked and labeling him a marked man. The prison was divided. Everyone had a group. The skinheads, the Hispanics, the white-collar cats, the Muslims, not to mention the COs. They each had their own circle with different rules. Rules inside of rules. Noah had to worry about it all and he had to constantly watch his back because he belonged to no one. He was a loner and he was just looking to do his bid without friction. There were niggas who came in and out of jail as if it were a revolving door. Five years was considered an easy stretch for some, but for Noah it felt like his entire life had ended before it truly had begun. If he had put in his time in the streets, sampled a taste of the good life, enjoyed the fruits of his hustle, he would have been able to take his time with ease. He would rather live enormous for a short time than struggle forever, but he had gotten pinched before any of his spoils came in. That was the part he couldn't wrap his mind around.

The medium-security prison gave the inmates just enough rope to hang themselves, but Noah wanted no problems. If all went as planned, he could be out with good behavior in thirty-six months. He was just trying to keep his head down and fly under the radar, but in a jungle where the men around him were facing life sentences, jealousy led to beefs unknown.

As he waited in line with a tray in his hand he frowned at the slop that was being placed on his plate. "Aye, my man, I don't eat meat," he said as he placed the tray on top of the counter and slid it back to the dude behind the serving line.

He chuckled, responded, "Good luck with that, G," and slid the tray back to Noah, who reluctantly took it. There would be no special requests made where he was. He was facing hard time. If he wanted to eat, he would eat what was served. Disgusted, Noah took his tray and scanned the room. He sat at the end of a table, avoiding interacting with anyone else, but his presence alone was enough to get him into trouble.

"Yo, did I tell you you could sit there?"

Noah looked down at the other end of the table where a group of men were congregating. Noah didn't respond as he looked down at his plate.

"This nigga don't hear me?" One of the men stood and Noah immediately assessed the situation. The dude was taller, appeared a few years older, but he had a bit of weight on him, which would slow him down. Noah gripped the sides of his tray as the loudmouth inmate approached. "You deaf, nigga?"

Noah stood without warning and slammed the tray into the side of the other inmate's head. Stunned, the man had no time to react before Noah's fist went to work and the commotion of the fight riled up the other prisoners. Noah was skilled with his hands and he knew when to take a win. He hit the dude with an uppercut that put him on his back before the guards subdued Noah, carrying him away from the fight before it got out of hand.

It wasn't until he was on his way out that loudmouth stood to his feet.

"You don't know who you fucking with, pussy! Just signed your death certificate!" he yelled angrily as he spat a mouthful of blood onto the floor.

Noah nodded his head and mean-mugged the dude until he could no longer see him. He wasn't one to talk big; he'd rather show and prove. As the guards dragged him away he didn't put up a fight, because he knew that he would see the dude again. Now was just the prelude to the show. Noah had swung first; there would be another bout to follow. Niggas in jail had reputations to uphold and something to prove. The hierarchy was based on your manhood and respect. Noah had just tested both of those and he knew there would be repercussions. It didn't matter to him. However and whenever the nigga wanted to do it, Noah would be ready.

"You haven't even been here a week, Langston, and already you're at it," the CO huffed as he tossed Noah back into his cell. He didn't respond. He hadn't been there long, but one thing he had learned was that nobody spoke to the guards. He could have easily shifted the blame, since he hadn't actually started the confrontation, but he said nothing. He simply mugged the guard as he watched the door shut. The click of the locks made his stomach turn. It was a cruel reminder that he couldn't just walk out of there anytime he wanted. He was a slave to this modern-day plantation and he hated it. He turned to find an envelope sitting on his bed. It was opened—normal procedure, as the guards had to inspect every single package that came for inmates. He snatched it off of the concrete slab and read the front. Seeing Bleu's name on the front, he opened it hurriedly, eager to hear from her. He had told her to stay away for her own good. It was just like her to be hard-headed, but today he was grateful to hear from her. He missed her like shit. After seeing her every day for years, her sudden absence felt foreign. Maybe that's why he had so much pent-up anger. His happiness had been forced out of his life. Now they were walking down two drastically different paths, his much more difficult.

He took a deep breath and took a seat as he flipped open her letter.

Noah,

I know you told me you didn't want to hear from me, but you had to know that I would reach out to you. You're my best friend and I miss you. I know I got weird with the "I love you" stuff. I don't know where that even came from. I've been through a lot. I don't know, just forget that part. I need you, Noah. You're my friend. The only person I have, and I just want to know that you're okay. As bad as your situation is, I feel like a brat for even thinking of being un-grateful about mine. I did it. I made it to Cali. I haven't even been here a full day yet and I already want to come home. Everything is so . . . well . . . it's different here. The chicks are different. They talk different and walk different. My roommate, I went through her closet and I swear her clothes cost more than my tuition. I'm out here with jeans and tank tops while the glamorous people are turning up their noses around me. I don't know. I just thought it would be different. I pictured a campus full of hungry students grinding toward the same goals, but these kids are definitely not starving. They drive BMWs and they don't eat at the cafeteria. They are spoiled. Like some for real 90210 shit. I guess I'm just out of my element, but then again, to you I probably sound crazy. You're stuck in there and I'm out here. The fact that I can't see you or touch you or hear your voice makes me sick. I don't know why you pushed me away, but I'm not going anywhere. Even if you never write me one let-ter, I'm going to send them to you regardless. I know you're scared. You'll never admit it, but I know you. You're as hard as they come, but who wouldn't be terrified of being sent away? You don't have to be hard with me. I just want you to be okay. I'm so sorry, Noah. I really am. You don't deserve this. I hate even thinking about you inside a steel box. Stay strong, and if you ever need me I'm here. I don't have any money, but when I do finally come up I'll bless your books. I promise.

Love always,
B

The letter tugged at Noah. He could practically hear her soft voice in his ear as he read it again to himself. He had no paper, no pencil. Even the smallest things in prison were a luxury. His mother was the only person he would expect to fill his commissary, but he would never fix his mouth to ask her. She had worked hard day in and out to take care of him and his younger siblings. He wouldn't take a dollar from her, not to finance a jail stint. He would never burden her in that way.

He folded the letter in his hands and tucked it beneath the tattered mattress. It had fueled him to hear from Bleu, but he knew that even if he had an envelope or a pen to reply, he wouldn't. His silence would be her only reply. For her own good, it was best if she stayed away . . . far away.

Bleu winced as she gently cleansed her incision site with warm water. It was a gruesome sight and would leave an equally hideous scar. It would forever remind her of the day that she had almost died. Without warning the bathroom door opened, and China came stumbling in. Bleu quickly grabbed her robe and tried to cover herself, but not before China caught a glimpse of her.

"Oh my God. What happened to you?" she asked.

Bleu tied her robe tightly at the waist. "It looks worse than it is. Don't worry about it." It was a blatant lie and they both knew it. Bleu grabbed her toothbrush out of the holder as suddenly the door opened again, and a dark-skinned girl with jet-black hair entered. "Apparently, nobody knocks around here," Bleu said.

"Don't worry about it. You'll get used to it," the girl said. She was gorgeous. Skin the color of hot chocolate and legs as long as stilts. She was the model type, flawless in her panties and bra, as she walked around without shame.

"I'm Aysha," she introduced herself. She was the first friendly face Bleu had encountered and Bleu returned Aysha's smile as she replied, "Bleu."

Aysha turned to China and said, "So much for your solo room, huh?"

"I guess so," China replied. China folded her arms as she eyed Bleu curiously. She pointed her finger. "How'd you get that?" China asked, motioning to the wound on Bleu's back that was far from healed.

"I told you it's nothing," Bleu insisted.

"Yeah, that type of stitch isn't nothing!" China shot back.

"What are you, a doctor?" Bleu shot back defensively as her brows dipped low. She walked back into her dorm room, and the other girls followed her.

"She's pre-med," Aysha informed Bleu.

"And I know enough to know that that wound is serious. You have to take care of it. It's not a small scrape. If you don't make sure it's clean, it'll get infected. Let me see it," China said.

"What?" Bleu replied.

China stormed over to her and snatched the belt off of her robe, causing Bleu to clutch it, keeping it together with her hands.

China gave her a look, and Bleu sighed, realizing that she wasn't going to take no for an answer. Bleu revealed herself and Aysha covered her mouth in shock.

"What happened to you?" she asked with worry, sympathy filling her gaze.

Bleu's body was healing, but it left gruesome bubble scars behind. They were purple, and the stitches that kept everything together made her look like Frankenstein. She knew it was ugly. It had taken weeks for her to get used to looking at the aftermath. It was hard on the eyes. The bullet had left a physical scar that she would carry for life, not to mention the mental one.

"I was shot. That's why I didn't start the term on time," Bleu admitted quietly, almost whispering.

Aysha shook her head as she frowned. "Damn, girl, somebody fucked you up," she said. "You sure you're even ready to be here?"

Bleu chuckled a little bit as her eyes watered. It took everything in her not to go in on them. These nosey broads were worse than the old hens who spread news through the ghetto grapevine back home. She couldn't, however, burn bridges that she might have to cross later. She knew no one here, so she might as well make an effort to get to know them. She would need allies here. The last thing she wanted was to beef out with the women she shared a living space with. She sighed and instead of going the "slap a bitch route," she decided to extend her trust. New friends were a rarity where she was from. If you hadn't been down from day one, you wouldn't get down, but she couldn't live by that rule anymore. What would she do? Stay holed up in her dorm for four years? Nah, she had to put herself out there. She had to start laying the foundation to live her new Cali life. "Y'all have no idea what it took to get here. I have to do this. That's why you two can't say anything. Not one word to anybody." She closed her robe insecurely.

Aysha held up her hands in defense. "I won't say a word, mama."

China nodded. "I won't say anything."

Bleu cut her eyes at China skeptically. She could just see China running across campus telling all her business as the opportunity arose. The bitch looked like a gossip. There was nothing worse than a chatty chick with loose lips, and China fit the description to a T.

"Hey," China protested, catching the shade. "I know I was in bitch mode last night. My bad. I won't say anything. You can trust me. If we're going to live together for the rest of the school year we may as well be cool, right?"

Aysha laughed and shook her head. "China's cool. She's kept bigger secrets than this."

China added, "To make up for last night, we'll show you around. Aysha is signed with Ford Models. Her pretty ass can get us into all the hot spots. VIP, bottle service, step and repeat, the whole nine. You should come out and let us introduce you to a few people. Might as well get accustomed to the vamp life. That's when the city comes alive."

"You model? Then why are you here?" Bleu asked curiously.

"Because this ass won't be this tight forever. Looks fade; my degree won't," Aysha said. "But while I'm this dope might as well enjoy the perks." She winked and flashed a smile before she added, "You in or nah?"

Bleu hesitated briefly before replying, "Yeah, I'm in."

Bleu tugged at her clothes insecurely as she stood in front of the full-length mirror. Jordans, a sleeveless, crop-top turtleneck, and black leggings gave her a sexy tomboyish look. It was the best thing that she had in her suitcase, but still it didn't quite feel good enough. She wasn't a stiletto type of girl, at least not yet. She had just graduated from high school less than six months ago. She was still in the realm of sneakers and backpacks, but clearly that attire didn't cut it here. She squirmed uncomfortably as she frowned at her reflection. She reached up and pulled her hair into a tight ponytail just as Aysha and China came bursting through the door. No one ever seemed to knock. Privacy seemed to be nonexistent.

"Nah, mama, hair down," Aysha said as she came up behind Bleu, giving her two cents.

"And what are you wearing?" China added. "We're going to a nightclub, not the mall. You're wearing sneakers. They won't even let you in without heels that are at least five inches."

Bleu turned and looked at the two glamazons in front of her. Her cheap threads were incomparable to the thousands of dollars' worth of labels they were wearing. Not only did she not look the part, but also she felt out of place. There was no way she could stand next to these two. It wasn't just a matter of money. Aysha and China had swag that was on a million. It was in the way that they spoke, commanding every eye in the room each time they opened their mouths. The way that they walked, heads high, shoulders back, hips swaying with precision. Bleu had thought college was the time to discover herself, to mature into a woman and blossom into her true being, but it appeared that everyone here had been there, done that. She was worlds behind. These socialites had been on. She was no longer the prettiest swan in the lake. She was playing in an ocean now and was swimming among sharks. She only hoped that she didn't get eaten alive.

"You are a little plain Jane, mama," Aysha said as she scrunched her nose. "Where's your makeup?"

"I don't wear makeup," she replied.

"What do you mean, you don't wear makeup?" Aysha asked. She shook her head and held up her finger as she sashayed through the bathroom that connected to her suite. She came back with a huge case and opened it. "I've been wearing makeup since eighth grade. Your mama never put you up on game? You don't leave home without putting on your face. A baddie must be beat at all times."

"Yeah, well, my mama wasn't really around like that," Bleu answered.

"Well, thank God for girlfriends then, right?" Aysha replied. "Don't worry. I'll get you together. That homely look might work where you're from, but out here everything is glam. By the time I'm done with your makeup and hair, it won't matter what you're wearing. You'll get in the club with no problem. The way you busting out of them leggings, I don't know a bouncer in town that will turn you away."

Bleu couldn't contain her laughter as she shook her head. She knew the effect her curves had on men, so she knew that Aysha was speaking nothing but truth. She closed her eyes as Aysha went to work.

"You bitches are killing my vibe. We aren't going to get there until after midnight," China said.

"Who ever gets there before that anyway?" Aysha shot

back. "Just sit back and relax. Let me work this magic real quick and then we out."

"That's Herve Leger, not one stain," China fussed as they exited her Mercedes truck and walked down the block toward the nightclub.

"Shut up; the girl ain't gon' ruin your dress," Aysha said as she sashayed, sitting pretty in her stiletto pumps. Bleu could barely keep up. She felt like their project. Nothing she was wearing belonged to her. From the too-big red bottoms on her feet to the dress, even her makeup . . . it was all borrowed. She tried to keep up, but her toes pinched together in the heels, rubbing against the toilet paper that she had stuffed inside to accommodate her small feet. She pulled at the hem of her dress, hoping that the draft she felt didn't indicate that her ass was popping out of it. "Don't fidget. You look great, hon. Just relax and follow our lead."

Bleu followed them as they passed the line and walked right up to the bouncer working the front door. "Hey, Aysha baby. Looking good."

"Thank you, boo. It's me plus two," she said.

"What up, China?" the bouncer greeted her as he lifted the velvet rope that separated the elite from the ordinary. "When you gon' give me some play?"

"When you own the club, not open the doors," China replied. She never seemed to run out of slick talk. In a town where the gift of gab reigned supreme it was an asset. She pecked his cheek with a quick kiss before stepping by.

Bleu gave him a shy smile as she followed China and Aysha in.

Excitement filled Bleu as soon as she was inside. The loud music drowned out all sound as she maneuvered through the thick crowd. The lights were dim, but the massive chandeliers that hung from the ceiling cast a slight glow over the room. Clubs back home had nothing on this. She was used to smoky rooms, ratchet bitches, and door-less bathroom stalls. This club was on an entirely different level and she immediately felt herself loosen up as they made their way to VIP.

"You clean up nice, huh?"

The voice in her ear caused her to blush as she turned to see Bree behind her. "I recognize that dress, shorty, but I can't lie; the fabric is hugging you better."

"You're full of game right now!" Bleu shot back with a smirk as she took a seat in the booth next to her friends.

"He can't help himself," China interrupted, slightly territorial as she leaned into Bree, planting her lips on his. "I let him indulge with the pretty girls as long as I get to play too."

Bleu's eyebrows arose in shock as she stammered a nervous, "Oh-h."

China smiled mischievously as she replied, "Relax, Detroit; you're not our type."

"I'm actually not from Detroit," Bleu responded, but China had switched her focus before she could hear the reply.

These bitches, Bleu thought as she shook her head. It was like they only listened when they wanted to. As soon as they grew bored, they tuned you out. What she pegged as rude was actually power. Aysha and China had a way of making her feel like they ruled the world. Their arrogance made her feel small, but she secretly envied their swag. They were living royal and no peasants were allowed. With borrowed clothes and insecure thoughts, Bleu knew she was a long way from having a place inside their kingdom. She was an outsider, and she couldn't help but wonder what it was like to truly be "in." They were just giving her a pass, being nice, because she was new. It was obvious that she didn't belong.

"Relax," Aysha whispered in her ear. "Here, have a drink." She slipped a champagne flute into Bleu's hand.

"How much is it?" Bleu asked.

Aysha waved her hand dismissively. "You're good. Have you seen yourself, Bleu? You're freaking gooorgeous," she sang playfully. "That ass, those hips, and that gap."

Bleu peered at her with the side eye, slightly offended. *Is she being funny?* She thought.

Aysha sensed Bleu's defensiveness. "I'm serious, Bleu. This is the land of picture-perfect. Every girl who has ever come to L.A. with a flaw that made her different has gotten rich. You don't want to look the same, dress the same, talk the same. Us Cali girls are paper-thin, with veneer smiles that hide a world of pain. You, your kind of pretty pays out here. You stick with us and you won't ever have to pay for another drink in your life. Watch this." She turned and reached for one of the bottles that were chilling on ice.

"Dom," she said. "It's a four-hundred-dollar bottle of champagne." She turned to Bree. "Thanks for the bottle, Bree!" she shouted across the booth.

His lips were occupied by China's kisses, but he still blessed them with a wink as he palmed China's ass with one hand and gave them a thumbs-up with the other.

"He doesn't care?" Bleu asked. "We won't have to pay him back?"

"You're cute, Bleu," Aysha said with a laugh. "Look, all these L.A. niggas are paid. If you ever have to buy your own drink you're doing something wrong. Come on; dance with me."

Before Bleu could protest, Aysha pulled her out on the dance floor. Aysha still held the huge bottle of champagne in her red-manicured hands. Her stiletto nails wrapped around the neck of the bottle as she swayed to the music. Her long, messy hair hung all the way to her ass, swinging behind her to the beat. She tipped the bottle to her lips. It was crazy how she did whatever she wanted whenever she wanted.

I guess this is how the beautiful people live. Who's going to stop her? Bleu thought.

Before she knew it, it was 4:00 a.m. and they were staggering out of the club. Bleu had just danced her ass off for hours, and to her surprise it had been the best night of her life.

9

"You. New girl in the back with her head on the desk."

Bleu would have heard her philosophy instructor's displeasure had she been awake, but she was suffering from the result of all-night partying. Her 8:00 a.m. class was not agreeing with her. While the professor was discussing Socrates and Plato, she had fallen asleep right inside of her book. It wasn't until she felt a tap on the shoulder did she become aware that all eyes were on her.

"Excuse me for interrupting your beauty rest. Ms. . . ."

Bleu cleared her throat and shifted uneasily as she replied, "Montclair. Bleu Montclair. I'm sorry."

"Since you feel confident enough to sleep through my lectures perhaps you can answer this question. Is the just person happier than the unjust person?"

Why did I not just stay in last night? She was mortified to be getting called out in class but took a deep breath and opened her mouth to reply. This was her arena. She might not have fancy clothes or Daddy's trust fund to fall back on, but in the classroom she was equal. "Since philosophy is not science I will give you my opinion on the matter. I believe the unjust person is happiest because they do not care about what others think of their actions. The unjust person lives only for their own gain and therefore has no standards outside of their own to meet. Socrates would argue that the just man is happier, but I disagree."

The professor was baffled as a small smirk crossed her face. She raised one brow and nodded in satisfaction. "Very well. Back to your nap now?" she asked.

"No, I'm up," Bleu responded with a smile, remembering why she was here all of a sudden.

The class ended and Bleu hustled out of the lecture hall, but before she could make her escape, her professor stopped her.

"Ms. Montclair?"

Bleu winced as her feet suddenly stopped moving, causing the student behind her to bump into her. "Sorry," she mumbled as she turned to her instructor. Professor Murial Davis was a hard-nosed, by-the-book instructor who knowingly had the hardest freshman course on campus. She was notorious for her hard tests and no-nonsense demeanor. China had warned Bleu about her, and as she walked over to her podium where the professor stood, marking up papers in front of her, Bleu was slightly intimidated. It felt like she was being called to the principal's office. The last thing she needed was to get on this old woman's bad side. She stood not even five feet five, but her presence was towering. Her red, fluffy hair was pulled back, held in place by a single pearl clip. A pair of cat's-eye reading glasses framed her blue eyes. Bleu stood there uncomfortably as almost a minute went by. She cleared her throat.

"This isn't some elective course, Ms. Montclair. The next time you fall asleep in my class I will kick you out, permanently. I don't think you want to be a sophomore repeating freshman philosophy simply because you couldn't stay awake, eh?"

Bleu shook her head as she gripped her book in front of her chest. "No, ma'am," she responded.

"I've seen your test scores. I've seen your transcripts. You're smart. I want to see that the scholarship you are here on wasn't wasted," she said.

"Yes, ma'am." Bleu felt like a child being chastised.

"Now run along. I have another class coming in. Unless you'd like to sleep through this one too," Professor Davis said.

Bleu shook her head and then practically ran out of the classroom. The lady was like the Wicked Witch of the West and Bleu made a mental note not to get on her bad side.

"Welcome to Picante. You can have a seat anywhere and some-one will be right with you, *mami, si?*"

The busy middle-aged woman spoke the words quickly as she passed Bleu with a round tray balanced on her palm. The smell of the Mexican restaurant was amazing, and immedi-ately Bleu's stomach growled, reminding her that she hadn't eaten. She wasn't there for food, however. She was looking for a job. After partying last night with Aysha and China and sleeping without linens when the night came to a close, Bleu quickly realized that she needed to make some money. Being in L.A. broke was next to impossible, especially when she had the Joneses to keep up with. She had taken a bus twenty minutes away from campus just to find the Mexican joint and she immediately noticed how popular it was. It was nothing special . . . sort of a hole-in-the-wall joint, but based on how thick the crowd was, Bleu knew that the food had to be good. The Spanish music playing in the background and the green and red Christmas lights that festooned the ceiling, despite the fact that it was nowhere near Christmas, gave the place a vibe all its own. She followed the waitress who was busy serving patrons, as she moved as if she had octopus hands. She was all over the place, refilling drinks, delivering food, settling bills for patrons. She seemed to be the only person working besides the chef, who was visible through the small food window as he slid plates of food through.

"Umm, excuse me, is Eddie here?" Bleu asked.

"Eddie's never here, sweetheart, but I could probably get him to come and help out if he knew a hot young thing like you was asking for him," the waitress said. She moved with swiftness behind the counter as Bleu followed her. "Who are you?"

"My name is Bleu," she answered as she practically chased her around the restaurant, trying to hold a conversation as the lady worked.

"Well, Bleu, if you are going to follow me, you might as well carry something," the lady said. "Here." She handed Bleu two plates and then grabbed four and with perfect balance headed to a table. "How do you know Eddie?"

"He was my cabbie the other night. He told me about this place. Said his wife owns it. Are you his wife?" Bleu asked.

"Marta," she said.

"Marta, I don't really need Eddie; I just came to see if you were hiring," Bleu said. "I'm a student and I could really use the money."

Marta stopped walking and wiped her brow with the back of her arm as she exhaled.

"This is family owned and run," Marta replied. "I work the floor and the cash register and my mama and papa cook the food. That's how it has been for ten years."

Bleu looked around at the packed establishment. "It seems like you could use an extra waitress. Or at least a dishwasher? I'll do whatever. I just need a job. I came out to California with nothing. I didn't know how expensive dreams are out here," she said.

The desperation in her eyes shone brightly. It was enough for Marta to sympathize with the young woman.

"Where are you from?" Marta asked.

"Michigan," Bleu responded.

Marta wiped her hands on her apron and then placed one hand on her hip. "Long way from home. How old are you?" she asked.

"Eighteen," Bleu answered.

"Fine," Marta answered in exasperation, giving in. "You can take orders, bus tables, help with dishes and trash. I'll pay you ten dollars an hour and not a penny more. You get to keep your tips."

Bleu's face melted into a smile of relief. It wasn't much, but her pockets would have more than lint in them, and for that she was grateful.

"Thank you," Bleu said.

"You're in school, right?" Marta asked. She was all business. A dark-haired, tan-toned Mexican woman, she wore her aging beauty well. She was fast talking and even faster moving; the crow's-feet around her eyes were every indication of how much sweat she had put into her business. Bleu could tell that the restaurant was Marta's baby.

"Yes, UCLA," Bleu answered.

"You can work nights then," Marta said. "There's an apron and an order pad in the back. You can start now. You don't work the register. I'm the only one who touches it, *comprende?*"

"Yeah, I got you," Bleu answered.

She pulled her hair up into a loose ponytail and retrieved the apron, wrapping it around her waist and sticking the pad inside. The restaurant was crazy busy, and as soon as she hit the floor it seemed as if she were pulled in a million different directions.

The location of the restaurant made it a popular choice with the night crowd. In the middle of West Hollywood, it was an after-hours hot spot when the clubs let out. The fact that it was an authentic Mexican family-owned business only added to its charm. It wasn't much, but it was a job.

Customers flowed in and out of Picante all night until finally at 2:00 a.m. they closed.

Bleu sighed in exhaustion as Marta walked up behind her. "I think you will work out well. I didn't realize how much help

I needed until now. Go home; get some rest. I'll see you to-morrow . . . six o'clock," Marta said.

Bleu nodded and then lifted her head when she heard the bell above the door ring.

"I'm sorry, we're—" She stopped speaking when she looked into his gray eyes. He was average height, but he had a big man's swag. His brown skin was smooth like cocoa, and the outline of his full lips enticed her. His attire was simple . . . designer khaki shorts and a sleeveless Lakers tank with fresh sneaks. A chunky diamond link rested against his shirt, his only accessory. She was speechless. His presence dwarfed her as he stood before her, handsome, suave, yet humble all at once. His arms and neck were covered in tattooed sleeves, rough-ening his pretty image slightly.

"We? I'm sorry, ma, but who are you?" he asked.

Marta came walking out of the back and answered the question for Bleu. "This is Bleu. I hired her."

"I've been telling you to get help around here for two years and out of nowhere you hire someone new?" he asked with a slight smile.

"She was persistent," Marta answered. Marta turned to Bleu and made the introduction. "Bleu, this is my nephew, Iman."

"Nice to meet you, beautiful," he said. There it was. The in-sincerity that came along with fine men like him. She had heard it all from his type. The lines. The flirtation. The whack little come-ons. It was all so predictable, no wonder all the ugly niggas were pulling all the women. They were the only ones with originality.

She pulled her lips together in a fake smile and replied, "You too." Just like that she was uninterested. She turned to Marta. "I'll see you tomorrow, Marta."

"Have a good night, Bleu," she returned.

Bleu walked out into the night air, relieved. All she wanted was a shower and her bed. She smelled like beer and corn chips. She had never worked so hard for $60 in her life. Those were her meager earnings for the night, and as much as she wanted to complain, she didn't. Sixty dollars would buy the linens she needed for her bed and towels for her showers. She had nothing, and anything was better than that. She looked up and down the block. The emptiness reminded her that the buses had stopped running hours before. She was too broke for a cab and she doubted that she would find another cabbie as friendly as Eddie had been. It would be a long walk back to campus. Her tired feet ached in protest as she started down the block. Just as she started off she felt a car pull up alongside her. She kept her head straight as the car crept. *I probably look like a hooker,* she thought as she picked up her pace. "Bleu! Do you need a ride?"

Marta's voice caused her to stop. Iman and Marta sat in the car awaiting her answer. "No, I'm good. Thank you," she said, too proud to accept.

"You can't walk all the way to UCLA, *mami*. Please get in the car. Iman can drop you off after he takes me home," Marta reasoned.

"I don't want to be an inconvenience," Bleu said as she continued to walk slowly. "I promise you, I'm fine. It's a nice night. I'll walk for a little while and then catch a cab the rest of the way."

The car stopped and Iman hopped out as Marta moved into the driver's seat. Bleu stopped walking as he approached and Marta pulled away. "What are you doing? Where is she going?"

"Home. There was no way she was letting me pull off and leave you out here this late at night, and since you weren't getting in the car . . ."

"This is stupid. You don't have to walk me," she answered persistently.

"Are you always this combative?" he asked with a smile.

"Usually," she admitted, causing him to laugh.

"The pretty girls usually are," he answered. She blushed and lowered her head, not sure of how to respond. *That line was a little original; okay, playboy, I see you*, she thought, making herself chuckle slightly.

"What's so funny?" he asked.

She shook her head and waved her hand dismissively. "Nothing," she responded.

He started walking, hands stuffed in his pockets as he strolled with a cool confidence by her side. "How did you get my aunt to hire you? She doesn't trust anyone with her restaurant. She wouldn't even let me bus tables, so how does a complete stranger win her over?"

She shrugged. "I don't know. I guess good people just recognize good people."

"That makes me bad people?" he asked, placing his hand over his heart as if she had wounded him.

She smiled and shook her head. "No, bad people don't get out of a new Mercedes to make sure that a random girl makes it home."

"So, tell me the truth. Why are we really walking?" he asked.

"I don't have money for cab fare. I barely had enough to catch the bus down here. I guess I didn't think of how I would get back," she admitted.

"That's a lot of trouble for a waitressing job at a taco spot," he answered, trying to figure her out.

"Yeah, well, I need the money, so . . ." She shrugged without finishing her statement. She didn't expect a guy like Iman to understand. He smelled like money. "A Richie Rich type like you wouldn't get it. I've got to work for everything I get. No silver spoons over here."

He stopped walking and grabbed her elbow to make her face him. "I understand, ma, and I respect it."

Those gray eyes pulled her in as she stared at his handsome features.

Suddenly he raised his arm, signaling the lone cab that was driving down the street. The driver pulled over and rolled down his window. "I'm not working! Taking it in for the night!"

Iman pulled out a Gotti knot, revealing the cash to the driver, enticing him to stop. It was true what they said; money made the world go round, because just like that the cabdriver was suddenly willing to pick up one last fare. Iman peeled off two hundred-dollar bills. "Get her where she has to go, a'ight?" He leaned down over the car and passed the money through the passenger window. Opening the back door, he held it open for her.

"You didn't have to do that," she said. "What about you?"

"I'll catch the next one," he said. "Where are you going?"

"Rieber Hall," she responded.

He leaned down and looked at the cabbie. "You hear that, my man? UCLA, Rieber Hall."

The man nodded and Bleu walked over to the door, hesitating as she stared him directly in the face. "Thank you," she said.

He gave her a wink, his charm undeniably sexy, as he replied, "Good night, Bleu."

She waved to him just before the cab pulled away, secretly wishing that they had taken that long walk to campus. He was someone she wouldn't mind spending a little extra time with. She wouldn't mind that at all.

Morning came too quickly and classes moved along too slowly as Bleu struggled through the entire day. She hadn't made it home until after 3:00 a.m., and with her first class being an early one it left little room for sleep. She was exhausted and on top of that distracted. She didn't know how she would balance everything out, but she knew that she would have to figure something out. She didn't come from money. There was no support system back in Flint, rooting her on and sending her care packages. All she had was herself, so she would have to play superwoman if she wanted to remain in L.A.

She made the long walk back to her dorm grudgingly, and when she arrived she stopped dead in her tracks. The familiar face immediately caused butterflies to form in her stomach. Iman stood, leaning against his white S-class Mercedes, arms folded across his chest. He wore Ray-Ban shades over his eyes and a fitted cap, but she immediately knew who he was. It was his aura that gave him away. She had never met a man who carried himself quite like Iman. He was a god, living among mortals. He was everything, and she instantly swooned over him in her mind. The giddy feeling that she got when in his presence told her she was feeling him more than a little bit, but she would never admit it aloud.

She frowned in confusion as she approached him slowly.

"What are you doing here?" she asked.

"It's a long walk to work. Let me take you," he replied.

"You came all the way here to take me to work? You didn't—"

"Have to," he finished for her. "I know. Are we going to repeat last night or are you going to get in?"

"I don't have to be there until six. You're kind of early," she said as she grabbed at the straps of her backpack.

"Then let's grab some food or something beforehand," he offered.

"Lunch?" She was unsure of his intentions and of her own, in fact. What was this? Why was he going out of his way to be nice? Where she was from, niggas who were that friendly wanted only one thing in return, and she wasn't paying her debts in pussy.

"It's just a meal, ma. It doesn't take that much thought," he said. Her uncertainty was written on her face, and he was perceptive to her doubts.

She looked down at her clothes. The sweatpants and tank top she had thrown on before rushing to class instantly filled her with embarrassment. He had caught her at her worst.

She pointed back at her dorm. "I just need to change. Do you want to come up?"

Iman gazed up at the building and then at Bleu. He nodded. "A'ight." He tossed his keys to a student who was walking by. The kid snatched them out of midair and looked at Iman, baffled.

"Bro?" the blond surfer boy asked as he held his hand up in confusion.

Iman pulled off a few hundred-dollar bills and placed them in the guy's hand. "Watch my car. I won't be long."

"Bet, bro. Thanks," the guy said in shock as he stuffed the money in his pocket.

Bleu shook her head as Iman came to her side. "You just have nothing better to do with your money, do you?"

"I could think of a few ways to put it to better use, but I don't think you would accept," he said slyly.

She stopped walking as she turned to him, slightly offended. "I'm not for sale."

"Girls like you usually aren't," he said. "I was talking about shopping, ma."

"Handbags and red bottoms won't work on me either," she replied.

"Who said I was trying to work on you?" he asked with a slick grin. The way his eyes creased when he smiled made Bleu's panties moist. He was too damned handsome for his own good, and he knew it. Oddly enough, she liked his cool air of confidence. It wasn't overbearing or obnoxious. He intrigued her with just the right amount of chivalry while still keeping his gangster.

"Now, if you throw dollars at my tuition bill, I'll twerk a little something for you," she joked.

He laughed, surprised. "So there's a sense of humor behind the hard façade?" he asked.

She cut her eyes at him and smiled before sashaying in front of him, headed for her room.

She walked inside. "You can sit on my bed," she said. He looked around at her bare walls, her bare bed. It didn't even seem like she had fully moved in yet. He took a seat as she she grabbed a simple sundress before rushing into the bathroom.

Bleu could have slapped herself when she looked in the mirror. She was just plain. Ponytail, no earrings, bags under her tired eyes. She couldn't believe he had seen her so rough. *The fuck?* she thought in frustration. His interest in her seemed odd, and she couldn't help but think he had a hidden agenda. He could undoubtedly have any girl in L.A. *Maybe he is just being nice. Why would he be interested?* she thought to herself. There was no umph, no glamour, no nothing about her that could possibly keep his attention. *Marta probably sent him here today.* Bleu slipped into the dress, her curves filling it out as they formed a dangerous silhouette. She left her hair in the high ponytail but switched it to a large bun and then added a pair of large hoop earrings. Within minutes she was ready, and when she emerged from the bathroom she held out her arms for inspection.

His smile was all the approval she needed as she followed

him to the door. He held it open for her, and before she walked through it she said, "Keep your eyes off my ass."

He laughed and shook his head. "That mouth real slick. A nigga can't even be nice," he said.

"Where I'm from accepting something nice from someone turns into a debt, and dudes back my way only want that debt paid one way," she replied honestly. She rolled her eyes and began to walk away until she felt his hand pulling her back. He pinned her against her door, standing so close that she became intoxicated by his Ralph Lauren cologne.

"I'm not that guy," he said. She felt the familiar bulge of a pistol that was tucked in a holster at his waistline, and her eyes widened in surprise. She hadn't pegged him as the type. His pretty-boy skater image had her confused, but clearly he had an edge to him and if she walked too closely to that edge, she could see herself falling . . . hard.

"For every guy that says that, there is at least one girl who would say otherwise. I don't trust words. I trust actions," she replied.

He nodded in understanding as he stepped back, giving her space. "I got you. I get it. Now can we go eat?"

Riding shotgun in his luxury whip, she stuck her hand out of the window as the wind blew through her hair.

"Where are we going? We've passed like ten restaurants," she said.

"I'm taking you to the beach. They ain't got those in Michigan, right?" he joked.

She cut her eyes and pursed her lips. "We have beaches," she replied sarcastically.

"Nah, those ain't beaches. If it ain't salt in the water it's just pretend," he replied, his eyes hidden behind his designer shades.

"I don't have that much time. I've got to be at work in an hour," she protested.

"Don't worry about work. You're with me, you're good," he answered.

As soon as he pulled up to the beach she immediately understood why Michigan beaches weren't worthy of the title. It was beautiful. Palm trees and tan sand were the backdrop to the light waves that broke at the shoreline. The pier stretched out into the water for what seemed like miles as happy faces skated and fraternized around her. There was no barbecuing, or project babies running around in soggy diapers. No 40-ounce Cîroc bottles in red coolers or picnic tables. It was just pure beauty all around her. Carefree and happy people, doing California shit. This was the life that she imagined before she moved west.

"Where are we?" she asked.

"Santa Monica Pier," he answered. "I like to come here to think. In the morning, when the sun is coming up and nobody else is around, I come here to plot my next play. The silence speaks volumes."

"I can only imagine how gorgeous the sunrise is here," she whispered.

"Now you don't have to imagine. You're here. You don't have to dream anymore, gorgeous. All you've got to do is live the life you want," he said. He opened his car door and she slowly climbed out.

She kicked out of her sandals as she walked onto the sand. Like a moth to a flame, she was drawn to the water. The smile that melted across her face was infectious, and he was amazed at how something so simple impressed her so much.

"I can't stay here long," she told him. "I just got this job; I don't want to lose it."

"You're pressed over that little money, ma? I told you, you don't have to worry about that," he assured her. "You would have made, what, seventy-five bucks today?" He peeled off ten crisp one-hundred-dollar bills from his knot and held it out for her. "This should buy me some of your time."

"I'm not pressed. I just need my job. I don't know if you noticed, but I don't have a lot. In fact, I don't have shit. So my job may be little to you, but to me Picante is a lifeline that I'm not trying to fuck up. I'm not a charity case. I don't need your money," she said as she stormed off. She turned back to him as she backpedaled away from him. "In fact, this was a mistake." Suddenly he seemed a little showy and his arrogance was turning her off. It was as if he thought he could buy the world. Little did she know, he had enough paper to damn well try.

"Bleu!" he called out to her, but her back was already turned to him as she went walking up the beach alone. "I ain't had to chase a chick ever, ma. You really gone make me start now?" he asked. He shook his head as he let out an exasperated sigh. She was work . . . a challenge, and he didn't know what made him enjoy the chase, but he did. Most women flocked to him, but Bleu . . . Bleu ran from him as if she was afraid to let him catch her. "We ain't doing this again, ma. You're a runner. You probably ran to Cali to get away from something the same way you're running now!" he taunted. "I thought you Detroit chicks were supposed to be tough!"

She stopped walking suddenly and turned toward him and walked up on him with fire dancing in her eyes. If looks could kill . . . "I'm not from Detroit, I'm from Flint, and you don't know shit about tough until you've come from where I'm from. Yeah, I ran. A nigga put a bullet through my chest and I ran as fast as I could, all the way out here. I'm not trying to go back, and right now Picante is all I have. I'm on a partial scholarship. It doesn't cover everything. I need books, clothes . . . basic shit. You get it? Do you understand why I don't have time to play on the beach with you?"

The desperation in her voice tugged at his heartstrings as he looked her in the eyes. She was exquisite. From the top of her head to the bottom of her toes, she was the most beautiful chick he had ever seen. Not because she was perfect, but because she was flawed. In a world where every chick was doing more and more to appear perfect, Bleu symbolized reality. She was a real young woman. Her curves, her face, her hair, her nails. It was all authentic, and what was even more exciting was the fact that the inside seemed to match her outer beauty. There were so many layers to her. She had a depth that he just hadn't encountered before. The shallow shit didn't matter to her, and his money didn't impress her. She was genuine, which was hard to find. In a world full of fakers, she was the realest chick he had found. She was rare and so different from every other pretty skirt in the bunch. She didn't have that L.A. ditz about her. She was born and bred somewhere else, a place where even the sun was afraid to shine, so she dulled her own.

She didn't even know how her presence brightened up a room, but he recognized it instantly, and he wanted that type of light in his life. He wouldn't push, but he had already decided that she would eventually be his.

"Yeah, I get it," he said as he nodded. He knew exactly how to handle her. She was so strong . . . had endured so much that the pressure was now unbearable. He would have to handle her delicately so that she wouldn't break. "Your job is safe. I own Picante. A'ight?"

She looked at him, surprised. "I thought?"

"Eddie and Marta got into some financial trouble with the bank about six months ago. I bought out the loan and came on as a partner. So the business is half-mine. Next time I tell you I got you, I need you to trust it. I won't ever lie to you, ma. You're good with me," he said.

This time, for some reason, she believed him.

"What do you do?" she asked as she looked at him in awe. "I mean you're what? Twenty-four? Twenty-five? You drive nice cars, have money, clothes, a business."

"I'm twenty-six and I make good investments, that's all," he said vaguely.

"Good investments?" she asked suspiciously.

"I'm a genius when it comes to a flip," he said. "I buy low and sell high."

"Smart man," she said while peering at him curiously. She could tell that he was holding back, feeding her only the information that he wanted her to know, but she didn't pry. She liked him. She hadn't meant to—in fact, she really didn't even want to—but his entire personality was appealing. "So what, are we going to have an imaginary picnic on the beach or are you going to actually feed me?" She smiled, genuinely smiled, and it felt so foreign on her face that she reached up to touch her lips. She realized that this had been the first day since getting shot that she had actually felt carefree.

He grabbed her hand and pulled her into him swiftly before tucking her under one shoulder as they walked toward the pier. "You not one of them diet girls, are you?"

"No." She chuckled. "I have to feed my curves." She stuck her tongue between her teeth and squinched her face jokingly, causing him to laugh. He pulled her in, kissing her forehead, sending chills up her spine.

"You're perfect, Bleu," he responded.

"You have no idea how false that is," she replied.

They walked onto the busy pier and each grabbed a burger and fries and on the open patio, taking in the breeze.

"You're definitely not the salad type. You wasn't lying," he cracked on her, causing her mouth to drop open in feigned offense. She threw one of her fries at him as they shared a laugh. She had never had so much fun. They ate and explored together and he allowed her to see the pier through a tourist's eyes, never losing his patience with her. Despite the fact that he had been there a million times, he did it all again without rushing her through the experience. Before they knew it, hours had passed. Time flew when in the presence of good company. As they sat at the top of the Ferris wheel, Bleu looked up at the setting sun.

"Sunrise can't be any more beautiful than this sunset," she whispered, sitting close to him as she stared out into the sky.

"I have a much better view," he replied. She looked up and caught him looking down at her; the way he rubbed her shoulders protectively made her move in closer. It was the most amazing day she had ever had. This connection with him was more than a spark. She could feel it in her bones.

She waited for him to kiss her, she silently screamed for him to make a move, but he didn't. He was trying the gentleman thing, but at that moment she just wanted to feel his lips on hers. She leaned into him, making the first move as her mango-flavored lips covered his. Her panties soaked instantly when his tongue slid into her mouth. Sensual, slow, seductive . . . he grabbed the back of her neck as he pulled her bottom lip into his mouth. She couldn't stop her heart from racing as pure attraction coursed through her veins. He made her feel like the prettiest girl in the world. The way his attention never wavered, the way he had walked all day with his hand on the small of her back, the way he touched her fingers lightly when they walked. It was as if he had to be touching her in some way. It wasn't overly mushy or corny, just a slight reminder that he was at her side. She loved the way he made her feel. They had just met; she could only imagine the way he would treat someone he considered to be his girl. *Wait*, she thought. *There is no way that he doesn't have a girlfriend. A girl like Aysha. Some model chick that I can't compete with.* She pulled away from him, suddenly tensing as the Ferris wheel lowered to let them off.

"What's wrong?" he asked.

"Nothing," she replied as she wrapped her arms around herself.

He could see her overthinking. He could see the stress in her shoulders as she stood and rushed off the ride.

"Bleu!" he shouted. The authority in his voice brought her to a halt.

She turned to him.

"Where are you at, ma? You went inside your head for a split second and came back different. What's the problem?" he asked.

She folded her hands across her chest and said, "Nothing, it's just getting late. I have an early class in the morning. Can we go?"

He closed the space between them and stood dangerously close. It was a habit that she was noticing. He never left her room to feel disconnected, and every time he touched her her breathing grew shallow.

"Don't lie to me, Bleu . . . ever . . . that's the one thing that I can't respect. Whether it's a small lie or a big lie, it's all the same to me. So tell me what's real or don't say nothing," he said.

She sighed and lowered her gaze, looking at her feet. He lifted her chin with his finger. He was so intense, so in control. "Today has been great. Being with you, kissing you. You make me feel like I'm your girl, but I know that I'm not. I won't ever be. You probably have some chick waiting for you to come home right now. A girl who wears makeup and who carries Chanel bags and wears six-inch heels. Some glamorous model or actress or singer probably. I can't compete with girls like that. I'm just a broke girl from the hood barely making it."

"If I wanted that, I could have that," he said. "But I'm here with you. I'm a busy man, Bleu. I don't have too many days open for lounging at the beach. I did this because I wanted to do it with you. I wanted to be a part of that memory for you. You're so different than any of these L.A. women. That's a good thing, ma. You talk about yourself like your dreams aren't worth shit. You're dope, ma, and I'm feeling the shit out of you. That whole broke, college-struggle thing is kind of fly. In a world of airheads and sack chasers, ambition and intellect are attractive. I'm not going to lie to you. My life is complicated. You're young. I don't really want to put these grown-man problems on your plate. If I could, I would erase you from my memory, but the truth is . . . I can't stop thinking about you."

"You have your pick and you choose plain Jane, huh?" she asked, wearing her insecurities on her sleeve.

"Other women can't compete where they don't compare, Bleu."

If he was gaming her, he was doing a good-ass job. He was talking that good talk, blowing up her head, and she was falling for every word. She kissed him and the way his hands wrapped around her behind, pulling him into her, made her moist with curiosity. It wasn't disrespectful or demeaning, the way most dudes made her feel. He was a grown man, and the way he held her made her feel like he was staking his claim. He made her want *it* in the worst way.

It was Iman who pulled back this time. Bleu was a young woman. He had almost ten years on her. She was so fresh-faced, so innocent . . . he almost felt guilty for being attracted to her. He knew that he would have to be extremely delicate with how he played things with her. Girls her age loved the hardest, and before he made her fall for him he had to be sure that he was going to catch her. It wasn't his M.O. to run around breaking hearts, especially not one as lovely as hers. He didn't want to be responsible for the change that came with heartbreak. If they were going to do this, he was going to move slowly, at Bleu's pace, and with extreme caution. So as much as he wanted to take her back to his place and explore the depths between her thighs, he resisted. He was walking a fine line. The media would slay him if they ever caught wind of his pretty little college girl. "You got that early class, right? I better get you back to the dorms," he said.

"What exactly are we doing?" she asked unsurely.

"I don't know, but whatever it is, I don't plan to stop unless you want me to," he replied. He had not been this intrigued with a female in a long time. Even vixens his age hadn't had the power to give him tunnel vision, but Bleu had caught him by surprise. He saw only her. "Do you want me to put the brakes on this, ma? I can't promise you dealing with me and my circumstances will be easy. So if you ever want me to step off, you got to tell me. Cuz when I look at you it's hard for me to walk away . . . it's hard for me to stop. Even though I know I should," he whispered, his voice pained, as if resisting her was torture. He caressed her neck, leaving tingles of pleasure on her skin.

"Why should you?" she asked.

"Because I'm no good for you. There are things that if you knew you—"

"There is nothing that I could find out that would make me

not want to be with you. I don't want you to stop, Iman," she replied, breathing heavy, as if the air had suddenly thickened.

He kissed her, attacking her lips as passion coursed through his body and pushed her against the rails to the pier. She hungrily kissed him back, the heat between them scorching.

"Agh," she moaned as he bit her bottom lip softly. Her head was spinning. "I have to go," she whispered. "Can this . . . Can we just do this slow?"

He placed his forehead against hers and exhaled. "Slow," he confirmed.

Bleu couldn't erase the smile from her face if she tried, and when Iman pulled up in front of her dorm she barely wanted to get out of the car.

"I'll talk to you later, a'ight?" he said. "Don't worry if I don't call soon. I have some business to take care of out of town. I'll check for you when I get back. Cool?" She nodded but suddenly grew insecure. She felt like she was being dumped, and they weren't even close to being anything official yet. He saw the look of uncertainty and he grabbed her hand, kissing the back of it. "I'll tell you what. Whenever I cross your mind, you call me. I'll answer," he assured her.

He leaned over and kissed her again before she exited the car.

He didn't pull off until she was safely inside. When she watched his taillights pull away she put her back against the door, swooning as she looked up to the sky in excitement. The energy between them had her giddy, and she jumped up and down in delight, having a mini dance party by herself.

Another student came walking by and Bleu snapped out of it, slightly embarrassed, and hurried up to her room while laughing at herself. It was like suddenly the pressure of being in Cali had lifted off her. It was then that she realized she had been shouldering the burden alone. For so long she had always had Noah to share her fears with; now that he was gone, she was overwhelmed, but Iman seemed to be the perfect substitute. She took out her student I.D. and swiped it on the door lock to her room.

"Umm, where the hell have you been? It's about time you came home. You need to find something to do with all this shit. It's like Christmas in this bitch," China said as she motioned to Bleu's side of the room.

Bleu frowned in confusion as she spotted the mess that sat on top of her bed. Gift boxes of all sizes took up the space, and she shook her head. "This has got to be a mistake," she said.

"Nope, two guys delivered all that stuff like an hour ago. They asked for you by name," China replied.

Bleu walked over to the gifts and began to open each one. She was baffled, as everything she could ever need for her dorm room rested inside the packages. There were bed linens, towels, notebooks, pencils, even soaps and personal items. A laptop and printer sat on her desk, while a new mini-fridge nestled underneath. Tears came to her eyes when she found the note that was buried under the chaos.

It simply read: *From Iman.*

She knew that he hadn't written it, because he had been with her all day, but he had made the arrangements and footed the bill for her to have everything she could even possibly think of needing. He had set her up for college, and these gifts were more thoughtful than any handbag or pair of shoes ever would be. He had noticed a need and fulfilled it. *Where the hell did this man come from?* she thought, feeling like the luckiest girl in the world.

"Who is it from?" China asked, slightly jealous as she looked at the expensive items. Iman had spared no expense.

"A friend," Bleu answered softly.

"What kind of friend does all this?" China asked skeptically.

Bleu turned to her and replied, "A good one."

10

Noah cringed as he stepped under the cold stream of water, his bare feet hitting the cruddy tile. He wasn't used to five-star anything, but the conditions of the prison were barely up to code. Being locked down made him feel like an animal. The inmates around him had the same distant look that he remembered seeing in impounded dogs. They were forgotten, unwanted, discarded. He knew years of being behind the wall would give him the same lost perspective if he didn't keep his mind together. He kept his back to the faucet so that he could keep his eyes on everything that moved around him. Without commissary he was living on scraps and barely surviving. His hands lathered his muscular body as his eyes stayed trained on the door. He had picked up a few pounds, but it was all muscle. He was his own team, his own army, and he trained his body daily to make sure that he wasn't weak. No amount of muscle in the world could fight off his new enemy, however. Noah's heartbeat rapidly increased as his internal radar sounded off when he saw the tough guy from the cafeteria walk through the door. Had he walked in alone, Noah wouldn't have been bothered, but with a gang of niggas behind him, Noah knew what time it was. The way that the rest of the inmates began to clear out and how the guard slyly eased his way out, Noah knew it was a setup. COs were as grimy as the inmates. His protection was in his own hands, and as he stepped out of the shower he felt naked for more than the obvious reasons. They had caught him slipping, and when he saw the sharpened end of a toothbrush slip from under the tan sleeve of the man he had beaten, he knew that this was an uneven match.

"Thought I wasn't gon' come back after that shit you pulled in the mess?" the inmate growled. "Bitch-ass nigga."

Again, dude was about talk. Unlike most, Noah didn't need to grandstand. He wasn't about the wordplay. When a nigga came at him talking reckless, he reacted. Usually the .45 he kept on his hip was enough to back any nigga down, but in here all Noah had was his one and two. He was grateful for all those project fights he had gotten into coming up. Growing up in the heart of Black Wall Street had hardened him to the point where he didn't even think twice. When somebody started yapping at him with the loud talk, he got it popping. Naked and all, Noah swung first.

He caught the dude's jaw with a clean two-piece and busted his nose wide open with a following jab. Noah could have easily taken this fight had it not been for the mob of dudes who grabbed him up. He bucked and fought against them, but they had the numbers on their side. They held him, one on each arm, as the dude rushed him. It only took a second for Noah to see the glint of the homemade shank, and his eyes widened.

Before his opponent made his move Noah gritted his teeth, preparing himself for the pain. He stared the guy directly in the eye and said, "Couldn't handle these hands, so you got to knife me up?" He taunted, "Better make sure you kill me, pussy."

The feeling of his flesh being punctured repeatedly was blinding as he saw flashes of white before his eyes. Each stab ripped through him. Had it not been for the men at his sides, he would have fallen to his knees in distress. He felt blood pouring out of him. They were trying to leave him leaking facedown in the showers. Sadly, he didn't fear it. Coming where he came from, making it to eighteen was a luxury anyway. His entire life didn't flash before his eyes; only Bleu's face appeared. There was something to be said about the last person you thought of when in the face of death. It was Bleu. It had always been about her.

"Hmm-hmm!"

The sound of someone interrupting caused the men to release him. Like children caught in the act they all turned to find three inmates standing at the doorway.

"You're done," one of them said as he walked up, breaking up the group.

"This don't concern you," the dude said.

"This concerns me because Khadafi says it concerns me."

The response broke the entire mob up as Noah staggered to his feet, clutching his midsection as blood seeped through his fingers. He couldn't even stand as he dropped to one knee while holding his bloody fingers in front of his face. So much blood. So much pain. He couldn't focus. The mob of men stood down, and it was as if the group of attackers had seen a ghost as they immediately deaded the beef. Just the mention of Khadafi Langston brought the bitch out of them, and as they conceded defeat the loudmouthed one spoke up. "You a lucky mu'fucka." He sneered. Noah met his death stare until he had left the bathroom.

Noah was weak and growing woozy as he stumbled slightly. His father's name had saved him. A dead man Noah had never gotten the chance to meet had saved him. How? Why did the name of a ghost carry so much weight? He had a hundred questions, but before he could open his mouth to ask even one, the entire room went black.

11

Her stinging, dry eyes told Bleu that it was a wrap. She had been staring at the same sentence for at least ten minutes, trying to force herself to read the words on the page before her. The library was the last place she wanted to be on a Friday night, but the hair tie on the outside of her dorm room door let her know that China had company. It was their code for, *I'm getting some dick, so don't bring your ass in here,* and Bleu respected it. She could keep herself busy. It had been three hours, and as she gathered up her books, she thought, *Fuck this. If she ain't done, she's about to be. The library is practically closing.* Bleu packed it up and made the long trek back to her dorm. The campus was still, which was odd for a Friday night, but no one seemed to be out. No fraternity boys staggering back to their rooms, no late-night nerds coming back from study-ing, it was just her and the night sky. In a city so big, on a campus so vast, she felt small. It was like UCLA had dwarfed her, turning her into this chick with insecurities and doubts. She was busting her ass working every day after her classes just to make a few ends meet. Her meal plan didn't cover the weekends, so she skipped meals or snuck food at Picante just to stop the growl in her stomach. On top of that, she just didn't fit in here. Aysha and China were cool—in fact, they had all become quite friendly—but she couldn't keep up with them. Their lifestyle, their tastes, their fashions, it was all just too expensive. They were glamour girls without a care in the world, but Bleu was burdened heavily. She was living the struggle life in L.A. and she couldn't help but wonder if she had made the right choice by coming to the West Coast at all. Perhaps the thug life back home was easier than the luxe life that she couldn't afford.

By the time she made it to her building she was more than tired. *I just want my bed,* she thought, but when she saw the hair tie still hanging from the doorknob, she sighed. *Fuck that. I'm not leaving. I'm about to bust up their little groove,* she thought as she used her key to open the door. She barged into the room.

"China, my bad, but this hair tie been on the door for hours and I'm—" She stopped midsentence and her eyes widened in shock when she saw what was laid out on China's bed.

"What the fuck? I thought you said she wasn't coming back anytime soon," Bree said.

"What are y'all into?" Bleu asked. "That's coke and a lot of it. That's at least fifteen bricks," she said, astonished. What the hell had she just walked in on? She wasn't green. She had lived around hustlers all her life, but she had never seen weight before. All the niggas she knew were moving ounces. If she had come across bricks back home, she would have come up on a lick. She knew niggas who would take that weight at the drop of a dime, but out here she was purely shocked. She didn't know how to react.

"Don't ask no questions. You pretend like you didn't see this and we're all good," Bree stated. He bent over the bed and began to stuff the packages into a large duffel bag before snatching it up and slinging it onto his shoulder. His aggravation was written all over his face. He stormed toward the door that she was blocking and she stepped out of his way. He stopped directly in front of her and said, "Are we cool here, Bleu?"

Silently she wondered what if she said no? The way he was ice grilling her told her that he was willing to do whatever to ensure her confidence.

"Yeah, yeah, we're good. I won't say shit," she said.

Bree reached into his jacket and pulled out a wad of rubber-banded money. He tossed it to her. "That should buy your silence. Just mind your business, Detroit. This don't have anything to do with you, a'ight?" he challenged her.

She nodded as he stormed out. She didn't realize that she had been holding her breath until she exhaled loudly as the door slammed. She had never been afraid of Bree before, but the look in his eyes intimidated her. Suddenly he wasn't so friendly. Now that she knew a secret of this magnitude she had become a threat, and she knew it.

"What the fuck, Bleu? You just barge in here?" China said as she threw up her hands.

"Bitch, I thought you were in here getting your back blown

out and you're in here doing . . . Wait . . . what was that? What were you doing?" Bleu asked.

"Something's got to finance the lifestyle," China returned as she pulled up her hair and peeled herself out of her clothes, preparing for bed.

"I thought your parents gave you money?" Bleu asked. "You said you're from Beverly Hills."

"Please," China scoffed. "My parents cut me off after my first stint in rehab. Everything you see I pay for. My tuition, my whip, clothes, all that—"

"How? You're selling coke?" Bleu asked in disbelief. Where she came from, the dope dealers weren't beauty queens. They were killers, and China didn't fit the mold.

"Hell no," China responded. "Look, I just move the product from Mexico to L.A. As long as I get it across the border I get paid. Twenty thousand dollars a trip."

Bleu's heart skipped a beat at the sound of that much cash. It was more than she had ever seen. "What?"

"It's good money. I put Aysha on when school first started. I've been down with Bree a bit longer, though," China finished.

Bleu was silent with disbelief. Here she thought these girls were shallow and spoiled when they were really like everyone else she knew, about their hustle. Money made the world go round and apparently there were no limits on how to get it. Even spoiled little rich girls had one foot in the game.

"What if you get caught?" Bleu asked. "Do you know what type of time they will throw at you if something goes wrong?"

"It never goes wrong. It's foolproof," China replied. She

frowned and then looked at Bleu seriously. "Look at you, Bleu. You work your ass off for peanuts. I see you trying to keep up, but that little taco joint isn't going to upgrade you high enough to play with the big boys." She walked with haste over to her closet. "Look at this stuff. Cavalli, Gucci, Fendi, Prada, Chanel . . . it's all here. I bought it. I've stacked a hundred grand in less than six months. This flip is real, Bleu, and if I were you, instead of turning my nose up at it, I'd be trying to get down. Bree is always looking for a pretty face to add to the crew. If you want me to, I'll bring you in. That's how Aysha got down. She ain't big-time yet. Those modeling checks are chump change compared to what she's making with me. Think about it. I mean, what do you have to lose?"

Bleu's mind was blown as she sat on the edge of her bed. Before China disappeared into the bathroom she added, "And next time knock."

Bleu leaned over the bar, her face buried in her textbook, but she could barely focus. Picante was abuzz with patrons, but she was clearly distracted. Every chance she got, she tried to read a paragraph of her work. She was juggling so many things that she was just waiting to drop the ball on one of them.

"Excuse me?" Marta interrupted. "You have customers waiting for you, Bleu. Table four needs their bill, and there are more people waiting to be seated."

Bleu looked up and noticed her tables were in chaos. "Sorry, I have a test. I was just trying to multi-task."

Marta sighed and said, "I tell you what. When we slow up, I'll give you an extra half hour for your break. There's a small studio apartment above the restaurant. You can go up there where it's quiet but stay focused. While you're on the clock I need you to do your job. I need your help."

Bleu nodded and closed her pen inside her book, marking her spot. As soon as she hit the floor she saw Iman walking smoothly through the door with a man trailing behind him. She smiled as he walked up on her, invading her space like he owned it. It was a habit of his that she liked. He was always in control. He didn't ask for what he wanted; he simply took it. Marta looked at the pair curiously and wagged her finger in chastisement. She could see the familiar look in Bleu's eyes. Iman had worked his magic on Marta's new waitress. Bleu didn't know it yet, but she would eventually worship the ground that Iman walked on. She had no wins against his swagger. Charming yet gangster, rich but with the humility of a pauper, dangerous, yet he had the ability to keep the ones he loved safe. Not to mention the mix of his Hispanic and black heritage; he had a face that looked as if it had been chiseled by Michelangelo himself. Bleu's heart didn't stand a chance. Marta had seen Iman break many hearts over the years. No woman could seem to keep him interested for long, and they always walked away having invested too much in a young king who valued them too little. Marta didn't have time to nurse the hurt feelings of one of her employees, but she knew that she couldn't stop the chemistry between them. What Iman wanted . . .

"No, no, no . . . she's at work and I need her here. You see this crowd, *mijo*?" Marta asked Iman. "You can sweep her off her feet after her shift, lover boy. What are you doing anyway?

You're too interested. You know your situation. Out of all the girls in the world, you have to choose her. She's a good girl. School girl. She doesn't have time for your type of trouble, Iman," Marta fussed. "All of a sudden you choose my favorite waitress to distract. Aye . . . *papi!*"

Bleu laughed as she blushed. "You heard her. She's the boss," Bleu said. "I get off at two."

"You get off now," Iman said. He pointed to the bulky guy behind him. "My sweet *tía*, you know Juice," he said, using the Spanish word for "aunt." Whenever he called her *tía* she couldn't resist. It reminded Marta of when he was a boy, cling-ing to her leg. Iman had a way of wrapping the ladies in his life around his finger and she was no exception. "He'll work her shift."

Marta sighed as she pointed a finger at Bleu's substitute. "Juicy, you better not drop one plate," she said, giving him a hard time.

"Is this okay?" Bleu asked seriously.

Marta nodded and gave Bleu a gentle smile. "Of course. My nephew likes you. I haven't seen him smile in a long time. He is so serious all the time. I like seeing him happy," she said. "Go ahead. You kids have fun. I'm going to put Juicy here to work."

Iman kissed Marta's cheek in appreciation. "You're still my favorite girl in the world, old lady," Iman said.

She held up a fist and shook it as she scolded him playfully. "I'm going to show you old." She pulled him in for a hug and then cupped his face between both her hands. She looked at him seriously and whispered, "Don't you start nothing with that girl that you can't finish."

"I never would," he replied. He turned and guided Bleu out of the restaurant, his hand placed comfortably on the small of her back.

Bleu looked at Iman. There was nothing that she would rather do than get to know him better, but the homework and notes that she had on her plate couldn't be ignored either. If Marta was going to give Bleu the night off, she wanted to use her time wisely. She let him lead her out of the restaurant, away from the noise, but she stopped walking as soon as they were outside.

"Hey, I know you probably have other things in mind, but I don't get a lot of free time these days. Between Picante and school, I can barely find time to eat. I have so much homework to catch up on. Would you mind if we just stayed in? You could come back to my dorm. It's actually kind of nice now. Somebody upgraded it by buying me everything I needed," she said with a huge smile.

"Somebody likes you, huh?" he replied coyly as he leaned against a white Phantom that sat curbside, illegally parked. It seemed Iman followed no laws but his own. He lived by his own set of rules and the world seemed to bend to his influence.

"I guess so," she answered as she walked up on him, standing between his legs as he wrapped his hands around her waist.

"Seriously. Thank you," she said. "But you didn't have to do that. You shouldn't have, actually. I don't like owing people."

"The fact that you wouldn't have accepted my help made me want to do it more. Don't worry about it. I'm not one of the tab-keeping type. It's nothing, ma."

He turned and opened the passenger door. "So you want to stay in and study?"

"I know, sounds boring, right?" she said.

"Nah, sounds interesting. You can study the books, and I can study you. That face, your eyes, your lips," he said as he took hold of her chin and pulled her into him.

She smiled before stepping into his car. It was going to be an interesting night.

"This is where you live?" she asked as she stepped out of the car and looked up at the huge gated estate in front of her. It was beautiful and sat on a large manicured lawn and a circular drive. The fountain that lit up the front yard looked like it belonged in front of a museum instead of someone's home.

"I usually stay at my condo in the city, but when I want seclusion and peace of mind this is where I come," he said as he hit a button inside his car, causing the gate to open.

He pulled into the driveway and parked directly in front of the front door before getting out to open her door.

She grabbed his hand as he escorted her into the house. "Buying low and selling high is working for you, huh?" she mumbled as she looked around at the marble floors and expensive furnishings. It was a castle, hidden in the hills of Calabasas, and for the first time she realized she was messing with a king. Iman's status was major, and she was beginning to wonder exactly what it was that this man did.

He smirked as he grabbed a remote control off the wall. With the click of a button he turned up the lights.

"Wow," was all she could say as she took it all in. "It's kind of big for one person, isn't it?" she asked.

"I suppose," he replied nonchalantly. "You can set up wherever you like. I won't interrupt you."

"I find that hard to believe. Everything about you is one big distraction, Iman," she said.

She walked up on him and rested her head on his chest as they embraced.

"Nah, can't have that," he said coolly. "Any nigga that distracts you from your goals is a dream killer . . . remember that. So you sit here and finish your work. That's the part about you that I like most. Can't lose your ambition hanging out with scrubs like me," he said as he gave her a wink.

Iman reached down and grabbed her bag off of the floor, then extended his arm to her. She took it, rolling her eyes as she walked over to the white leather couch.

He gave her space, and before she knew it she was in her zone. Books fed her mind. It didn't matter the type or the subject matter. Studying, reading, writing, adding, subtracting, logic, it all fed her insatiable brain. She wasn't dumb . . . she knew that she came from the bottom and that the people born at the top had an advantage over her. But the classroom was a level playing field. It didn't take money to be smart. Intelligence couldn't be bought, and in that arena she was more than capable. Physical features faded and were hard to change. If you were ugly, you stayed ugly, but if there was something that her mind lacked, she could change that. She could learn more, acquire new skills. As she dug into her books she felt him watching her, admiring her, but she was on her level. Once she focused in on something it was hard to distract her. Hours passed and she didn't stop until the pages in front of her became a blur. Finally she closed her book and looked around, but Iman was nowhere in sight.

She heard the clanging of pots and pans as the smell of something divine invaded her senses. She followed the clues to the kitchen to find a man in a chef's hat working busily over the stove.

"Oh," she said as she jumped slightly. "I'm sorry. I didn't know anyone else was here."

"You're perfectly fine. You can have a seat in the dining room. I'll bring dinner right out," he said, his eyes never leaving the stove. She turned and walked curiously into the dining room, where Iman stood, popping the top off a bottle of champagne.

"I thought you would get hungry, so I called over my chef. I'm not too good in the kitchen," he said sheepishly as he ran his hands over his wavy hair. She walked over to the table completely impressed. This wasn't the game of a young man. Dudes her age thought wining and dining meant Applebee's and a movie. Iman was pulling out all the stops to sweep her off her feet. Little did she know, everything Iman did was on a large scale. He didn't small-ball. Whether she was present or not, he lived on this level daily.

"Yeah, I am starving, but a pizza would have been fine," she replied with a smile.

"It's the simple shit about you that makes me want to shower you with complexity. If I got it I spend it, and when I find someone to spend it on, I don't take shortcuts. So, nah, pizza is a no-go," he said.

He took his seat at the head of the table; then Iman nodded at her. "Come here," he instructed her. She walked to him slowly until she stood beside him. He pulled her into his lap and she laughed.

"The other end of the table is too far. I'm addicted to you like shit, ma," he admitted.

"Good," she answered. "I just can't help but wonder how many other chicks have gotten this five-star treatment."

"None," he replied.

She looked at him skeptically, cocking her head and pursing her lips. He was older than her, more experienced. She knew that there had to be someone. With men like him it was always a competition.

"If there was somebody else in the picture, I would tell you. I'm not into making fools out of people," he said.

She straddled him and wrapped her arms around his neck as she kissed him slowly, her soft lips pulling his full ones into her mouth as her tongue tasted the champagne on his tongue. She had never felt this way before. The closest she had come to love was the connection she felt with Noah, but even that couldn't compare to the mixture of lust, infatuation, and wanting she felt for this man. Her womanhood clenched as he gripped her ass with one hand while fisting her hair with the other. He handled her with expertise as he alternated between kissing her lips gently and tasting her tongue. Bleu's body was on fire and she could feel the hardness building, growing, under her as she moved her hips slowly . . . sensually. Their clothes were the only barriers stopping the flow, and as if he couldn't take it anymore, Iman lifted her onto the table in front of them and spread her legs wide. The fabric of her panties held up no fight as he ripped them off of her, exposing her shaven treasure.

She gasped when he put his mouth on it. Inexperienced in this level of intimacy, she immediately became insecure. She had never dealt with anyone his age. The furthest she had taken sex was to let a high school boyfriend play with her clit. They had never taken things to the next level, and by the time he had attempted to, she had thought he was too lame to even deserve it. She was untouched, unspoiled, and ashamed that at eighteen she was still hadn't chosen to give herself to a man. She wasn't a virgin, Larry had taken her innocence long ago, but she had never given the gift of her womanhood to any other. After living with the man who had molested her, she had grown confused about so many things. She had blamed herself for years for what had happened to her, which made it hard for her to ever allow any random boy to make a move. She was prudish by hood standards. Around her way, chicks got their cherries popped early . . . fifteen at the latest, and high school boys definitely weren't about that head life. Suddenly she realized the age gap between her and Iman. She couldn't even enjoy the magic that he was performing because she was too busy wondering if it was what he was used to.

Does it taste okay? Is it funky? Should I have shaved it bald? Then she thought of her body, the hideous scar that was still healing on her abdomen. She hoped he didn't think she was childish. She was in her mental, and the fact that her legs weren't putty in his hands gave her away. Her body was tense. He stopped, and as soon as the tickle on her clit went away, she wanted him to start all over again. He stood to his feet and looked down at her, cupping her face.

"What's wrong?" he asked.

"I'm not like other girls you've been with," she said, giving him a glimpse of her insecurities.

"And I love that," he responded.

She slowly let the strings of her dress down as she peeled down the top, exposing her body from the waist up. The scar was jagged and had bubbled slightly from where the doctors had sewn her up. It ran from her pelvic bone all the way up to the middle of her chest. He bent over and she placed her hands on his wavy hair as he planted a gentle kiss on the most hideous part of her.

"Who did this to you?" he asked. Anger flooded him, his gray eyes darkening as he stared at her.

"I got caught up in a robbery," she admitted. "I don't know who they were, but I'll never forget their faces. I still have nightmares about that day." She shivered slightly as she remembered the searing torture she had felt that day. Iman noticed and he pulled her close.

"You know you're safe here, right? In L.A., I mean. You're thousands of miles away from the people that hurt you and not a nigga in this city will touch a hair on your head if I put the word out. All you've got to do is give me a reason to put that word out, ma. Say you're mine. Say you belong to me. I protect what's mine," Iman whispered.

"I don't know if you deserve me just yet," she flirted, with a smile. She began to slip her arms back into the spaghetti straps of the dress, but Iman only thwarted her plans to dress by pulling them back down.

"It's ugly," she whispered, referring to the scar.

"I don't think anything belonging to you could be ugly, ma," he said.

His lips covered hers and the fountain that gushed between her thighs told her she wanted him just as much as he wanted her. He was so good at this, however, that it intimidated her. It was as if he had read the instruction manual to her body and he knew what buttons to press to cause her the most pleasure.

She was nervous as she wondered if her amateur ways could allow her to reciprocate. She was insecure and positive that she was an unfit contender in the fight for his attention. *He's going to fuck me and then realize that I'm not even on his level,* she thought. She was out of her league and she knew it. He was nothing like the dudes around her way, the ones she ran circles around and dismissed without a second thought. He was a boss. He was a man. He would break her heart with rejection once he realized they were worlds apart.

"I've never done this before, not willingly," she finally admitted, barely saying the words loud enough for him to hear.

Girls her age wished they had more experience, but real women knew that men cherished a woman with very little. Finding a woman with none at all was like hitting the lottery. She was uncharted territory and not only did he want to explore her body, but he had an interest in her mind and heart as well. Her words rang in his ears. *Not willingly?* he thought.

He pulled back because he knew what the statement implied. She was wounded, scarred, in more ways than one.

"I'm sorry, ma; we can stop," he said, his voice deep, guttural, as if it would be the hardest thing he had ever done.

"Please don't," she replied. "Just go slow."

He looked her in the eyes, wanting to take things further. Their sexual chemistry was on 10 and his body urged him to conquer her, but the innocent look in her eyes caused him to stop. He kissed her lips softly.

"I'm not rushing. You can only experience your first time once. I want you to be certain that you want to share that with me."

The heat that was building between her legs told her that she was sure. This felt like love. Or was it lust? She didn't know, and because of that she nodded her head in agreement. "Thank you for being patient with me," she whispered.

"Thank you for giving me something to be patient about," he replied. "You're a gem, youngin'," he said.

The chef came in with their food, interrupting their moment, and Bleu climbed down off the table, slightly embarrassed.

"I'm going to wash my hands for dinner. The bathroom?" she asked as she cleared her throat, her face burning with shame.

The chef chuckled slightly as she headed out. "That way, sweetheart. Second door on the left, past the stairway," the man instructed.

Iman hid his smile behind his hand as he rubbed his chin in amusement. Everything about Bleu was endearing.

When she was out of the room the chef said, "Be careful with that one. She's a good girl."

"Indeed she is," Iman responded as he turned and took a seat at the table.

Bleu sighed in relief once she was tucked inside the safety of the bathroom. She was so hot and bothered. A part of her wanted to tell Iman to finish what he had started. He had certainly turned on her body's faucet, causing her waters to flow and her love button to plead for attention. She looked underneath the sink and found a stack of washcloths. She quickly took a birdbath, refreshing herself before hurrying back to the dinner table.

"You good?" Iman asked.

She nodded. He motioned for her and she crossed the room to go to his side.

"Are you mad? I don't want you to think I'm playing games," she said.

"I'm not a clown, Bleu. I'm a patient man. When it's right it will jump off. I'm not applying no pressure to you over nothing petty. That's your temple. I respect that you respect it. It makes me respect you."

"I didn't want to say no, but—"

He placed a finger over her lips to silence her. "You're young, ma, so you feel like you need to justify yourself. When you tell a nigga no, nothing has to come after that. Learn to say no without explaining yourself. That's that grown-woman shit. You're out here by yourself, no family, no nothing. You'll be better off once you realize that you don't owe anybody shit, including me."

He pulled out her chair for her and she took a seat, feeling empowered by the game he had just given her.

They sat like king and queen at opposite ends of the table as they dined on a five-course meal. They laughed with each other as if they had been acquaintances forever, and it was through conversation that they realized how kindred their spirits were. Iman was protective and serious, brooding in a way that was extremely intriguing. It took a lot for him to lower his guard and allow himself to be vulnerable with a woman, but Bleu was stripping him of his defenses. He was feeling the shit out of her, and his willingness to let her in terrified him. Who was this young chick from the Midwest who was putting a claim on him without even trying?

She stood and picked up her plate before rounding the table to collect his.

"What are you doing? The chef can take care of that," Iman said. He was clearly spoiled by luxury.

She scoffed as she frowned. "I think I can handle the cleanup. I've washed a dish or two in my lifetime. Where I'm from we don't have personal chefs and housekeepers," she said with a laugh.

She waltzed into the kitchen and placed the dirty dishes in the sink. The chef was still moving around the space, and he paused when he noticed her begin to work.

"I've got that," he said.

"No, please let me. The food was great. I think you've earned the night off," she said. "What's your name?" she asked.

The dark-skinned man was tall, with a big belly and a shiny bald head. His friendly face was illuminated with a smile because in all of his years of cooking he had never had a client do the dishes behind him.

"Leslie," he replied. "Iman here calls me Big Les."

Iman nodded as he stood in the doorframe watching Bleu's and Les's interaction.

"Well, Big Les, I think I can wash a dish or two. I think you've earned the night off, right, Iman?" She turned to him.

Iman nodded in confirmation. "You heard her, man," he replied.

Big Les chuckled and replied, "I guess there's a new queen in the castle." He gave Bleu a wink before heading out.

There was just something about a woman taking care of his home that Iman found sexy. The view from behind Bleu was breathtaking. The way her hips spread out beneath her thin waist teased him, but he resisted his need to pursue her. When she was ready she would come to him, but he had to admit it would be a struggle. Bleu didn't even realize the power she had over him, and for that Iman was grateful. Bleu was the type of girl that was impossible to resist.

It wasn't until the sun peeked through the blinds that Bleu even realized that she had spent the night. After dinner Iman had given her the tour of his home, and they had eventually settled into his comfortable king-size bed. They had fallen asleep like only new lovers could, wrapped in each other's arms. It wasn't until things got old did a nigga push you to the other side of the bed for their own comfort. She had lain comfortably, head on his chest, all night. He had been a perfect gentleman and not once had he let his hands slip. It was more intimate than any night of passion. They had connected emotionally, mentally . . . and she had loved every minute of it. She eased her way out and reached for her cell that sat atop the nightstand. The numbers 12:32 slapped her in the face, causing her to panic.

"Oh my God, oh my God!" she whispered as she covered her face with her hands. Her distress awakened Iman, who pulled her back down with him.

"I didn't mean to stay the night," she revealed.

"If it was up to me, you'd stay every night," he replied as he kissed the top of her head without opening his eyes.

She smiled at the thought. To be young and in love was amazing. With young emotions came the thought of forever. Despite how unrealistic it actually was, she felt like she wanted to feel like this until the end of time. Iman made her feel . . . beautiful? Perhaps irresistible? Or was it irreplaceable? She didn't even know what this feeling was. It was so unfamiliar that it almost intimidated her. All she knew was that it felt good and she didn't want it to end.

"I can take you back to campus so you can handle your business," he offered.

"I don't want to leave, but I've got to," she said.

Iman climbed out of the bed, his washboard abs tightening with his every movement as he stretched his arms overhead. "Let me take a shower and I'll drive you back," he said.

She nodded as she watched him head toward the master bathroom. The sound of his phone vibrating on the wooden nightstand grabbed her attention as she crawled across the bed.

She picked it up and a sickening feeling consumed her as she looked at the picture flashing on the screen. One of the beautiful people was calling him. One of those California model chicks . . . the type that made Bleu feel so ordinary. Tan was her name and it felt like someone had knocked the air out of her lungs. She carefully placed the phone back where she had gotten it. Her kind of pretty wouldn't cut it in L.A. and it definitely wouldn't keep a man like Iman interested for long.

I'm not even fucking. This virgin shit is going to get old quick, especially if hoes like this bitch are throwing it at him left and right, Bleu thought. She wasn't fancy and there wasn't anything about her that said expensive or exclusive. In fact, the words "Bleu" and "high-end" didn't even belong in the same sentence. She didn't call purses "bags" or even own one worth mentioning. She was an ordinary girl, and in the race to win the heart of an extraordinary man ordinary didn't win.

It was in that moment that she decided that it was time to up her game. China had given her an open invitation to get down with her hustle, and Bleu did need to make some real money. At first she had dismissed it, but now she was reconsidering. She couldn't keep living the struggle life out here, not when there was money on the table practically waiting to be picked up. Picante couldn't finance the lifestyle that she desperately wanted to be a part of. She was about to dive headfirst into a deadly game, just so that she could afford the luxe life.

12

"Blake Jackson?" Bleu questioned as she looked down at her fake I.D. "I don't even know what a real passport looks like. How do I know this even looks like the real thing?"

Bleu fanned herself as she felt her temperature rise. Her nerves were all over the place. She had a million reasons to back out of this. Her gut was telling her that she was headed toward trouble, but it was just like a young girl . . . she knew all the reasons why this was wrong, but still she was going to go through with it. Knowing that the fire was hot wasn't reason enough not to touch it; she had to feel the burn . . . learn the lesson the hard way.

"You have got to calm down. You acting hot," China said as she drove the rental car down the highway. "We're headed to San Diego; we'll cross over into Tijuana there. You don't even have to be nervous yet. The hard part is getting the bricks back. Going there is just like any other drive."

Aysha sat up from the backseat and added, "Just consider this a vacation. We'll get a little sun, meet a couple boys, have a few drinks. On the way back we pack something extra in the suitcase and forget that it's there. No big deal."

"No big deal," Bleu confirmed, but she was unconvinced as she tried to relax. She wasn't beat for this. What was the point of escaping the hood if she was going to put herself in hood situations anyway? She could have stayed in Flint; at least there she would have been closer to Noah. Her thoughts wandered as she thought of him and suddenly her breathing calmed. He had not written her back and a part of her felt slighted. *I don't even know if he got the letter,* she thought. *He couldn't have. He would reach out to me. I hope he's okay.* Hours passed and Bleu was silent as Noah consumed her thoughts. She missed him. Like lungs needed air, like a flower needed the sun, she needed him. She didn't realize how much she loved him until she had been forced to let him go. Now she was just going through the motions. Without him, she felt like a piece of herself was missing. Noah was locked up and with him so was her heart. He was her very best friend . . . the one person in the world who understood her.

"Hello? You in there?" China called as she waved her hand in front of Bleu's face.

She snapped out of her thoughts and pushed China's hand aside. "Yeah, I'm here," Bleu answered in irritation.

"Crossing into Mexico isn't the problem," China schooled her. "Just keep it cool and hand me your passports."

"What if they can tell it's a fake?" Bleu asked, worried.

Aysha placed her passport on the center console. "They won't. This isn't our first time at the rodeo, Bleu. Stop tripping. You're making me nervous, damn," she said.

Within fifteen minutes and after a routine check at the border they were passing into Tijuana. "I told you," China said. "Now it's time for the fun part."

"The fun part?" Bleu questioned.

"The beach," Aysha concluded.

"What? Shouldn't we get the stuff and head back?" Bleu asked. She was truly green to the game and it was showing. "I have to work tonight and I have a class tomorrow morning."

"Well, that's too bad then. Every time we come here we stay three days," China informed her.

"I can't stay for three days! I have classes," Bleu protested. Ditching would throw her all the way off track. "Why wouldn't y'all tell me we would be gone long!"

"Well, we can't cross the border too frequently. That will throw red flags. Nobody comes to Tijuana and then leaves in a few hours. So consider it a vacation," China schooled her. "This is an entirely different ball game, Bleu. That good-girl shit has to go. Fuck class. We're playing with the big boys and they'll eat you alive, so get your shit together and let's make this money."

The first thing that Bleu heard when she stepped out of the car was the sound of the gentle waves as they broke on the shoreline. As she looked out onto the water the view took her breath away. This was it. This was what she had always thought paradise looked like. While the rest of Tijuana was a myriad of outdoor markets and run-down infrastructure, the beach was the complete opposite. The shoreline was beautiful. The golden sand met the turquoise water and painted a perfect picture before her. It was a little piece of heaven on earth, and the hundreds of people who were out in the water looked like they were having the time of their lives.

Aysha immediately peeled off her clothes and tossed them in the trunk. Her long lean body was the perfect canvas for the Burberry two-piece she wore. It was more of a string than anything, and she was flawless in it.

"I didn't bring a suit," Bleu said.

Aysha shrugged as she released the ties on her top, allowing it to fall into the sand. She shrugged as she revealed her perky breasts. "So don't wear one," she said with a carefree laugh as she immediately headed for the water. Bleu shook her head in amazement as she blushed slightly.

China laughed. "You only live once, right?"

Bleu's skepticism was written on her face. She wasn't the girl with the perfect body. She was fine with her curves and she knew that many had admired her voluptuous nature, but she wasn't without insecurities. Stripping down to her essence wasn't her idea of fun. She had scars. Scars that no one needed to see. Ones that would expose the fact that she didn't belong in this bubble of an L.A. world. She was flawed.

BEEP! BEEP!

They turned at the sound of the car horn, and she watched

as a man climbed out of an F-150. He was handsome, young, and flashy. The blinding watch on his wrist told a story of wealth as he approached. He seemed to like excess. Everything about him was a bit overdone. Too much jewelry, too many women hopping out the back of his truck, too much arrogance in his stride as he approached. He was attractive, but conceit dripped off of him. She could tell that he had never heard the word "no." He was sexy and powerful. Everyone on the beach seemed to flock to him, paying respect as they surrounded him like groupies.

"That's Cinco," China said. "That's who we're here to see. He's the man that makes it snow in L.A."

He was younger than Bleu had expected. When she thought of the Mexican Cartel, she envisioned old Mexican men in linen suits and full beards with beer bellies. Dude before her couldn't be a day over twenty-three. He gave new meaning to the word "kingpin." He was the new generation of a powerful ruling family in Mexico. With a mother from South Central L.A. and a father who reigned over one of the most powerful cartels in Mexico, Cinco had more hustle coursing through his veins than Nino Brown himself. Cinco's cartel ties were only the tip of the iceberg; he was also affiliated with the street gangs in L.A. He was heavy in the streets and known for his murder game. Coke wasn't his expertise. He simply had unlimited access, so he might as well make his money flip. His familial ties made him powerful. His father was a notorious supplier. Cinco would have made the perfect man in charge if it wasn't for his hot head. So his father appointed someone else to the throne, and Cinco acted as the shooter. He was so good at being bad and Bleu's intuition told her that he was danger personified.

"You brought a new face with you. One that's easy to look at," he said as he greeted China.

"This is my girl Bleu," China introduced.

Cinco walked by China, his gaze fixed on Bleu as he approached her. He stood directly in front of her. She thought to lower her gaze but decided against it, as she realized he was purposefully trying to intimidate her. He was used to people bowing down just based on his status.

"You're a beautiful girl, shorty," he said.

"I've been told that," she replied.

"Take off your clothes."

The words were so direct that they confused her. *Damn.* He didn't even wet it before he fucked her.

"Excuse me?" she asked with an attitude.

"I haven't had to repeat myself in a long time!" he shot back, the look in his eye slightly threatening as an arrogant smirk crossed his face. Her breath caught in her throat as he placed his hands on her thighs and worked his way north.

"I don't know you, shorty. You could be the feds," he said.

"I thought Bree vouched for me," she replied in confusion, slightly shaken as Cinco's hands ran up her thighs as he felt her up.

"Bree's word don't mean shit to me. I like to know who I'm dealing with myself," he replied. The smirk on his face told her he was enjoying watching her squirm. He played with the outline of her panties as his fingers dipped dangerously low.

She grabbed his hand. "I'm not wired, and if I was it wouldn't be down there," she said as she slapped his hand away forcefully.

"I like you," he said as he chuckled obnoxiously. "You're feisty."

"And you're an asshole!" she shot back. She was so offended that she shook with rage, but her flip lip was attractive to him. No one had ever spoken to him sideways and lived to tell about it, but she did it without thinking twice, all in the name of self-respect. All of his minions watched, silently trying to gauge what his reaction would be. The air was tense and China moved toward them, but he put his finger up, halting her.

"I've heard that before," he said, reiterating the comeback Bleu had given him earlier. She wasn't beat for the bullshit. He could dig that. Already she was more interesting than half of the people in his circle. Yeah, she needed the money, but she wasn't willing to smut herself out in order to make it. Most chicks would have jumped at the opportunity, but she was a different breed. Her V didn't have a price tag on it. No amount of money could buy her. Already she wasn't feeling him. She had met niggas like him before who thought their reputations were enough to get them anything they wanted. She also knew girls like the one he was mistaking her for. He had her confused however. Yes, she was impressed by the money, by the intrigue of his affiliation, but his status didn't give him an all-access pass to her body. She was not easily conquered, and, more important, she was selective about whom she kept time with. "Take your hand off my thigh please. I'm here to make money. If you're not talking about that, you're not speaking my language."

She sounded tough, but on the inside she quivered. She was in another country, popping big shit to a nigga who could easily leave her slumped. Bleu was from the murder capital, but she didn't have the same bite as the rest of the dogs from her litter. Her bark was fierce, but she hadn't ever had to back it up and she certainly didn't want to test her gangster now. She knew that she was out of her league, but she wanted to make it known that she was here strictly for business.

Cinco's eyes lit up in amusement before he turned his back to her. "Get shorty a drink," he said to China. "We need to lighten her ass up."

The devil's playground. That's what this was. As Bleu sat in front of the bonfire under the night sky, listening to the sound of the ocean, she realized that nothing this wrong had ever felt this good. Her discomfort slowly dissolved as the red cup full of Cîroc and papaya slowly seduced her into relaxation. Cinco and his people were circled around the fire, popping bottles of champagne, making it flow like water. Candy bags full of pills were passed around and the smell of Kush filled the air as everyone chased their own kind of high. They were living by their own set of rules, and in Mexico not even the authorities could stop them. This was that outlaw shit and Bleu had to admit that it felt kind of good. She had always played by the rules. She sat in the front of the class, paid attention, tried to remain good when the world was full of bad, but not tonight. Tonight, she was lawless. As the liquor hit her system, all her reservations about what she was stepping into melted away. *Fuck it.* She needed this. No one was financing her dreams, so she had to finance herself, and a shitty waitressing job wasn't going to cut it. It was worth the risk . . . at least, that's what she kept telling herself.

"Hey, girl, you all right?" Aysha asked as she took a seat in the sand next to Bleu.

The glazed-over look in Bleu's eyes caused Aysha to laugh. "I'm good," Bleu replied.

"You're fried," Aysha said as she shook her head.

"Pretty much," Bleu said with a smirk.

"You're doing better than I did my first run. I was a hot mess. My nerves were out of control," Aysha said. "I thought I would pee on myself the first time I met Cinco."

"You're not afraid of getting caught?" Bleu asked, turning serious suddenly. "I know the money is good, but I keep thinking what if—"

"Don't think about the 'what-ifs.' Think about 'what is.' Cinco isn't stupid. He's been running this flawlessly since he was sixteen. He is cartel," Aysha said, whispering. "They aren't amateurs. Every precaution has already been taken to make sure we make it across the border. Don't worry about it. We'll be fine," Aysha said.

Aysha and China were so certain that Bleu blew out a deep breath. They knew this business better than she ever would. They understood the politics of it all and, more important, they knew exactly whom they were dealing with. Cinco was a young king in Mexico. The police wouldn't dare interfere in his operation. It wasn't until the drugs hit U.S. soil that things became risky, but in Mexico Cinco and his entire empire were untouchable. His youth contributed to his legend. Where most kingpins kept a low profile, Cinco wanted the spotlight shining brightly on him. He basked in it as if God were personally shining it for him to perform. If he had to play by the old-school rules of secrecy and seclusion it would have killed him. A real boss was untouchable and at most times undetectable, but Cinco lived for the clout and attention. He needed to be among his workers so that he could exercise his power. It was his yes-men who kept his ego fed. They made him feel like a god. Without the feeling of control, he was nothing. It wasn't the dollar or the flip that he was addicted to; it was the influence . . . the fear. There were more than fifty people around him. Yeah, they were having a good time. Liquor and drugs were in excess, providing them a gangster's buffet, making the mood light. But at the end of the day, they were all there under Cinco's rule. They were his workers and he was the boss. He wasn't worried about being touched because it was known that he was gruesome when it came to punishment. Besides, the shooters he had strategically placed throughout the crowd ensured his safety. He was unbothered and it showed as he sat, enjoying the night.

Bleu could feel his eyes on her as she sat hugging herself while staring into the fire. She looked up, meeting his gaze, and he raised his cup to her. He nodded. She did too and it was all the invitation he needed to make his way over. He was attractive, but it was overshadowed by the fact that he knew it. Arrogance was the ultimate turnoff for her. His flamboyance annoyed her intensely.

"Take a walk with me," he said as he held out his hand to help her up.

Aysha looked at Bleu and nudged her shoulder. Bleu rolled her eyes and took his hand as he pulled her up out of the sand. She dusted off her behind before stepping away with him, and headed up the dark beach, away from the group. He handed her his cup, and she frowned as she looked at the dark liquor inside.

"I'm good," she responded, declining. "If I drink any more I might throw up on your feet."

"You're not good, shorty. I don't fuck with nervous mu'fuckas. You acting like the feds," he said. The glimmer of danger in his eye made her reach out and accept the cup. She took a sip and he smirked. "That will loosen you up. You're wound a little tight, shorty."

She took several gulps this time, drinking until it was gone. She gave him a sarcastic smile as she tipped the cup upside down, proving it was empty. "Is that better?"

"Much," he replied with a laugh. "What is somebody like you doing here?" he asked.

"I don't know what you mean! Somebody like me?" she responded.

"This life isn't yours. You've probably never stolen a candy bar from a corner store in your life! Girls like you don't traffic dope. You're too clean-cut," he said, meaning it as an insult.

"I'm not like Aysha and China. I come from the bottom. I need the money. Not for shoes or handbags, either," she replied vaguely.

"You're just trying to eat," he concluded. He sat in the sand and patted the place beside him. She placed her hands on her hips as she looked back toward the bonfire. They had walked about a half mile down the beach, and nothing surrounded them but darkness.

She didn't know him and her stomach was in knots as she replied, "Maybe we should go back where everybody else is." She could tell he was used to getting his way, and he seemed to want his way with her.

He grabbed her hand, pulling her down into the sand. "You scared of me?" He seemed amused at the thought. He got off on fear. Fear, in his eyes, made him powerful.

She sat beside him and watched the moon light up the night sky. The darkness that settled over the ocean barely allowed her to see where the beach ended and the water began. Her heart pounded. Partly from fear, partly from nerves.

"I'm afraid of what I'm getting myself into," she admitted.

He gripped her chin and turned her face until she was staring into his eyes. "It's that innocence that is going to make you so good at this, *mami*," he said. Her chin tingled where he touched, and she moved her face out of his grasp.

"Don't run from me, Bleu. Come here," he said flirtatiously as he turned over on top of her. "You're so fucking sexy, shorty. Those lips . . . I've been wanting to kiss you all day. I bet that pussy's fat."

His words were playing with her head as she felt her nipples harden. Her head spun and, despite the cool air rushing in over the night sea, she felt her temperature rise. She was hot . . . too hot, and slightly nauseous as she tried to stand. *What the hell is wrong with me?* she thought as she placed a hand on her head, feeling her clammy skin. Her world had turned into a merry-go-round and her legs wobbled like twigs as her vision blurred. She fell back to the ground, disoriented.

"Wait," she whispered as Cinco's lips covered hers and his hands palmed her breasts. The weight of him pushed down on her as her back hit the sand. "Wait," she repeated. "I'm dizzy, Cinco. I don't feel good."

"I can make you feel right, shorty," he whispered as he licked her neck while simultaneously sliding her panties down. "Just relax. Stop fighting it. Just roll with the E, shorty."

There it was. Like a bomb, exploding in her mind, his words rang out. She was rolling on Ecstasy. He had drugged her. Cinco had slipped it into her drink and now her body was betraying her. Right felt wrong and bad felt good. That's why his touch turned her on so much. While her mind screamed in protest, her body was putty in his hands.

"Please stop," she cried. His pursuit was relentless as he slipped a finger across her swollen clit. He rubbed her wetness between his fingers.

"I don't think you want me to stop, shorty. That pussy begging for me." The lustful tone in his voice and determination in his eyes caused her to tremble with regret. This was her fault. She had let him walk her up the beach, away from her friends, and now he was going to take what he wanted. Her protests didn't matter.

"No!" she shouted. "Cinco, no!"

Her hands pushed against his chest to no avail, and her panic soared when she realized he was going to take it. Her sex, her treasure, her pussy, her feminine gold . . . she had said no and still he parted her thighs. This was rape, and when the reality smacked her in the face she cried. Her tears mixed with the sand as she felt his hardness on her inner thighs.

"Please, don't do this," she whispered.

"I get what I want, shorty, and I want you. This is a part of the job," Cinco said with a sinister look in his eyes.

"No! No! No!" Her hands flew as she tried to fight him off, scratching him across the face as her long nails drew blood.

"Agh, fuck!" he shouted as he sat up suddenly, nursing his face with his hands.

Bleu scrambled to her feet, but the Ecstasy had her out of sorts. Her legs were weak, and she couldn't stop the beach from spinning around her. Suddenly she was falling, and it felt as if a thousand pounds hit the sand as he threw her back to the ground.

"Bitch, I was tryna be nice to you and take my time. You like it rough, I'm going to give it to you rough," he growled between gritted teeth as he flipped her onto her stomach. "Get on your fucking knees before I snap your neck, bitch."

Bleu sobbed. She thought about running, but her legs wouldn't carry her very far. The gun that he had casually taken off of his hip lay just a few feet from her. She looked at it.

"Bitch, don't even think about it," he growled. He snatched up the 9mm pistol and pointed it at her. "Turn around and get on all fours." She had no choice but to do as she was told. The sand dug into her bare knees painfully.

"Please don't do this," she pleaded. She raised her head. She could see the bonfire blazing in the distance and the people dancing around it. She was so far away that they looked like dots on the beach. She wanted to scream, but she knew that her voice wouldn't carry that far, and it was a good chance he would keep his promise and kill her before anyone came to help. Besides, who was going to stop him? He was a boss among pawns. She was at his mercy, and because of that she was doomed. Cinco wrapped one arm under her as he slid inside her depths. There was no condom, no protection, between them as she felt his bare skin invading her most personal space. He hit it, doggy-style, and with every thrust of his hips she died a little more inside.

"You're on E, bitch; just enjoy it. Stop fighting me and take this dick," he groaned, completely gone off on the euphoric feeling he got as her tightness pulled on him as he slammed into her. With every pump she cringed. She hated this. She hated that she had walked herself right into harm's way. Her sixth sense had been telling her to stay away from him as soon as she laid eyes on him, and still she had found herself in this predicament. She cried silent tears as he degraded her, pushing her face into the coarse beach. Facedown, ass up. It was the ultimate disrespect, and all she could do was wait until he chose to let her up. He finished on her backside and stood up, adjusting his clothes as he looked down on her in amusement.

"I never met a bitch who didn't like it, shorty. Save them tears," he spat arrogantly with a grin of amusement. She lay on her side, sobbing hysterically. He scoffed and shook his head as he made his way back up the beach.

She didn't move until she was sure he was gone. The smell of him lingered all over her body, making her nauseous. She took off her dress and then crawled across the sand until she touched the water. She just wanted him off of her. The semen he had left behind, the smell, the touch . . . she wanted to erase it all from her memory. She walked until the dark water covered her bottom half and then dipped her entire body underneath. The cold shock slapped her with sobriety as she emerged, gasping for air. She let the ocean wash away her sins as she walked back up to the beach. With shaky hands she slipped back into her dress, leaving her soiled panties on the ground. A mixture of embarrassment and fear caused her legs to shake uncontrollably. This had not been the plan. Everything was all fucked up. How could she move work for a ruthless dictator? He was a narcissistic asshole. She just wanted to go back home . . . to cross the border and be back in her dorm room, but she was too deep in to change her mind now. If she didn't go through with it, her sudden departure would arouse suspicion and Cinco would come for her head. He wasn't some Hollywood playboy. There was nothing pretend about Cinco. He was cartel. He was dangerous, and if she made the wrong move it could very well be her last. She knew too much not to go through with this run and he had taken too much from her already. She might as well finish what she had started; otherwise she would return to L.A. with a wet ass and empty-handed.

13

Arms extended, legs spread, Bleu shook as Cinco's goons taped bricks of cocaine to her body.

"Why do we have to carry it on us? I thought it would be in the trunk or something," she whispered to Aysha, who stood next to her, going through the exact same routine.

The goon stopped and smirked menacingly as he turned to Cinco, who was standing above their heads, overseeing everything from the second-story loft in the massive warehouse.

"*Bonita* here wants to know why we're taping the product to her," he said.

Cinco smirked as he began to saunter down the steps slowly as he stared at Bleu. She could see the hint of laughter in his eyes. He liked the fact that he intimidated her. He made her skin crawl, and as he approached, she silently regretted ever asking the question. He rubbed his hands together and then stood directly in front of her, causing her to shift her gaze. She didn't want to look him in his condescending eyes. He made her feel dirty as images of him inside of her flashed through her head. Her breathing became shallow and nausea plagued her. Cinco made her nervous, and not in a good way. She didn't trust him . . . in fact, she felt a twinge of fear. Narcissism and power rarely mixed. She didn't want to see Cinco's bad side again. She could tell he had a fetish for inflicting punishment when things went awry. She just had to play his game and get his coke across the border. One time . . . and then she would never have to see him again.

"I want you to value my cocaine like you value your life. You can ditch a car, a bag, a suitcase. You're going to make sure you make it back. My kilos will make it back with you," he said.

"And if we're searched?" she asked boldly.

"You do your job right and you won't be," Cinco replied.

"What if we're caught?" she asked.

"You rot in a jail cell, because if you talk I'll cut out that talented little tongue of yours," he said. He looked her up and down menacingly, causing her to shake. "This is the risk you take. You take the money if it goes right, so you have to take the consequence if it goes wrong." Cinco stopped speaking as he stared Bleu directly in the eyes, inspecting her, watching her shake slightly as she held her breath. "You act real jittery, ma," he observed.

"She's good; she understands," Aysha said, speaking up on Bleu's behalf. "It's her first run. It's just the nerves."

Bleu wanted to back out, but she couldn't find her voice to speak up. Instead she stood there, tears accumulating in her eyes as the goon finished taping her down. She had never been this afraid in her life. She had always believed in following your first mind, and her gut was telling her that this idea was the worst.

"Yeah, okay," he said sarcastically as he casually walked away. "Have Bree holler at me once y'all cross the border," he said.

Bleu didn't realize she had been holding her breath until she exhaled in relief when Cinco and his goons exited the door.

"I can't do this," she whispered.

China shrugged her jean jacket over her shoulders, covering the bulkiness of the kilos that were taped to her body. "Put your big-girl panties on, bitch. You're spooking everybody with this goody-two-shoes shit. Let's make this money. Don't make me look bad for putting you on. Get it together."

China stormed out and Aysha gave her a sympathetic look. "Stop worrying. We have done this before. We'll be fine. Just don't think so much," Aysha offered.

Aysha walked out as well, leaving Bleu standing unsurely as her thoughts ran rampant. Being caught was her greatest fear, and the butterflies in her stomach were setting off an internal alarm. *It'll be fine. Everything will be okay. Just get through this one time,* she kept coaching herself, trying to will up the courage to be an outlaw. She wasn't the girl who broke the rules. She didn't live on the edge. She had done everything right up until this moment, and she was quickly realizing that she wasn't about this life. As the sun beamed in through the open door, illuminating the darkened warehouse, Aysha peeked her head back in. "You coming or what?"

Bleu nodded. "Yeah, yeah, I'm coming," she replied as she pushed her reservations to the back of her mind and followed her friends, headed for disaster.

The six-lane highway leading to the border was crowded with weekend traffic, headed back into San Diego.

"Once we cross over, it's only a few hours to L.A. This is the hard part," Aysha said.

"More like the boring part," China mumbled as she rested her foot on the side-door panel as she painted her toes.

The smell of exhaust thickened the air from the hundreds of cars that were lined up. Cinco had twenty mules crossing simultaneously. The girls didn't know that they were the ones Cinco had decided to throw to the wolves. A sacrifice was made each time Cinco moved weight from Mexico into the States. On every run there was always one load that never made it back. The smallest shipment was always caught, and while a big fuss was being caused over the arrest of the small fish, the big fish eased into the States without notice.

Tension settled into her shoulders as she tried to swallow the lump of uncertainty that had formed in her throat. She was sweaty. The plastic-wrapped kilos of cocaine were making her hot and a sweaty sheen formed on her forehead. Her gut was screaming at her to turn around. As her eyes scanned the long line of cars she felt cornered. She had always had a knack for listening to her intuition, and this setup just didn't feel right.

Border patrols had the canines out and walked them between the standstill traffic, on leashes, in attempts to sniff out drugs.

"Are those police dogs?" Aysha asked, sitting up in her seat.

"Shit just got real," China said. "What do we do?"

"I thought y'all said this would be a cakewalk. Nobody said shit about dogs," Bleu protested. "There's no way this car is going to make it across that border."

"It's never been like this before," Aysha said nervously as she turned to look behind them, instinctively searching for an escape route.

China gripped the steering wheel. "They're on alert. We've done this a dozen times, and not once was there dogs. Somebody tipped them off. They know that there will be drugs trying to come across the border today. What do we do?"

"Oh my God, oh my God," Aysha panicked. "We're going to get caught."

"We're not going to get caught," Bleu said, practically shouting. She couldn't afford to be caught. Aysha and China, on the one hand, had rich parents and powerful families who could probably get them out of a jam if this thing went bad. Bleu, on the other hand, had no one. If she was caught her life would be over. Her mind started spinning as she leaned over anxiously between the two front seats.

"I need you to ease off of this highway. Pull over right there to that rest stop," she directed.

It was the only exit between the dogs and them. If they didn't stop they would be caught.

"We're getting off? Getting off and then what?" China asked snidely.

"I don't know; just get off!" Bleu said, barking the order as if she were the boss. "Unless you got a better idea."

"Just do it," Aysha said, voice shaking.

China maneuvered the car across four lanes, complaining the entire way. "Do you bitches know what happens if we don't get this shit across the border? Cinco isn't a play gangster. It's all or nothing with him. He will kill us if we ditch these kilos."

Bleu felt all eyes on her. China was staring at her intently in the rearview mirror while Aysha had turned around in her seat. They both wanted answers. How Bleu had suddenly become the ringleader she didn't know, but she would rather take her fate into her own hands than depend on either of them. They didn't understand her struggle. They didn't know where she came from and why she never wanted to go back. The silver spoons in their mouths kept them well fed. They were making runs for fun, whereas Bleu was doing it for survival. No matter how many times they had done this before, they would never be as streetwise as Bleu. She was groomed for it because she had lived it. It was innate for her. F-city had taught her well, and now it was time to show and prove.

China parked and the girls got out, looking over their shoulders as they made their way inside of the women's restroom. China went through pushing open the stalls to make sure they were all empty as Bleu flipped the lock on the bathroom door.

Bleu paced back and forth as she ran her fingers through

her hair. She blew out a forceful breath of air, exasperated. *What the fuck were you thinking?* she wondered, but it was too late to beat herself up. She was in the thick of it and she needed to keep her cool so that she could think clearly.

BANG! BANG! BANG!

The girls jumped out of their skin when someone knocked at the bathroom door.

"Is anybody in there? I've got a busload of people who need to piss! What the hell?"

Bleu sighed in relief as an idea sparked in her head.

"Grab the bags out of the trunk and hurry," Bleu instructed.

She went to the door and unlocked it. A white man wearing a blue driver's uniform stood, disgruntled, on the other side.

"You done in there, lady?" he asked.

She nodded and then stepped to the side as a few of his passengers began to file in. She held up the handicap bathroom until Aysha and China returned.

The three of them went inside.

Bleu didn't speak. The restroom was full of tourists. No one could overhear her, Aysha, and China's plans. They were taking risks that could put them away for life. Anonymity was of the utmost importance. Instead, she lifted her dress and began to remove the kilos from her body. She neatly stacked them into the duffel bags as her friends did the same. Thirty bricks. It wasn't major weight, but when Cinco had two hundred mules moving across the border daily its worth summed in the millions.

"Just follow my lead," Bleu whispered as she grabbed one

of the bags and exited the stall. She walked right up to the side of the bus and lifted one of the doors, exposing where the luggage was stored. She tossed the bag underneath.

"Are you crazy?" China asked.

"You wanna stand out here and argue about it or nah?" Bleu asked.

Bleu was coming up with the plan as she went along, but they didn't have time for second-guessing. China stuffed her bag underneath and Aysha did the same. They discreetly lowered the door. The crowd of passengers was too thick for anyone to really take notice. The women didn't act hot, so they didn't get caught.

Bleu turned to one of the passengers. "Hey, where is this bus headed?" she asked.

The woman was distracted, holding a fussy baby on her hip. As the woman replied, "San Diego," she didn't even look Bleu in the eyes.

"We'll meet the bus at the terminal," Bleu said to her friends as she headed toward the car without looking back.

"And what if someone takes the bags? Or they find out what's in the bags? This isn't smart. You heard Cinco. He wants us to cross the border with the product," China said vehemently.

"Well, I don't see Cinco out here! He's not the one that those dogs are going to pounce on or the one who has to do the time if we get caught. Fuck Cinco right now. I'm moving my own way. As long as I get it there he shouldn't have no problems," Bleu spat. She sounded tough on the outside, but inside she was quivering. The risks had changed, but the stakes were still high. If something went wrong . . .

She shook her head, not even wanting to think about the repercussions.

There was only one hiccup in Bleu's plan. The buses had a special line that they went through in order to get back into the country. She maneuvered through the thick traffic as she tried to stay on the bus's tail, but she was quickly diverted to a different lane.

"We're losing it," Aysha said eagerly. Bleu was now the driver. She was in control, and as much as she wanted to keep her eyes on the product, she had no choice but to merge into the lane with all the other cars. The wait was ridiculously long, and she gritted her teeth as the bus eased through customs and out of sight. A slight panic set into her bones. Her anxiety was at an all-time high. China and Aysha had hollered "easy money" so much that Bleu had never expected anything to go awry. She had forgotten Murphy's Law. "Anything that can go wrong will go wrong." In fact, it had gone to shit.

"We will meet the bus at the terminal. Just relax," Bleu said.

It took two hours to get to the Greyhound station, and the ride was so silent that Bleu could hear each beat of her trepid heart.

"That bus been back," Aysha stated as they pulled up across from the bus station. "I'm not going in there. They probably went through the bags and everything by now."

Bleu eyed her surroundings, scanning the streets, searching

for any signs of a setup. She knew that it was very possible that the police had been called. Her bags had been sitting for hours, unclaimed. The stupidest thing that she could do was step inside to retrieve them, but she didn't have a choice. She popped open the door.

"You're going in?" Aysha asked.

"Somebody has to," Bleu said as she looked left, then right before crossing the street in haste.

She walked into the station wearily, inspecting her surroundings. Everyone seemed suspect. It all felt like one big conspiracy. She tried to keep her cool as she walked up to the ticketing counter.

"Excuse me, where can I find unclaimed luggage?" she asked.

Without even looking at her the woman said, "Lost and found is in the back."

Bleu located the office and peeked her head inside. No one was around and a pile of lost luggage sat unattended. Bleu just wanted to get out of there as soon as possible. Although no eyes were on her, it felt as if she were being watched. She spotted the three duffels and grabbed them quickly, struggling as she flung the straps over her shoulders. The weight of the cocaine caused the straps to dig into her shoulders, but she kept it moving.

"Ma'am! Excuse me!"

Bleu froze as she turned around, eyes widened and filled with guilt as her stomach flipped. This was it. She was caught. Her bold ass had walked right into a place of public transportation and scooped three bags full of drugs. Her eyes stung and she could feel the tears coming as the man said, "You need some help with those? It seems like you're having a hard time."

"Help?" Bleu breathed out in relief as she chuckled nervously. "You want to help me? That's all?" She realized that she was on edge and jumpy. "Thank you, but I'm fine," she said as she rushed out of the doors. She practically ran across the street to the car.

"Oh shit, you got it?" Aysha said, impressed.

"Pull off. I almost shit on myself in there," Bleu said.

China looked in her rearview mirror and said, "I guess this will be your first and last run?"

This close call should have been enough to scare her away from the game, but now that it was over, the thrill of it all had her floating on a natural high. She wouldn't dare go on the same dummy mission again, but she would do it again . . . her way. She had found a better way to get bricks across the border and she was going to put it to use.

It took everything in her to keep her cool. She had never held so much money in her hands at one time. *Twenty thousand dollars, for one run to Mexico. I'll do that all day,* she thought as she flipped through the bills, making sure she hadn't miscounted. She felt like she had been to hell and back, but she had to admit it had been worth it. In a short weekend she had made more money than most people see in an entire year. All of her worries had gone out of the window. She clipped off a small stack for herself and then set aside $1,000 for Noah. She made a mental note to drop it on his books before placing the rest of the money inside a white envelope. Taking a pair of scissors, she lifted her mattress and cut a small slit under it, then stuffed the money inside. It would have to be her makeshift safe until she purchased a real one, but she wasn't worried. China and Aysha had been at this a lot longer than she had. They didn't need to steal from her; they had their own dough.

A knock at the door interrupted her. "One second." She flipped her mattress down and smoothed out her blanket before rushing to the door to answer it.

"I fucking love you!" Bree shouted as soon as she opened the door. He rushed her, picking her up at her waist and running with her until he slammed her on top of her bed. China and Aysha came waltzing in behind him, smiling as positive energy filled the room. "That shit you pulled at the border was genius! If it wasn't for you, the run would have been a bust, Detroit," he stated. He pulled a knot of money out of his True Religions and tossed it at her. "That's for being on your shit."

She snatched the money out of the air and thumbed through the bills in disbelief. Bree played with hundreds as if they were singles. In fact, all the women did. They were reckless and carefree with their spending, as if they had the seeds to money trees.

"Pretty soon you'll be so good with the paper you'll know how to count it on sight. That's five racks," Bree said.

"For improvising?" she said in shock.

"For improvising," he confirmed. "If it wasn't for you, those bricks would have never crossed the border and all three of you would be sitting in a federal jail right now. You made the right move. There's a reward for that. Cinco sends his appreciation."

The mention of Cinco made her cringe. She didn't want anything from him. Was this a gift to make up for his forcing himself on her? No amount of money could make up for the fact that he was an asshole. She started to decline the extra money. She wanted no favors from Cinco, but this was what she had done it for. The paper. It was all about the money, and she had earned it. *Fuck Cinco,* she thought.

"You ready to burn down a mall, chick?" Aysha asked. "Now that you've got it, you can retire them clothes you been wearing. Time to step your game up, mama."

"I can't. I have class and then work," Bleu replied as she frowned while biting her bottom lip. She had already missed three days in a row. She wasn't paying tuition at UCLA. They would pull her scholarship just as quickly as they had given it to her if she didn't keep up her end of the bargain.

"Okay, well, while you're in class, we'll be riding with the top down on Rodeo," China said.

As she watched them leave, she thought, *One more day isn't going to hurt. I can always call in sick to Picante.* She rushed to the door and stuck her head out as she yelled, "Hey, I'm coming. Just give me ten minutes. I'll meet you in the lobby!"

She rushed to her desk and gathered an envelope and a piece of paper before pulling out her chair. Almost as soon as the money graced her hands she thought of one obligation she had to meet. Noah. She owed him, and she wanted him to know she had his back. The first dollar that she spent would be on him. She jotted down the words quickly before placing it in the envelope and stuffing it in her jacket pocket and rushing out the door.

14

Noah,

I don't even know if you're getting my letters. I've written you before and you didn't write me back, so I'm going to keep this one short. I put $500 on your books. It's against the rules to deposit any more than that per month. I'll keep sending it, though. On the first of every month until you're home. I miss you so much. So much has happened since I last saw you. I wish I could talk to you and hear your voice. Tell you what's been up with me. Things are finally good with me. I miss you every day. L.A. is everything I thought it would be and everything I never thought it would be all at the same time. I wish you were here. I hope you're okay.

Always,
B

Noah folded the letter and placed it under his mattress. Hearing from her was like tasting a little bit of freedom. She was his rib, and their separation only intensified his feelings for her. He wouldn't let her know, however . . . he couldn't. Putting himself out there and telling her what he was feeling would only make her come running home. Without anyone on the outside to keep her safe she would be easy prey. He smiled as he thought of the money she had sent. Bleu was real. She had kept her word and he loved the shit out of her for that. There were women twice her age who couldn't hold down a nigga during their bid, but so far Bleu was proving to be thorough. He was grateful for the money because finally he could get himself right.

Since he had found out that he was Khadafi Langston's son, things had turned around dramatically. Noah's father had never done a thing for him in his life, partly because he had no idea he existed, but now that it was known, his last name carried enough weight to guarantee his protection. He had been brought into the fold of Khadafi Langston's empire . . . an empire that Noah would inherit upon his release. He was young, so a lot of the old heads hated him from afar, but for the most part he was doing an easy bid. He had an army of goons behind him, which meant protection. On behalf of his father Noah had been labeled street royalty. Nobody wanted those types of problems and the few who did hadn't stepped to him since the shower incident. A quick stay in the infirmary and a few stitches had put him back on his feet. Inmates and even a few of the guards had offered him gifts just to show respect. Goods were just as valuable as money inside. Everything from food and soap to razor blades had been offered to him as a show of good faith. Once word of who he was spread through the prison his status became legendary, but he wasn't naïve. Nothing was given freely. If he accepted any of the handouts from any of the other inmates he would owe an unspoken debt. He wasn't that desperate. Bleu's $500 would come in handy because he was going to flip it. The prison's drug trade was practically nonexistent. No one had figured out how to get product on the inside. There was a void in the market, and Noah was looking to fill it. It was the only way he would be able to keep his head above water during the five years. He wasn't sure if Bleu would ride out his entire sentence with him. Surely she was struggling herself; he had no idea of the newly acquired hustle she had attained. He didn't want to be a monthly bill to her, so he would flip her money once, which would allow him to eat repeatedly.

He turned to his cellmate. Noah hadn't said anything to the old man. In fact, Noah didn't even know him. Noah's original cellmate had been moved out in the middle of the night and the old man had moved in. When the switch had occurred only a few words had been spoken.

"I'm Bookie. I used to run with your pops," he had said. "You need anything, you let me know."

That had been weeks ago and the two hadn't said much since. Noah kept to himself, as did the old man, both keeping a comfortable distance in the tomb-like cell. It wasn't until now that Noah actually broke the silence.

He sat on the edge of his bed, elbows resting on his knees as he folded his hands.

"You hunched over in contemplation, young buck, might as well speak your piece," Bookie said as he sat, reading a book, his glasses hanging so far off his nose that they looked as though they would fall off. He had gotten his nickname because his head was always stuffed in a book.

"You said you know my father," Noah said.

"Everybody knows your father, young buck. The whole city. They respected him. Loved him," Bookie said.

"The thing I can't figure out is why you sometimes talk about him in the past tense, but other times . . . times when you slip up, you talk about him like he's still alive," Noah said.

Bookie looked up from his book but quickly diverted his eyes back to his reading. "Slip of the tongue, I guess," he dismissed.

"I want to see him," Noah said in a hushed tone. "I don't know why he faked his death, but I know he's out there. Niggas is too scared and his reputation is too strong for him to be six feet under in a grave somewhere. He owes me. I've never asked him for shit. He's never done shit for me. I've never even seen his face. I want one sit-down. That's it. Tell him to come for a visit."

Bookie didn't respond, just kept reading his book as their usual silence fell over the cell. Noah didn't need a response, however. Bookie had heard him and he knew that Khadafi would get the message. All he had to do was wait.

A couple days of stunting and flossing turned into an entire week, and as Bleu walked inside Picante, she felt horrible about flaking on Marta. The woman was always busy. She juggled the duties of the busy restaurant as if she had octopus arms, doing eight different things all at once.

"Nice of you to show your face, Bleu," Marta said as she took a moment to stop and place her hand on her hip. She was exhausted and she looked at Bleu sternly. "What is all this? You're fancy fancy now?" she asked as she motioned to Bleu's upgraded appearance. The girl in a tight-fitted Burberry button-up with Prada heels was not the same young struggling college student Marta had hired. "You hit the lottery?"

"No, it's just a few new clothes," Bleu replied.

"And a new car?" Marta said with a raised eyebrow as she motioned to the Mercedes that Bleu had parked directly in front of the establishment.

"Did Iman buy you that?" Marta asked.

"No!" Bleu replied, louder than she intended to. "God, no! It's just . . . I bought it. . . . I—"

Marta held her hand up. "No. I don't want to know and I don't want you to lie to me, so just stop. You haven't been here but a few weeks. You were just broke and begging to get this mediocre job, now you're driving around in foreign cars and wearing five-hundred-dollar shirts," Marta said. "I don't want any trouble in my business, Bleu. Perhaps this wasn't a good fit after all. You clearly don't need the money anymore, honey."

Bleu nodded because she couldn't see herself working for the measly pay when all she had to do was make a run to Mexico to make racks at a time. Marta was right. Bleu's brief time at Picante had come to an end, but she didn't want to leave Marta hanging.

"I can stick around until you find someone new," Bleu offered.

"It's okay, Bleu," Marta said. It was as if she could see through Bleu. Marta didn't know exactly what Bleu had gotten involved in but wasn't a fool. She had seen how the city of L.A. could turn a good girl bad. "You be careful and you take care of yourself."

Bleu nodded as she hugged Marta. "Thank you, Marta. I'll stop by from time to time to check on you. Those tacos are my favorite," she said with a soft smile.

"You do that, honey. I'll always have a warm plate waiting for you," Marta replied. As Bleu walked out, she felt like she had disappointed her own mother. She turned and waved as she hopped into her new Benz and pulled out into traffic. She was living large. A small taste of the good life was enough to turn her out. Now that she knew what it was like to live enormous, she could never see herself living dormant ever again.

15

Bleu sat in the bus terminal, her eyes dancing around the room as she made a mental note of everything around her. She didn't know why no one had figured it out before her. Cinco had girls going across the border with ten bricks, fifteen at the most, when he could have had each girl carrying ten times that much. When Bleu had retrieved the luggage from the first run she had noticed how unsecure the bus station was. There was no security checkpoint, no checking of the bags. They hadn't even checked her I.D. when she had picked up her luggage from lost and found. It was literally a smuggler's dream. She wasn't foolish enough to move anything without testing it first, so as she sat with her bus ticket to Tijuana in her hand she observed everything.

"Bus Eleven-Twenty-Eight now loading for Tijuana. All passengers please make your way to gate seven," the voice came over the loudspeaker, and Bleu jumped to her feet and grabbed her bag. That was the one perk about bus travel. She carried her own belongings all the way to the door of the bus. It wasn't until she was ready to board did a carrier take it from her. She watched intently as they put her bag under the bus. *They don't scan it or nothing,* she thought in amazement. There were no dogs, no X-ray machines . . . nothing. Bleu could practically see the profit she was about to make. She had gotten twenty thousand for a light run. With the type of weight she was planning to move she would see a hundred grand easy for every trip she took. She took a deep breath as she took a window seat. The thought of so much money gave her anxiety as she leaned her head back against the headrest. Champagne dreams filled her mind as the bus rolled away from the station.

Tijuana and its dirty streets, its run-down buildings, and its corrupt government intimidated Bleu, and as she stepped off of the bus she started to second-guess herself. At least when she had come with Aysha and China she had them to back her up. Now that she was solo she felt like a sitting duck. She was trying to play a big boy's game, but she was vulnerable . . . she could feel it, and her senses were kicked into overdrive. She didn't want her name to be flagged by customs, so she knew that she had to at least spend one night in Tijuana. She hadn't thought of what she would do to occupy her time, and now that she was here she knew this couldn't be a dry run. *Fuck a test trip.* She had seen all she had needed to see to know that she was coming back across the border with bricks. *Why waste the opportunity?* she thought.

She walked with her duffel bag slung over her arm as she

made her way up the desolate street. She had no idea how to get in contact with Cinco, but she was here now. It was too late to turn back.

I have to call Bree, she thought, knowing that he was the only person who could put her in touch with Cinco. Bree organized the runs. He was the one Cinco did business with. If she was going to dive in headfirst, she would have to go through Bree. It was only right. He was a distributor. Once the cocaine made it into the States, it went to Bree, who then played middleman to various dealers around the city. Once the dope was sold, Bree kept his cut and then sent the majority of the cash back across the border to Cinco. Bleu hadn't yet handled the money, partly because Bree didn't trust her with it. He always sent China to pay Cinco, and Bleu was good with that. They all had their parts to play, and if all went as planned, Bleu's role would be moving weight. She could feel herself becoming good at it. She was a thinker, and once she had gotten her footing in the game she would be able to come up with a better strategy. She didn't want to be responsible for the money. That was too much temptation.

She walked into a run-down hotel and she frowned at its appearance. Its once-white walls were now a pale yellow and the smell of mold reeked in the air. She traveled light, with just enough money to eat and sleep. The last thing she needed was to be robbed in Mexico. She wanted to be discreet as possible. She already stuck out like a sore thumb; being flashy would only get her into trouble. She walked up to the front desk.

"Hola, señorita. *¿Puedo ayudarte en algo?*" the clerk said.

Bleu didn't know a lick of Spanish, and the confused expression on her face gave her away. "I just need a room . . . one night?" she said as she held up a finger as she frowned, hoping that he understood.

"*Si, si,*" he replied. "*Cincuenta dólares.*"

She was lost, but she heard something that sounded like "dollars" and figured it was time to pay. She pulled out a hundred dollars, figuring that the run-down establishment wouldn't charge more than that. Placing it on the front desk, she said, "Keep the change."

She walked up to her room, and when she arrived at her door she saw a girl smoking a cigarette sitting on the hallway floor.

"The fuck chu looking at, *puta*?" the girl asked.

Bleu didn't respond. She simply put her key card in her door and walked inside. She set her bag on the raggedy furniture and cringed when she saw a cockroach crawling up the wall. She didn't even know what she was doing here exactly. She had an idea of how to expand her hustle in her head, but she wanted to scope out the scene first. To her, China and Aysha's operation was too elementary. They had almost been caught, and Bleu wasn't with risking her freedom. She was more into paying people to do the hard work for her. The sound of sex filled the air as the headboard from the next room began to hit the wall. Bleu peeked her head out into the hall, looking left, then right. The girl was gone, so Bleu could only assume that she was the one making sex sounds. She was clearly a prostitute; in fact, Bleu had passed a couple of them on the way in. A smile spread across her face, and she walked next door. She knocked on the room door.

The girl with the shitty attitude answered. "What the fuck do chu want?" she said with a heavy accent.

"To help you make some money," Bleu responded with a smirk. "And you ain't got to lay on your back for it either."

Bleu recruited ten women, all prostitutes with nothing to lose but everything to gain, and she waited patiently for them to get their paperwork together so that they could cross the border. She spent her first twenty thousand, investing in them. She cleaned them up, fed them, housed them, and when the time was right, she put each of them on a bus with a bag full of dope as her luggage. Bleu paid them $2,000 each on the back end of the deal. The women were so used to making 40 bucks at a time that the quick lick was enticing for them. Bleu hired her own mules, and with the lack of security on the bus systems she moved hundreds of bricks at a time. So while Aysha and China were making $20,000 a trip, Bleu was clearing $150,000. She didn't go too often. She limited her trips to once a month, but when she did it, she did it big, and it didn't go unnoticed. She was moving so much weight that she became Cinco's breadwinner. Everyone had underestimated Bleu, but she was in the business of working smart, not hard, and it was paying off.

16

It didn't take long for Bleu to acclimate to the world of the rich and infamous. She was young and getting it. "New money" was an understatement.

She had never had anything, so when she acquired everything she didn't know how to act. Clothes, shoes, a brand-new C-class Benz that she had leased without thinking twice, she had it all, and within the blink of an eye she had run through the money. It was crazy how quickly the money had gone. It had burned a hole in her pocket. When you spent it by the thousands, twenty grand truly didn't go far. She was no longer on a beer budget, she had upgraded to champagne, and all of her purchases reflected her new tastes. Now she was playing on the same level as China and Aysha. There was no hierarchy. Bleu was no longer the poor little Flint chick on scholarship. Now they were peers and the material possessions on her back made her feel like they were equals. They defined her worth, and if the price tags that she popped were any in-dication of her value . . . she was quite expensive.

The three girls sat in the VIP booth of one of the city's most exclusive clubs, popping bottle after bottle in celebration. "To being young and reckless!!!!" China screamed as she held up an entire bottle of Rose champagne. *Fuck glasses.* They didn't need them. They were balling out as Aysha added, "And beat and unbothered!" She raised her own bottle. "And faded and upgraded bitches!" Bleu shouted over the music as she put her bottle in the air. The girls took the champagne to the head as if it were water, and Bleu swayed to the Kendrick Lamar lyrics that were blaring through the speakers. With her hands in the air she two-stepped coolly.

"You're a new bitch, with a new whip, and some new shit!" Aysha screamed drunkenly. "Might as well stunt. Get your pretty ass up here!" Bleu laughed as she watched Aysha climb atop the table and put her hands in the air as if she owned the club. Bleu looked around, waiting for security to tell her to chill, but no one ever came. Pretty women ran the world, or at least L.A., and Aysha did what she pleased. As Bleu looked down at her new appearance, a confidence she had never known bubbled over. She climbed up onto the table with China right behind her and the three women danced the night away. The evil eyes from the broke chicks in the club only added fuel to their fire. The threesome sparked every man's curiosity because not only were they beautiful, but they also were ordering bottles of champagne nonstop, and at $500 a pop they were letting it be known that they were paid. They were burning through more paper than people saw on their paychecks and it didn't go unnoticed. Every dope boy, jack boy, and fly girl in the building was looking, whether they wanted to or not. The attention fed Bleu's ego like no other. She had never been a part of the elite or considered to be a part of the inner circle. Even in high school she hadn't been a part of the popular crowd, but this feeling . . . this bad bitch, center of the universe, do whatever, whenever feeling . . . it was the shit. It was definitely something that she could get used to. She had lived dormant for so long. Walking a straight line had led her to boredom, and she had known nothing but struggle. As soon as she took a risk, she had begun to live, and the enormity of it all was intoxicating . . . wait . . . or was that the liquor? Either way, she was feeling it and didn't plan on giving up this new hustle anytime soon.

The smile faded from Bleu's face when she noticed Cinco and his yes-men entering the club. Her ears went deaf to everything around her, her feet came to a stop, as she stared at him from across the room. The fear that crept into her chest was crippling. Their eyes locked and Bleu felt as if he was a predator . . . she, his prey. It was like he could smell her fear. An arrogant smirk crossed his lips, and he nodded, causing her to climb swiftly down from the table. "I've got to go!" she yelled to her friends.

"What?! Now? But we're celebrating!" Aysha protested.

Bleu's hands fumbled as she reached into her new Chanel bag and pulled out a wad of money. She unrolled a thousand dollars and placed it in China's palm to cover her tab.

"Hey, what up? Why you leaving? We're just getting started," China said as she held up a small vial of cocaine between her fingers. A mischievous grin accompanied the sparkle in her eye. "There's nothing like catching this high and then riding the wave. You have to stay!"

Bleu was stunned momentarily. It wasn't like she hadn't been around drugs. Her mother battled an addiction to crack cocaine, so it wasn't foreign to Bleu; she was just surprised that China freely admitted that she used it. Back home that shit was not the business, but in L.A. it was the drug of choice. Everyone who was someone floated high on "something." A weekend thing . . . a party favor . . . whether it be Ecstasy or molly, hitting lines or popping pills, syrup or a little weed . . . everyone enjoyed the rush. There wasn't anything taboo about it among the stars and socialites. She had just been inducted into the "famous for no reason at all" club. She was young, gorgeous, and now paid. She was expected to partake and the temptation was real. Maybe it would numb the disgust she felt from allowing Cinco to play her. She still hadn't told anyone. A good high would erase her shame, even if only for the night.

"Come on, Detroit," China urged.

Bleu looked back and saw Cinco drawing near. She shook her head. "I've got to go. I forgot I have a paper due tomorrow morning," she lied. She looked over her shoulder and could see Cinco crossing the room. Her skin crawled as she thought of him between her legs. She cringed. "I'm out of here."

"Are you even okay to drive?" Aysha yelled, concerned.

Bleu nodded, but she was unsure of that herself. An entire bottle to herself had her stumbling through the crowd. She could barely walk a straight line as she made a beeline out of the club in her stilettos, but she would take her chances. She just wanted to get out of Cinco's sight. She had made the mistake of getting too close to him before, and as she slipped out of the club she vowed to herself that it would never happen again. She had forgotten that this was his world, he reigned supreme . . . she would have to tread lightly to stay off of his radar. She knew that she should go back to campus, but when Iman's name illuminated her cell phone, she found herself hopping on the highway, headed his way. He hadn't invited her, but she wanted to do more than hear his voice. She wanted to see him, feel him . . . she needed comfort and, more important, she wanted to show him that she could compete with all the fancy girls who had owned a spot in his heart before her.

As she pulled her new car up to Iman's home she quickly checked her reflection in the rearview mirror. Smudging her MAC-covered lips, she inhaled sharply. She was a whole new bitch. Iman was a high roller around town and had countless women auditioning for the main role in his life. She now looked the part, and she couldn't wait until he laid eyes on her. There was something to be said about $1,000 extensions and Italian threads. The enhancements seemed to bury the old Bleu. She was happy to put the homely version of herself to rest for good. *That girl didn't have a chance in this world*, she thought. She feathered her hair with her hands and shook it into place as she stepped out of the car. Confidence on 10, she was riding a natural high as she sashayed in her new Loubs until she reached Iman's door. Instead of knocking, she called him. He wasn't expecting her and she wanted to surprise him.

He had hit her up only once while she was away. She figured he wouldn't be the type to chase, and in all honesty she hadn't given him much to pursue. She wasn't the most beautiful girl he had ever been with. Her body wasn't the best. Her smile wasn't the prettiest and she definitely wasn't the most glamorous. Little did he know she was working on becoming all of those things. Money had opened up a world of possibilities. As she stood on his doorstep, butterflies dancing in her stomach, she realized that she had never been this girl. She wasn't the pursuer; she didn't make bold moves. As a result her dating life had been put on pause. She had never been down to let a nigga pay to play or up for competing with chicks over one guy, but here she was on Iman's doorstep, throwing her hat in the ring for his time and affection.

"Hello?" he answered.

The sound of his baritone melted her face into a smile. "You wouldn't believe how many times you crossed my mind these past few days," she said.

"Is that right?" he replied. "I find that hard to believe, seeing as how you're just now hitting me back. I was starting to think you wasn't feeling me. You quit fucking with me already, ma?" His tone was playful and she chuckled softly, blushing as memories of his face between her thighs came rushing back. She wished that they had taken things all the way that night. She wanted to feel him inside of her. She wanted him to make love to her . . . so that she could lock him down and get rid of all the other girls who were undoubtedly in his life. She needed to prove that she was better, prettier, more loyal. She just wanted to be his girl. Her Flint mentality had her thinking that she wasn't good enough by L.A. standards. But as she tossed her twenty-four-inch weave over her shoulder she reminded herself that she now looked the part. There wasn't a bitch in town giving her a run for her money, not tonight at least. She wore her new money well.

"I don't think I could ever quit fucking with you, Iman," she admitted.

"Don't speak too fast. There's still a lot about me you don't know," he said, suddenly serious.

"Doesn't matter," she said surely. "I know how I feel when I'm near you, and that's enough for me." She rang the doorbell and then said, "You expecting company or something? Am I interrupting something?" She placed her hand over the tiny camera that was within arm's reach above her head. She didn't want him to know it was her. Surprising him, drunk and sexy, in the middle of the night was more spontaneous. She couldn't wait to see what he thought of her new look.

She heard the hesitation in his voice as he replied, "Nah . . . nobody even knows I rock like that out here. Hold up a minute." He paused and she frowned as she heard him moving about on the other end of the phone. "Let me hit you back."

CLICK.

Bleu looked at the phone, taken aback, suddenly feeling like a pop-up visit wasn't a good idea. She was playing games, trying to be coy and cute, but clearly Iman took his privacy very seriously. "I should have called first," she whispered.

She raised her hand to ring the bell again, but before she could, the door flew open and she found herself staring down the dark barrel of a 9mm pistol.

"It's just me!" she screamed, terrified, as her hands went up and she dropped her new Louis clutch.

Iman immediately lowered his gun and breathed a sigh of relief. "What you doing, ma? I almost blew your fucking top off," he said in exasperation.

"I'm sorry. I was trying to surprise you!" she shrieked. Her voice was shaky as her heart raced.

He looked her up and down, noticing the dramatic transformation. She held out her hands with a hopeful smile. "Well, surprised?" she said unsurely. Embarrassment flushed her face as she suddenly felt like a little girl playing dress up. "You like it?"

"I like," he replied, not knowing how to take the drastic change. He grabbed her wrist and pulled her into the house, swatting her gently on the ass as she walked by him. The smell of her perfume awakened his senses as he felt his manhood jump. He admired the view of her voluptuous ass before walking up behind her and putting his arms around her small waist. He pulled her into him and placed gentle kisses on the back of her neck. "I love the heels, the dress, all that, but I also really really *loved* the skinny jeans, flip-flops, and backpack. That simple shit is sexy, ma."

"When I'm standing next to you I want to look like I'm supposed to be standing next to you," she replied. She turned toward him and wrapped her arms around his neck. "It looks good, though, right?" she asked as she pulled her head back so that she could stare in his eyes.

Iman could have told her that he found the slick ponytail she normally wore prettier than the weave. He could have said that when she didn't try so hard she drew his attention more. He could have just spoken up and said he preferred her plain face to the one before him that seemed to be hidden under makeup. She was like a Barbie. Everything in place, sucked in, tucked, drawn on, accentuated. What she didn't realize was that he loved her simplicity. She was trying to fit into the crowd and she did it well. She looked fine, but it was just more of the same. He wanted to tell her, but he didn't want to embarrass her. She had tried to up the ante for him and he wasn't in the asshole business. He would roll with whatever she liked; as long as the inside didn't change he could deal with whatever aesthetics she preferred.

"It looks good, ma," he replied, giving her a reassuring kiss.

She felt like an adolescent, because whenever he put his hands on her she creamed instantly. She could feel the silk as it melted from the folds between her thighs and she shuddered. Her body was his. He owned it, and not just because he had claimed it first. He moved with expertise, and as he reached down and began to rub on her pearl, she shuddered, wrenched with pleasure, and found her orgasm without even trying.

"What are you doing to me?" she whispered, amazed at how she reacted to him.

"Pleasing you, Bleu," he replied. "Can I have you, ma? Tell me you're ready."

The way he said it made it seem as if he would die if she deprived him any longer. "You can have me, any way you want," she whispered, the liquor in her system making her bold.

Her taut nipples were now victims to his fingers as he used

her own wetness to tease them. She didn't even know how her dress had gotten on the floor. He moved with such finesse and skill that he had disrobed her without her even noticing. He had her drunk with lust. He got on his knees; she gasped, and her chin hit her chest as he pulled her throbbing cherry into his mouth. As her head fell back in complete bliss she realized there wasn't much she wouldn't do to keep this man. He was new, exciting, and she had a feeling that he was more dangerous than she thought. The thought alone made her come on the spot. He stood and scooped her up like a caveman, tossing her over his shoulder, causing her to shriek as he ran with her upstairs. She laughed uncontrollably as he tackled her onto his bed. The last time she had been in it they had kept it PG, but tonight things would be R-rated.

"Play with it for me," he said as he removed his clothes. He wasn't shy, and for good reason. His body was amazing and she silently wondered if he would hurt her with what he was packing.

Lust thickened the air, making it hard to breathe. Nerves made her body feel electrified as butterflies danced in her stomach. He eased between her legs, parting them like the Red Sea. He was her Moses. Her body needed no prepping. She had been waiting for this moment for eighteen years. She was wet, ready, wanting, but still she trembled.

"You okay?" he double-checked.

She nodded.

"No head movements, ma. Tell me yes," he whispered as he kissed behind her ear.

"Hmm," she moaned. "Yes . . ." was her reply.

He thought about putting on a condom, but he wanted to feel every depth of her unspoiled treasure. If he put a baby in her, it would only be a plus. Iman wanted her . . . forever. He knew that as her first official lover, however, he was setting the stage for how she would allow a man to handle her afterward. For that reason alone he paused and reached into the night-stand by the bed. Iman was clean. Iman meant her no harm, but he couldn't say the same for the men she might encounter should they not work out. He ripped the foil package and slid it over his length. "Make me strap up every time, ma. This is your temple. Make a nigga respect it," he whispered as he po-sitioned himself over her. He was an unselfish lover, as he slid into her gently. When he felt her tense, he paused. "Relax, Bleu. Just talk to me. Tell me how I'm making you feel," he said, distracting her.

"It feels so . . ."—she wondered if it would be as good as she anticipated—"good," she whispered breathlessly as he pushed his way inside of her. She gasped; so did he at the tightness that enveloped him.

"Oh shit," he moaned as he ground in . . . then out. Bleu felt the addictive mixture of a little pain and a lot of pleasure as she matched his thrusts. They were hungry for each other and sounds of passion filled the air. No one had ever made her feel this way. His body inside of her made them feel like they were synced. This was the ultimate exchange of energy, and it was in that moment that she realized what she had just given him. She couldn't understand how women slept with man after man with no remorse. To have a man inside of you was giving him a part of you. To spread herself thin by giving herself to everybody would be absurd. No wonder bitches had no idea who they really were. Some had given away so much that they had nothing left for themselves.

Bleu could feel his heart beat as it thundered against her breasts. She had never experienced the earth-quaking sensations that he was causing. Somehow he was the conductor to her body's orchestra and together the melody they created struck the perfect chord. She was love struck and he made her feel wanted. He made her feel . . . feel—

"Agh!" she cried out as something erupted inside of her. Not all men could bring a woman to her peak, but Iman was skilled in his lovemaking. He made her orgasm and he didn't go for his until he felt her body go limp beneath him.

He lay behind her, their sweaty bodies spooning as he breathed in her ear. "Thank you."

"Thank you for what?" she asked as she looked back at him, confused.

"For giving me you," he replied. He kissed her lips and then reached around to play with her clit. It was time for round two, and Bleu had no complaints at all as her body turned to putty in his hands. It was going to be a long night indeed.

17

Late nights and early mornings only felt good in love songs. As Bleu pulled herself out of Iman's empty bed she groaned. Her head banged with the onset of a hangover, and before her feet could hit the plush carpet she felt the liquor in her stomach. She didn't remember much. She was surprised she had even made it to Iman's home. "Faded" was the understatement of the century.

How the hell did I drive? she thought. *And where is Iman?* She turned to see that half of her face had been left on the pillowcase. She was missing a false lash and everything. She shook her head as she tore the linens off the bed and piled them in a heap on the floor before rushing into the adjoining master bath. One look in the mirror told her the story of the night before. She was a wreck. Her once flawlessly beat face now looked like a clown show from a rough night's sleep and her hair was all over her head. She showered quickly, peeling the layers of insecurity off of her face until there was nothing left but Flint-town Bleu. She then stepped out of the shower, borrowed the robe that hung on the back of the door, and wrapped it around her body. When she stepped back into the room, Iman sat on the edge of his bed. His presence always took her breath away.

Why is he so fine and why is he smelling this good? she thought, knowing that he was her weakness. He was dressed in Armani jeans and a V-neck Ralph Lauren fitted T-shirt, but even when he was casual, he commanded the room. He suffered from the fine-nigga syndrome. He could literally do no wrong.

"There's my lil' mama," he said, admiring her in her natural state. "I almost didn't recognize you last night."

She smiled and closed the space between them. She stood between his legs as his hands instinctively wrapped around her waist and rested on her behind while his head lay on her stomach.

"What's up with the Benz? The expensive clothes? You rob a bank while you were M.I.A.?" he asked as he stroked her hair.

"No, I just came upon some money," she lied. "I applied for a loan and decided to buy a few things, that's all."

He looked at her skeptically but didn't push.

"I can pay you back for all of the things you bought me," she said.

"You're good. Keep it for a rainy day," he replied. "Tell me you can stay all day here with me," he said.

"Of course I can," she replied, not thinking twice about any of the classes she would be missing.

He untied the robe and kissed her stomach. Goose bumps formed when he removed his lips. Her body was slowly becoming his. "What's with you, Bleu? You've got school. What I tell you about a nigga that wants to distract you from that?" he asked sternly but softly as his kisses went lower.

"Hmm," she moaned as her river began to flow. "It's just a few classes. It's no big deal."

"It's a big deal," he stressed. "I don't care who it is . . . including me. You put that first. I know L.A. seems like the big-city life . . . the pace . . . the lights . . . the people . . . it's exciting, but don't lose you. I'm kind of digging you. You would be doing yourself a disservice if you switched up too much," he said.

As he schooled her, his lips came closer to her pleasure until finally he hit his mark. He wasn't big on putting his mouth on a woman, especially the type that Bleu so desperately wanted to become, but with her it was different. He had a thing for this young woman and he loved the way her scent lingered on him all day; despite the shower he routinely took after sex, the hint of sweetness followed him. It was like she had him spellbound. Iman wasn't a stranger to pussy or to women thirsting after him. With money and power came an assortment of women at his disposal. All races, all ages, all flavors, they wanted him . . . but he wanted her. A part of him wanted to keep this thing with Bleu to himself. He wanted to cherish it, keep it private so that the streets couldn't corrupt it. Bleu was a good girl. He didn't want to be the reason she turned bad, but being with him, she would eventually see the bad side of things. He wanted her to be far removed, which was why he always brought her to Calabasas instead of the condo he had in the city. There were parts of his life that she couldn't be exposed too just yet.

"Oh my . . . Iman," she whispered. His name on her lips. His mouth on her body. Her heart unknowingly in his hands. It was all so right, and as he brought her to the peak she trembled.

She pushed him back onto the bed, eager for more, but he resisted. He flipped her over, taking control as he planted a kiss on her forehead. "Go to class, ma," he said sternly. The buzzing of his phone against his hip caused him to rise off of her and almost instantly the mood changed in the room. She caught a glimpse of his phone. *Tan.* It was the beautiful one again. Bleu was starting to wonder who this girl was. Apparently she called frequently, and although Bleu knew that it was too early for her to question him about it, she still couldn't help but feel jealous. He sent the call to voice mail before refocusing back on Bleu. "I've got a little business to take care of anyway. I'll check for you later, a'ight? I've got to go, but you can take your time and leave when you're ready. The cleaning lady is here, so don't worry about locking up behind you."

She sat up, nodded, and watched as he left the room, suddenly in a hurry. She bit her bottom lip as confusion plagued her. *Who is Tan? And why did he rush out after she called?*

"Ms. Montclair, a moment of your time if you will?" Professor Davis said as the students filed out of her lecture hall. Bleu had missed half the class thanks to the morning traffic from Iman's Calabasas palace, but it was better than missing class altogether. She gathered her things and approached the wooden desk anxiously. She hated these one-on-one sessions. They were never good, and she took a deep breath to prepare herself for whatever curveball her instructor was about to throw her way.

"Let me be frank with you, Bleu," Professor Davis said without looking up. She never seemed to look Bleu in the eye when they spoke. It was as if the professor didn't even think Bleu was worth wasting a moment of her time on. She busied herself with papers that sat atop of her desk. An assignment that Bleu had forgotten to do. *Is that what this is about?* Bleu wondered. "When I first learned that you would be a part of this class I looked forward to teaching you. The guidance office lobbied on your behalf for you to start extremely late and I pulled your file personally to find out what the fuss was all about. I've been highly disappointed, to say the least," she said.

Bleu shifted uncomfortably but remained silent as Professor Davis continued. "You barely show up for class and when you do, you don't participate; you're distracted. . . . I accepted you under the terms that you would make up the work that you missed. I've yet to receive the back assignments and you have missed a few of the current ones as well. Do you want this, Ms. Montclair?"

Bleu felt sick to her stomach as she listened to how much she had dropped the ball. "I've wanted to come here since I was a kid," she admitted.

"Well, you're about to blow it," Professor Davis said. "You're a smart girl, but UCLA isn't a cakewalk and right now you're failing every class. You have exactly two weeks until the semester ends. If you don't make up your work for not only this class but the rest of them too, you'll lose your scholarship. You need to maintain a B average to stay here. You need to screw your head on straight or you'll be out of here. Am I clear?"

"Crystal," Bleu responded. She rushed out of the class and practically ran back to her dorm room. Tears clouded her vision as she thought of all the work she had neglected to do. Yes, she was hustling, but she was hustling so that she could maintain herself in college. It was all for the greater good . . . to help her achieve the ultimate goal. She had lost sight of that and now her entire dream was in jeopardy.

"Fuck, fuck, fuck!" she mumbled as she burst into her dorm room.

China came out of the bathroom, wrapped in a short housecoat while a bath towel was twisted around her wet hair. "Hey, chick," she greeted Bleu, blasé as she removed the towel, shaking out her dark tresses. "What's wrong with you?"

"I fucked up," Bleu replied. "If I don't keep my grades up, they will kick me out of the university. This is my dream. This drug thing is just a hustle. I don't want to do this forever. If I get kicked out, I lose everything." The last thing Bleu wanted was to retreat back to Michigan with her tail tucked between her legs. She had nothing to go home to. This was it. It was all or nothing. Somehow she had forgotten that. She had gotten so sucked in by the lavish life, by Iman, by the excitement of the hustle, that she had let school fall to the wayside. "I'm in trouble."

China waved her hand and replied, "That ain't nothing."

Bleu frowned and shot back, "Bitch, it's everything! What are you talking about?"

Bleu wouldn't be surprised if China was eager to see her

lose her place at the university. Although they were cool, Bleu could sense a slight tension between them. They were more like frenemies, or associates. Bleu didn't extend the word "friend" easily and she had never been blind to sneak disses or ill intent. It was Aysha whom Bleu rocked out with. Her friendship with Aysha was heavy and genuine, but there was low-key hate running through China's blood. She and Bleu kept it friendly, but underneath it all there was a bit of discord between the two. Aysha was their common denominator, and now that Bleu had taken to the game like a duck to water, she sensed that China felt a type of way about her sudden come up. One run had gotten Bleu praise that China hadn't yet received, planting a mustard seed of jealousy.

"Like I said, it's nothing. Don't worry about it. I've got something for you that will get you through finals and help you catch up," China said. She walked over to her desk and opened the drawer. She pulled out an unlabeled pill bottle and tossed it to Bleu. "It's Adderall," China said. "It'll get you through the next few weeks. You'll fly through that homework with no problems, trust me."

Bleu hesitantly took the bottle. "You take these?"

"This is UCLA. The curriculum here is hard as hell. Half the kids here pop pills to get by. You would be surprised," China admitted. "Try it. If you don't like it you can give them back, or if you need something a little bit stronger, let me know. No biggie."

Bleu closed her fist around the bottle reluctantly. She wasn't in the position to turn down anything that would help her get back on track. "Thanks."

. . .

Iman didn't want to be the bad guy, but he was, and as he put his key into the door of his L.A. high-rise, he felt conflicted. His gut tightened as the smell of Chanel perfume filled the air. It was her signature scent, and over the years his reaction to it had gone from sugar to shit. He had loved her once upon a time. When they were young he thought she would be the love of his life, but puppy love had quickly expired. By the time he realized he wanted out, they were married, with a kid on the way. He had been trapped, but her family connections had secured him a lucrative place within the Mexican Cartel. His entire empire depended on his relationship with her.

"Finally decided to come home?" Tan's voice was like ice as she looked at him through the reflection of the vanity mirror, where she was seated. She brushed her long dark, hair with precision as she cut her dark eyes at him.

She was beautiful. A Mexican *mami* with a sharp tongue but even sharper curves, every man's fantasy except the man she called her own. There had been many women outside of their marriage, but hell, there had been side niggas too. Men weren't the only creatures who liked to have their cake and eat it too . . . the problem was her cake was stale. She was blatantly aware that Iman had lost interest. She could always sense when a new chick was in his ear, but what Tan didn't know was that this time Iman's heart was involved.

"We need to talk," he said as he stood in the doorway to the plush bedroom. White on white decorated the space.

"So talk," she replied.

"I'm moving out," he replied honestly. "We both know this thing between me and you has been done for a long time."

Tan turned around and peered at him through the slits of her menacing glare. She had known him long enough to read him like a book. "You've met someone?"

"This isn't about a bitch," he replied as he swept over his face with his hand, suddenly feeling as if he were choking. "This is about you. You walk around this bitch miserable, ma. The love ain't there no more. You just want me because of who I am, not how you feel for me. You know I'd never beat you, Tan. If you think I'ma leave you dry, don't worry. I'll bless your accounts with enough to take care of you for life."

Tan laughed lightly, as if she had heard a joke. "It's because of me that you have the money you have. You think my account depends on you to maintain seven figures. This is about you and whatever bitch . . ."—Tan paused, throwing the insult with emphasis—"has you thinking the grass is greener on her side. The grass is greener where you water it, Iman."

"Is it worth watering, Tan? If you tell me this is real for you and that you love me like you used to, I'll drop everything. Is the girl who went against everything and everyone for me still in there? If she is, I'll leave the game, I'll leave the women alone, and it'll be me and you. It'll be like old times. But you just got to say one thing to me, ma. Tell me you love me and that's it's us against the world," he said. His voice was even because he had no hope. He knew that she was with him out of convenience. Her silence resounded loudly, wounding him slightly, but his face was unmoved. "Exactly," he finished. He turned to walk away, but her voice halted him.

"There have been bitches before. What's so special about this one? Keep the whore out of sight. She's a side bitch, so keep her in her place. You will grow bored with her just like all the others," Tan said, unbothered as she stood from her seat, the Chinese silk robe she wore hanging from her shoulders like a regal gown.

She was such a fucking lady . . . a boss by birthright. She was the daughter of Lisbon Sandoza, the head of one of Tijuana's most dangerous and powerful drug cartels. It was her connections, her lineage, her blood, that made Iman so powerful and untouchable. When they were fifteen years old they had fallen in love. It was young and hot. Like Romeo and Juliet their forbidden love was unstoppable. When her father caught wind of the intense teenaged affair, he up and moved his family back to Mexico, leaving L.A. behind and with it the troublesome boy who had his daughter's heart. Iman wasn't pure-blood. He was mixed. Black and Mexican-born, he wasn't the ideal match for the Mexican princess. He was a mutt and Sandoza had no desire to accept Iman into the fold. When Tan took an entire bottle of sleeping pills to punish her father for moving her away, Sandoza realized that he would rather have a daughter who loved Iman than no daughter alive to love anyone at all. He moved Iman to Mexico and brought him into the operations of the cartel. It wasn't until he was twenty-one years old did Iman move back to L.A. When he did he came with a street army that the city had never seen, and he took over the drug trade, crowning himself king. Tan and Iman married a year later, and they were supposed to live a thug-life version of happily ever after until tragedy struck. Seven months into her pregnancy, their unborn child died in the womb and Tan was forced to deliver a dead baby into the world. She had not been the same since; their love hadn't been the same since. Of course, they tried again and again, but repeatedly she miscarried. Her womb was ruined and it had turned the once-sweet young girl into a coldhearted wife. Now, three years later, they were both drowning in unhappiness. In fact, Iman had become numb. Numb to pain, numb to joy, numb to emotion . . . until he met Bleu . . . she made his heart flutter, and although he had promised her there was nobody else for her to worry about, he knew it was untrue. Tan wasn't competition; she was the fucking judge, jury, and executioner. He had to end his marriage before Bleu caught wind and before his wife felt threatened enough to try to destroy her.

18

Fuck, it was the only thought that came to his mind as Noah was snatched out of his sleep. He had been caught slipping, and after months of sleeping with one eye open he had briefly allowed himself to become lax. A potato sack was placed over his head and he bucked in protest as he was roughly pulled to his feet. The haze that the sandman had placed over Noah put him at a disadvantage, rendering him useless as he tried to fight off his assailants. Before he could even get the chance to holler or get one of the COs' attention, Noah felt a crack to the back of his skull that sent him right back to la-la land. Right before he passed out he thought, *Damn, I'ma die in here.*

The dim lights of the prison flickered as Noah came to. He grimaced, touching the back of his throbbing head. As he pulled his hand away he noticed blood on his fingers and he staggered to his feet. The empty cells around him let him know that he was in the abandoned cell block. The state couldn't afford to keep the entire institution up and running, so this portion went unused, undocumented, and unrecorded. It was completely isolated from the rest of the blocks, so he knew that if someone had brought him here to die no one would hear his screams. Every other single nook and cranny of the prison was taped but this space; it was almost as if it didn't exist at all.

The sound of hard-bottomed shoes echoing against concrete alerted Noah, and he stood defensively as he waited. If he was going to die he would go out fighting, and he prepared himself for it mentally as his heart pounded in his chest. In that moment, when he was cornered and at his weakest, he knew that there was no fear in him. He had always believed that a man was defined by the way he behaved in the face of danger, and if he hadn't known before, he knew now. There was no bitch in him. He was all g as he prepared himself for the worst.

"You can relax, Noah."

The voice came from behind him as the warden appeared in front of Noah and he had to swivel on his feet to see how it was possible.

Behind him stood a man dressed in a gray Gucci suit. His expression was serious as he stood with one hand tucked away in his slacks. Noah looked back to the warden. "What's this about?"

"This conversation never happened. You understand?" the warden asked, looking Noah square in the eye.

He nodded, still uncertain about what exactly was going

on. The warden looked at the man behind him. "You have twenty minutes," he said. He then walked off, his shoes echoing again down the corridor until he was no longer in sight.

Noah turned to face the man, finally focusing on him. Adrenaline pumped through Noah as he identified his features. They shared the same eyes, the same nose. . . .

Is this—?

Before Noah could process the thought the man spoke.

"Hello, Noah. I heard you've been asking for me," he said.

Noah had always wondered about his father. As a young boy Noah had watched his friends form bonds with their own that he knew nothing about. He had learned it all on his own. How to hoop . . . how to fight . . . how to drive. The things that fathers showed their sons Noah had missed out on. There was only so much that his mother could do for him. At the end of the day, he had been a little black boy, and no matter how much she tried to provide, she couldn't teach him how to grow up to become a great black man. This man's absence had contributed to Noah's current predicament whether intentional or not.

"Khadafi," Noah whispered. "They said you were dead."

"The streets say a lot of things. Sometimes the illusion of death is the only way you can truly live, son," Khadafi replied.

Noah stiffened and replied, "We ain't got to play them roles. Only one person has called me son my whole life. I'm cool with that."

Khadafi nodded. He was composed as he stood, both hands in his pockets now. Shoulders squared. His salt-and-pepper goatee revealing his wisdom. "I respect that, but just so you know, I didn't know about you. If I had, things would have played out much differently, believe that."

Noah nodded, but he didn't need condolences. There were no words that could make up for what had occurred. It was too little too late.

"When I heard there was a young boy here asking questions about me, I did my research and discovered that you were my son. It seems your mother told you about me at least. For that I am grateful," Khadafi said. "I assume there is a reason why you wanted to see me?"

"I'm all I got in here. I don't got much time, but it's enough. I don't want the walls to start feeling like they're closing in on me. I need to get my legs under me. Establish a consistent flow of paper coming to my books. It's a lot of luxuries that's missing in here. Stuff that niggas will pay to get their hands on," Noah said, not wanting to speak too candidly.

"You sure you want to do that? You're only in for five. With good behavior you'll be out in three. Keeping your nose clean would be—"

"According to the legend, hustling is in my bloodline," Noah interrupted. "Can't give me advice you didn't follow yourself, old man."

Khadafi chuckled and nodded as he replied, "Okay. Consider it done. Bookie will discuss my percentage and prices with you."

Noah nodded and was about to reply when the warden stepped back in with two guards at his side. The brief meeting between father and son was over. They had never gotten a chance to know each other as family, but now they were in bed in business. Khadafi didn't even dabble in small drug deals, but this was a debt that he owed to his son. He couldn't refuse. He extended his hand to his son and Noah accepted it as Khadafi pulled him in for an embrace.

"Naomi Porter," Khadafi whispered in his ear. "Add her to your visiting list."

Noah nodded and made his way over to the guards. Khadafi's voice called out once more. "Warden? Are these the guards that escorted him here?"

"Yes," the warden replied as he frowned, unsure of the purpose of the line of questioning.

"The way they roughed him up didn't go unnoticed. Fire them," Khadafi demanded.

Noah smirked but couldn't hide his shock as the warden nodded obediently. *Damn,* Noah thought, surprised at the amount of pull Khadafi had. As Noah was escorted back to his cell his mind raced. Heroin was a big deal behind the wall, but it was so hard to get inside that it was rare that inmates ever got their fix. Prison was a hard walk of life, and every man had his own way of dealing with it. A nice high would be more valuable than gold inside and give Noah a way to finance himself for the next five years. If he was caught, five years could become a lifetime, but it was worth the risk. He didn't know how long Bleu could or would fill his commissary, and he refused to put the burden on his mother. He had to do what was necessary. Noah had to survive.

Bleu blazed through the pages of her history book as if she were reading for pleasure. She hadn't realized just how much she had been skipping class until it was time for her to make up all the work. She was supposed to be catching up to the other students. She had started late and the university had taken a chance on her, but she had been so caught up in other things that she had forgotten why she was there in the first place. The Adderall gave her a leg up. The amount of focus she felt was incredible, but she still couldn't help but feel overwhelmed. She was buried in reading assignments and late papers. She had been stuck in her dorm room for three days and hadn't slept once. Still her progress was slow, and her heart concerned.

If I don't get this work done they're going to kick me out, she thought. *The fuck?*

Tears flooded her eyes and she planted her hands on her face. She felt like screaming. The stress that she felt was driving her crazy. She was a prisoner to these damn books. History. Philosophy. Math. Chemistry. Weeks of it! It was all too much.

"Agh!" she finally let out as she swept her notebook off her bed.

Startled, China jumped as she removed her earbuds and looked at Bleu in concern. "Umm, okay? You mad or nah?" she asked sarcastically. Her normal wit wasn't amusing to Bleu. In fact, she was so on edge that it irritated her. Bleu cut her eyes at China. If looks could kill . . .

Catching the shade, China added some chill to her approach as she said, "It can't be that bad. Do you need help? You're taking the Addie, right?"

Bleu nodded her head and replied, "Yes, I'm popping them

like candy, but it's only so much they can do. Yes, I focus, yes, they help me stay up, but it doesn't make me move any faster. And even though I've been up for days, my body is dragging. I get why people take them, but I need some shit to turn me into Superwoman." She shook her head. "How the hell do you and Aysha keep up? Between hustling and school, I'm lost."

"We pay the geeks to finish our work," China replied, "but we do still go to class, Bleu. You just stopped going altogether."

"I got caught up," Bleu whispered in despair.

"Well, I hate to tell you this, I know the timing is off, but we need to make another run," China said. "The connect wants to meet us. Bree said we're moving a lot of product across the border and dude is curious, I guess."

Bleu's interest was immediately piqued. Another flip was just what she needed. Bleu blew through her cash almost as quickly as she made it. She only had $2,500 left from their last run. If UCLA did in fact kick her to the curb she needed some money to survive. She couldn't, under any circumstances, go back home with her tail tucked between her legs. "When?" she asked.

"Friday," China said.

"All this shit is due Friday," Bleu complained.

"So finish it beforehand. All I know is that you can't miss this run. It's important, and if you don't go, it makes us look hot," China replied.

Bleu shook her head. Like water running through her fingers she felt like her dream was slipping out of her hands. She just didn't have enough time to play catch up. There was no way she could get everything done by Friday. She was jittery and completely fatigued, but her mind was highly alert. Still, it didn't make the work get done any faster.

"Look, Bleu, I have something stronger than Adderall. It will help you finish by Friday, but the shit is no joke. You have to be careful," China warned. Her eyes were suddenly deathly serious and she spoke at a whisper, as if there were someone else in the room.

"What is it?" Bleu asked, desperate for an easy fix.

China arose from her bed and hurried over to her desk, where she snapped open her Gucci clutch. She pulled out a small Baggie. She tossed it to Bleu.

"What the fuck is this?" Bleu asked as she held it up. "Glass?" She had never seen it before. The tiny clear crystals sparkled slightly as she poured a few out into her hand.

"It's just a little meth," China said dismissively.

"Meth?" Bleu said as she frowned. She didn't know shit about meth. All she knew was that it was a "white people" drug and anyone she had ever seen on it had fucked-up teeth.

"Don't judge, bitch," China replied with a knowing smirk. "Do one line and all of that work you stressing over will be done before Friday. A few students here swear by it. I have a good little side hustle going on with it, so I know it works. You think you haven't slept now? This shit will have you speeding through life at eighty mph. You might crash at the end, but it will get you through the weekend."

Bleu's entire body shook. She didn't even smoke weed, so the thought of using meth scared her. She knew the power of addiction. As a little girl she had witnessed her mother tee-tering between sober and strung out. There had been no in-between. Addiction ran through her veins, and Bleu feared it like the plague. She didn't want to start something that she couldn't stop. She shook her head, declining. "I'm good."

"Oookayyy," China said as she shrugged her shoulders. She took the Baggie from Bleu and placed it in her desk drawer. "Well, I'm going to give you some privacy and let you get back to it. I'm going out with Aysha. We'll check in on you later, a'ight?" She bent down and picked up the notebook that Bleu had tossed to the floor and then extended it to her roommate. "You've got this."

Bleu nodded as she accepted the notebook. "Thanks." She watched China make her departure, wishing that she could tag along.

When she was alone the walls seemed to close in on her. School was sucking the life out of her. She hadn't spoken to Iman in days. Every time he rang her line she buttoned him. He was a distraction . . . a welcome one, but still a distraction all the same. "I have to get out of here," she said to herself as she suddenly began stuffing her books into her backpack. A change of scenery was needed. The air in her small dorm was starting to suffocate her, and if she didn't get out of there, she would drive herself insane. Considering that she hadn't left her dorm in a week, she decided that the fresh air from an evening stroll would do her some good. She left her Benz parked and took the long walk across campus.

The library was unusually deserted for a weekday and Bleu was grateful for the peace. It was just something about being in a room full of books that put her heart at ease. In another lifetime she must have been a librarian, because her love for words and the faded pages of novels ran so deep. She was a smart girl. She had always been. She didn't know why she craved to be one of the stupid ones so badly, but smart girls never had any fun. They weren't the girls who got the guys . . . especially not a guy like Iman. They weren't the center of attention. They were just . . . boring. The thrill of being a red-bottomed, champagne-popping, club-hopping diva appealed to her. What she didn't realize was that smart girls grew into smart women, and smart women ruled the world. So while she was chasing material things and craving shallow praise, she was cheating herself.

Bleu sat at the table in the corner and pulled out her books as she yawned. Her phone beeped loudly and she quickly silenced it. She picked it up.

TEXT MESSAGE
IMAN

You're hard to keep up with, beautiful. Should a nigga take a hint and get lost?

Bleu smiled. If only he knew exactly how much she was feeling him. It slightly amused her that a man with his experience with women was tripping so hard over her. She was flattered, to say the least.

TEXT MESSAGE
BLEU
I'm sorry. I'm getting ready for finals. Been studying
for like a week. At the library. I promise I'll call you
tonight when I make it back to my room.

She waited for his response, but when she received none she turned off her phone and opened her books. The thought of him made her smile as she tried her hardest to concentrate. She powered off her phone, because as long as it was on she would be anticipating his next words. She yawned again and this time she noticed exactly how exhausted she felt. Her eyes were starting to blur. Days without sleep were beginning to catch up to her, and the bags she felt as she rubbed her weary eyes only confirmed it. She rested her head on her clenched fist, forcing herself to read the pages in front of her. Stopping wasn't an option, at least not a voluntary one, but when her eyes began to close without her even realizing it, there was no use in fighting it.

I just need to rest my eyes for a minute. . . .

Then minutes mistakenly became hours.

"Hmm-hmm."

Bleu snapped out of her sleep in alarm as she felt the presence over her shoulder. She turned around, slightly alarmed until she saw him. Iman. He towered over her, handsome as ever as he gave her a charming wink.

"What are you doing here?" she asked as her face melted into a smile.

"I know you're busy with the school thing and all, but I figured you got to eat, right?" he suggested as he held up a bag from the best burger joint in town. "Last time you said I was too fancy with the chef and all that, so I opted for a college-girl meal." He winked. She smiled. Iman grabbed her hand. "You look tired, ma; everything a'ight?"

She thought about telling him about how she had slipped up, how her scholarship was in jeopardy, but decided against it. It wasn't his problem and she didn't want to weigh the air down with negativity. "Everything's perfect now that you're here," she assured him.

Iman looked at her for a moment, letting time skip a beat as he took her in. She was back to her normal self, although her fashion had stepped up quite a bit. True Religions, Converse kicks, a UCLA hoodie, and a Polo hat. Her long weave was pulled into a ponytail to the back. She was casual, resembling the small-town girl he had first met. He loved her in this state.

"What?" she asked as she fidgeted from his intense stare.

"You're dope," he complimented.

"I know," she chuckled in response.

"Is there somewhere more private we can go? The little librarian gave me the death stare when she saw me come in here with this food."

Bleu laughed as she gathered her stuff and stood. "Yeah, we can go upstairs to the third floor. There shouldn't be much of anybody up there this time of night," she responded.

He placed his hand on the small of her back as they made their way. "You got me out here like a lovesick teenager, ma," he said. "I feel like I'm sweating you and shit."

"That's a bad thing?" she asked. They stepped onto the elevator and she leaned against the wall as he invaded her space.

"I don't even do young chicks, the mind-set ain't right, but with you everything is different, Bleu. You make me feel things I haven't felt in a very long time. I've been through a lot. Seen a lot. Lived a lot. I want to be honest with you about everything. There are a lot of things you are unaware of. Things you should know before you give me your heart," he said. He caressed her face as he spoke, and his eyes told a story of pain that made Bleu's heart beat nervously in response.

"I think it's too late," she answered. "I've never been in love, so I don't know if that's what I'm feeling, but—"

She didn't even have a chance to finish her sentence before Iman's lips covered hers. Their kiss was slow, like a forbidden dance. He held her so gently that she quivered. She was young, and she knew that Iman would throw her entire world off track, but nothing . . . absolutely nothing had ever felt this good. It was too hard to stop from falling down that slippery slope. He lifted her leg around his waist and palmed her ass. He needed her. She could feel it . . . this energy between them thickened the oxygen around them, making it hard to breathe. This thing of theirs was magnetic, and if souls really could mate they would produce generational love for years to come. They were so wrapped up in each other that they didn't even notice the elevator doors open until . . .

"Ms. Montclair."

The even tone of disdain belonged to Professor Davis. Bleu immediately pulled away from Iman in embarrassment, straightening her clothes as her eyes widened in horror.

"Professor Davis . . . I . . . umm, we—"

"I'm glad to see you're using your time wisely, Ms. Montclair," Professor Davis said sarcastically. "One would think you would at least try to keep your place here, but apparently it isn't a priority."

Bleu and Iman exited the elevator as Professor Davis entered.

Bleu had no response. She knew how bad things looked. She was blowing her opportunity at UCLA. She and the professor both knew it. Respect was earned and Bleu had none reserved with Professor Davis. Bleu had done absolutely nothing to prove that she even deserved her scholarship. As the elevator doors closed she wanted to say something in her own defense, but what could she say? At this point she had to show and prove. Words meant nothing and the look of disgust on her professor's face spoke volumes. The doors closed and Bleu sighed as she placed her hands over her face.

"I'm such a fucking idiot," she said aloud as tears overwhelmed her. She was tired as hell, edgy, embarrassed, and completely in over her head. A breakdown was inevitable.

Iman pulled her into him. "Shh, it's okay, ma. I'm sure you're not the first student she's caught kissing her boyfriend in an elevator," he said. He was clueless to her dilemma. Her entire life had been one long struggle, and she was about to earn a one-way ticket back to Flint.

"You don't understand," she whispered.

"Can I do anything to help?" he asked.

She nodded as he wiped her tears with his thumb. "You can give me a ride back to my hall? I can't do this with you. Not tonight. She's right. I should be focused. Finals are in a few days. I know this seems young and dumb to you, but it's important and I have to focus."

He nodded and wrapped his arms around her. This young woman had his heart on a string. There wasn't much that she could ask of him that he wouldn't oblige. He could see that she needed him to fall back for a while. She seemed like she was wound tight, obsessing and stressing over her schooling. He could dig it and he would play the game by her rules in order to make things easier.

The amount of cloud smoke that Bleu was hit with as she entered her room slapped her in the face. China sat near the open window, blowing trees. The smell of weed was so potent that Bleu knew what was going on before she even stepped inside. The towels that had lined the bottom of the door did little to keep the scent inside.

"I can smell that shit all the way from the hall," Bleu said as she flung her backpack toward her desk. "Why can't you do that in Aysha's room? You know I don't smoke."

China waved Bleu over and patted the spot beside her. "Relax, Bleu. You're wound kind of tight. It's finals week. Everybody in the dorm is probably doing the same thing right now. There's nothing wrong with taking the edge off and getting a little pick-me-up."

China inhaled a blunt filled with "purple" Kush. She held it in her lungs before choking it out with a cough and a laugh. "For you to be from the hood, you're real square, you know that, Bleu?" she asked.

Bleu scoffed and shook her head. "Not square; weed isn't my thing, though. Have you seen niggas roll blunts? All that spit is digusting."

China put out the blunt and hopped off the windowsill as she pulled at the boy shorts she wore. "Well, lucky for you I've got a pipe," China said. China went over to her desk and prepared the pipe before coming back to the window.

"Just relax, girl. This will make you forget all of those worries. This is that good shit. Just close your eyes and inhale," China instructed.

Bleu thought about saying no, but honestly, getting high sounded like the perfect solution to her problems. She just wanted to zone out for a while.

"Just do it. It's just a little smoke," China convinced her.

Bleu closed her eyes and wrapped her lips around the pipe as China put the flame underneath. She inhaled and then instantly choked and coughed as the vapor seemed to burn her lungs.

China held the pipe to Bleu's lips again. "Hit it again," she coached. "You'll get used to it."

Bleu swept a loose hair behind her ear and leaned over the pipe again.

This time she didn't choke, and as the seconds ticked by she felt a warmness flow through her.

Instant gratification.

Bleu's mind became a blank canvas as the pressure she felt miraculously dissolved. Her nipples pressed against the fabric of her T-shirt and her clit swelled.

"It's hot in here." She moaned out the words as her body

slipped into a euphoric state. "This is some good shit," she whispered as she licked her lips. "I never knew weed could feel this good."

"Weed can't," China said. "You just hit meth."

Suddenly it sounded as though China were speaking French as Bleu's eyes blurred. Fear of the unknown seized her.

"What?" Bleu asked. "Why would you—"

"Relaaaax," China said. "You hit it now. No point in tripping. Just enjoy the high and thank me later. The high with meth is amazing, but the comedown is rough. Especially for your first time. When you start feeling like crap, sleep it off."

Bleu wanted to be mad, she wanted to go off, but the good feelings that were coursing through her convinced her that she couldn't be too upset. *Besides, I can't get hooked after one time, right?* she thought. *Anybody can quit something that they've only done once.*

Bleu's mind was in a happy place because although she was pissed she felt anything but. Her week had been hard and this mental break was much needed. *Fuck it, this could be my last week in L.A. If I fail these finals I'm out of here anyway. Fuck Professor Davis. Who gives a damn what she thinks? Might as well enjoy the little time I have left here,* she thought. She wasn't even tripping when she watched China refill the pipe; this time she didn't hide the glass shards. Wasn't any need for further trickery. Bleu wanted more of this bliss . . . this ecstasy. It was like someone had handed her the key to happiness. Her heart skipped a beat in anticipation as a light sweat developed on her forehead as she watched how China prepared the pipe. Bleu fanned herself as her body temperature rose in reaction to her first blast. China held up the pipe once more. Bleu's first hit had been under false pretenses, she hadn't known what she was smoking, but this time she was more than willing as she sucked the vapors into her lungs. Her head fell back in complete bliss as she closed her eyes.

"It feels like my arms are going numb," she whispered. She began to scratch at them as she felt tiny legs crawling up her skin.

"Don't scratch," China schooled her. "Just rub. There isn't anything there. It's just the high. The last thing we need is you digging holes in your skin, walking around looking like a meth head. Be discreet. As long as you don't fall into the traps, no one will ever know you're using it."

"I'm not using it," Bleu said quickly, defensively. "You make it sound like I'm hooked."

China held up her hands innocently. "I didn't mean it like that. I'm just saying . . . I'm trying to look out for you."

"This is a onetime thing," Bleu said.

"How do you feel?" China asked.

Bleu stood up and hung out of the window as she looked over the campus and shouted, "I feel alive!" She burst into a fit of laughter as she climbed up on the windowsill. "Whooo!!" she shouted, feeling as if she could finally breathe a sigh of relief. Nothing had changed, but the drugs had warped her mind into believing that her problems didn't exist. "I don't want to sit in this dusty-ass room. Let's go out. Call Bree; where's Aysha? Let's get into something."

"Chill, party girl. Everybody's wrapped up in their own thing. We all have finals to get ready for," China said.

She passed Bleu the remainder of her stash. She supplied Bleu with an eight-ball, more than any beginner was ready for. "Can you handle that?"

"I told you, I'm not doing this again," Bleu replied.

China nodded and then put her stash back into her drawer. "Okay," she said while giving Bleu a skeptical look. China knew how easy it was to get caught up in the euphoric rush. She noticed the stars in Bleu's widened eyes. She was tweaking and in outer space. China had just introduced Bleu to an abusive lover. It was making her feel good now, but it wouldn't be long before the pleasure eventually became pain.

19

Thirty-six hours later

Bleu's fingers cramped as they moved across the keyboard at lightning speed. Her brain was working harder than it ever had but, with the help of her new secret weapon, she didn't sweat it. She had written three research papers so far. What had taken other students an entire semester to do she had done in hours. What she had promised herself would be one hit had turned into a run of repeated doses. She didn't know that the high would last for a while, so in fear of it disappearing she kept re-upping. This new level of productivity was addictive and the rush was unlike anything she had ever felt before. Every time it felt like it could be going away she itched for more. It was like good sex or good food; one taste had her coming back again and again. The Adderall had made her focus, but it hadn't been enough. She had still felt tired and the effects of no sleep had made her feel like a walking zombie. With meth, she felt limitless. She didn't even realize that she hadn't slept. Between the days on Adderall and now the meth, she was coming up on day six without rest. It didn't matter that she had bags under her eyes or that her appearance was slightly disheveled. She didn't even care that she had forgotten to eat. She felt like Superwoman and as long as she was flying through the schoolwork she had no complaints. She was geeking and going through life at a hundred miles per hour without brakes.

Giddy with excitement and anxiety, she reached for her bag, removing her books. As she began to read, the words jumped off the pages. She flipped the paper so quickly that she gave herself paper cuts. Every sentence made perfect sense. Every word she typed sounded like pure genius. It felt like she had just discovered a miracle drug, and there was no doubt in her mind that she would be able to finish everything on time. Meth had made the impossible possible. She no longer had to worry about losing her scholarship, but in the process she had lost her soul. It was in the devil's hands now, and it would be a long time before she would get it back.

Forty-eight hours later

Slowly, as her high faded, the weight of the world was placed back on her shoulders, and this time it was heavier than ever before. Regret and shame gripped her as the reality of what she had done hit her under sober pretenses. Finally, after three and a half days of nonstop work and after almost a week of no sleep, the aftermath hit her. As she lay curled under her covers, with her hands over her ears and a beauty mask shading her eyes, she felt the misery that was inevitable. The overdose of dopamine that had flooded her system now was stopped altogether and she was left feeling empty, void of all emotion. She was a shell, but the inside had been carved out. All she wanted to do was sleep, but every time she closed her eyes she pictured herself wrapping her lips around a glass pipe. Then she saw her mother wrapping her lips around a glass pipe. It was too familiar and, in the depths of Bleu's soul, she feared the repercussions.

What the fuck was I thinking? she asked herself as she clenched her eyes shut. Things were out of control. If she had felt the need to turn to drugs just to help her manage her time then she was doing something extremely wrong. She was letting L.A. get the best of her. Yes, she had made up her work. She wouldn't receive her semester grades for at least another week, but she knew that she had aced her finals. The meth had done everything that China had promised, but had the trade-off been worth it?

The ringing of her cell forced her to lift her head as she reached for the nightstand where it rested. Even Iman's name didn't excite her. The fog that had settled over her life was too thick for even him to break through. She buttoned him, sending him to voice mail, and then clenched her eyes together trying to force them to stay shut. Her mind wanted to sleep, but her body wouldn't let her. She was up and down, her emotions all over the place. She couldn't control them if she tried. The sound of China walking into their room, followed by the voices of Bree and then Aysha, caused Bleu to grimace. She just wanted some privacy . . . time to process what she had done. She wasn't ready to face them. Surely they looked at her in an entirely new light. If she was judging herself she knew that they had to be. Again she thought, *What the fuck was I thinking?* The stupidity of her decisions was immeasurable and she was sick to her stomach just thinking about it. Or was she sick to her stomach from the meth? She didn't know at this point.

"Damn, girl, you a'ight?" Bree commented as he reached down and pulled the covers from over Bleu's head. "Fuck you get into last night?" he asked.

"She's fine," China said with attitude, not appreciating Bree's interest in Bleu. "She just went on a little meth run."

Bree's face turned cold as he sat down on the edge of Bleu's bed. "You didn't give her nothing to help with the comedown? Come on, ma. You know better than that!" Bree barked as he pulled Bleu up. Her body was so fatigued that she was like a rag doll as he leaned her back against the wall.

"Hmm-hmm, just go away, Bree. I feel like shit," Bleu groaned.

"And you gon' feel like shit unless you take something. You can't fly high and then dip this low, baby girl," he said.

Aysha stood back, a bit taken aback as she watched Bree force Bleu to sit up. She covered her mouth in disbelief. "How much did you give her? Meth, China?" Aysha asked. She had dabbled in many things, but crystal meth was something that she vowed to never do. Ever. She had seen the monstrous things it could do.

"Not that much. She's fine. It's just her first time," China snapped.

Aysha went into her purse and pulled out a pill bottle. She popped the top and passed Bree one of the magic downers inside.

"Take this," Bree said as he pinched the sides of Bleu's face, forcing the pill into her open mouth. "It'll bring you down, relax you, and help you sleep. I need you good for the weekend. I have never even met the connect before, so this is big. I need you at your best."

She took the pill and Aysha handed her a bottle of water to wash it down.

"I have more if you need 'em," Aysha offered. "I have fucked-up anxiety, so my doctor writes me a regular prescription."

China huffed loudly. "My God! She's fine! She's high as fuck! When she comes off of that shit she'll be okay. Can you lay out the lick this weekend or are you gonna baby her all day?"

"Relax, China. Should have never gave her the shit from jump. Fuck was you thinking?" Bree asked.

"I was thinking that I was helping her ass out," China snapped. "You know what? When you're done babysitting, call me."

Suddenly she couldn't contain her jealousy and stormed out as Bree shook his head in frustration.

"Go after her," Bleu moaned as she lay back down. "I'm good."

"Are you sure?" Aysha asked.

"Yeah, I'm positive. I'll be ready by the weekend," she mumbled.

Two days. She missed two whole days of life, and when she finally came to she frowned, as her covers stuck to her wet body.

"Did I pee on myself?" she asked, disgusted as she felt the warm, wet bedding beneath her. She was grateful that she was alone and she jumped up, embarrassed, as she snatched the soiled sheets off of the bed. She peeled herself out of her clothes and swept her messy hair out of her face. The world was hazy, and although she had just awakened, she felt like she could lie right back down and drift back into dreamland. Her body was tired, sore even, but slightly unsatisfied. It was like she had an insatiable urge to smoke just one more time. She shook her head, trying to gather her wits as she stuffed her sheets into the dirty hamper before making her way to the bathroom. Tension had found its way back into her shoulders. The false sense of security that she had felt faded away and she was left with a nagging feeling of worry. She lowered her head, not caring that the water was destroying her hair as it sprayed down on her. She was overwhelmed with the reality of what she had done. She had stooped to a low place and, as she watched the water swirl down the drain, she wished she could rinse her sins away. She squeezed her eyes closed as the beads of water beat down on her back, kneading the stress out of her shoulders with every drop.

Did I even pass? she thought, worrying that the drugs had made her overconfident in her own ability. *Who takes final ex-*

ams high? I probably fucked up any chance I had of passing, she thought. She washed her body, mind cluttered with guilt from what she had done, as she hurriedly dressed. She was bothered by the uncertainty of her fate. She couldn't sit around and wait for semester grades to be posted. She needed to know now. *I can just ask my professors,* she thought as she hurriedly dressed. She grabbed her handbag, threw a Polo hat over her wet weave, and headed out the door. The guessing game would kill her if she waited. She had to know how she had done. The actual test was such a blur that she silently feared the worst. She drove across campus, flying at top speed like a bat out of hell and then parked directly in front of the building. She rushed in to see Professor Davis.

She knocked on the door timidly, almost afraid to hear the results.

"Ms. Montclair, come in," the professor greeted her, never wavering from her serious, no-nonsense reserve. The woman intimidated Bleu, and if she passed this class she would never have to deal with her again. "Relief" would be an understatement.

"Good morning—"

"Good afternoon . . . ," the professor greeted her back.

Bleu rolled her eyes as she shifted her stance. *She enjoys torturing me,* she thought. "I was wondering if you could tell me my semester grades. I studied really hard and—"

"You passed—"

"Yes, yes, yes!" Bleu exclaimed as she breathed a sigh of relief.

"Every class except mine, Ms. Montclair," Professor Davis finished.

Bleu's face fell in confusion as her excitement ceased instantly. "What does that mean?" she asked.

"As you know, it is a condition of your scholarship that you keep a 3.0 GPA. You passed your classes, but you didn't ace them, and with the 1.5 you attained in my course your overall average fell below a 3.0."

"What is it?" Bleu asked, heartbroken.

"2.65," Professor Davis responded. "The university won't be renewing your scholarship next semester. If you want to stay here you will be responsible for your own room and board, plus tuition and fees. I'm sorry."

Bleu's world crashed. Even after taking the meth, after pulling the all-nighters, after going to the extremes just to catch up, she had still come up short. "Please, I busted my ass—"

"For finals, Ms. Montclair. You busted your ass for finals. There are students who bust their ass every day. They work tirelessly, day in, day out. You only gave your best effort when you were in jeopardy of being dismissed from the university. You say that you want this, Bleu, but you don't act like it," the professor said. "I must say I expected more." Professor Davis spoke condescendingly, her voice dry and unflinching. She never even looked up from the stack of papers in front of her.

Bleu was devastated. Her eyes watered in disappointment. *How did I let this happen?*

"Is there a reason you're still here?" the professor asked.

Without responding, Bleu rushed out of the office, and when she was in the hallway she leaned her back against the wall, letting her head fall back as her tears fell. She had been so stupid. So reckless. So ungrateful. She had fumbled her dream and for what? To pop bottles in a club? To rock the flyest shit? Be the flyest bitch? She had joined a plastic world where money and status reigned supreme. She had been so busy assimilating to the lifestyle that she had forgotten why she had come to L.A. in the first place. Stupid. That's how she felt. Like a superficial, airhead, ass little girl. The big-city lights had blinded her, but now that school was no longer an option her newfound "it girl" status was all she had left. At a time like this a girl would think of her parents . . . of making that dreaded phone call and explaining how she had blown it. Bleu didn't have that. The only person she thought of was Noah. The moment he crossed her mind her heart fluttered. She was supposed to make it for both of them, and despite the fact that he wouldn't judge her, she felt as if she had let him down. He was her best friend, her soul mate, and the one whose heartbeat matched her own. She loved Noah with every inch of her being, and although she was with Iman, she knew deep in her heart that he was just a beautiful distraction. Iman's presence made Noah's absence affect her less, yet she still missed him. There was no one who knew her better or knew how much she truly wanted to live this California dream. If he were out, he would have been the one to remind her not to blow the opportunity that had been given to her. He would have kept her balanced. She needed his kind of normal to remind her of where she came from, but with him locked away she was transforming into someone different. A girl who wore makeup, drove a Benz, chased mental highs, and popped pills to recover from the self-induced lows. Bleu was changing, and although the pace of her new lifestyle was exciting, the fact that she had flunked out of her classes was proof that she couldn't keep up with it all.

"This is some bullshit! She just got here. I put her on and now she's the one who gets to meet the connect? Bleu don't even know how to handle no shit this big! She had to get zooted just to get through fucking final exams! All of a sudden she's Escobar or some shit!"

Bleu stood on the outside of her dorm room as China's irate voice blared through the closed door. "She's new and I've been down with you since day one."

Bleu entered the room, interrupting them as she stood in the doorway. "What's up? Clearly we have some things to discuss, because I can hear you screaming my name all the way down the hall. What's going on?" she asked.

Bree sighed. "The connect only wants to meet you," he informed her.

"And that's a problem?" she asked as her brow furrowed in defense. "Before I came on y'all was moving fifteen ki's a week. Thanks to me we're moving five hundred."

"We take the risks with you," China spat.

"Do you really? Because I don't recall you renting the charter bus in your name. If we're ever stopped and searched, the police are taking me in; they're asking me the questions. I take all the risks, but even still I split the profits equally with you and Aysha," Bleu responded.

Aysha stood off to the side, leaning against the bathroom door as she watched her two friends go head up over the crown.

China wanted to be queen bee, but since Bleu had come into her own, it wasn't so evident who was leading anymore. "As long as the money flow don't change up, I'm good. I don't care who goes," she said with a shrug.

"You in it for the paper, not the recognition," Bree said to a seething China. "Remember that. You can go, but we'll fall back . . . stay at the hotel while Bleu handles the meeting."

"Yeah, whatever. Next thing you know the paper gon' be distributed differently too. Mark my words," China said as she stood up abruptly, storming out.

"When do we leave?" Bleu said as she flipped her hand dismissively, immediately changing the subject.

"You sure you good with this?" Bree asked. "You can say no if you not with it."

The thought of being in Cinco's presence alone again spooked Bleu. It wasn't just about intimidation with him. He frightened her. There was something about the look in his eyes that made his black soul shine through. The opportunity was too good to pass up, however, and if she didn't do it, there were a million girls behind her who would. Now that she had gotten herself kicked out of UCLA, she would have to keep hustling to survive. It was no longer about material things. She needed stability. She would have to put her big-girl panties on. This was a new level of the game. She was a mule and was making good money, but her position was the lowest. Mules were expendable and easily replaced. She felt it in her bones that after this trip her value in the "dope game" would increase and with it so would the amount of respect and money she earned. She needed to meet the man behind Cinco, because, at the end of the day, even he had a boss. Nobody even knew the name of the connect. The fact that he had requested her presence spoke volumes. That meant money was about to flow. She wasn't trying to make a career out of this, but she wasn't against a nice flip. She needed the money. She had gotten used to the finer things. She didn't want to go back to ordinary after experiencing the extraordinary.

She nodded. "Yeah, I'm good," she replied. "I'll be ready."

20

"Inmate, on your feet!" the CO called out aggressively as he entered Noah's cell.

Noah sat, playing cards with Bookie. He looked up in annoyance as he asked, "What's the problem?"

"You're signed up for the new college program!" the CO shot back.

"Nah, that ain't me. I ain't sign up for no shit like that," he responded coolly.

"You're on the list, so on your feet," the CO demanded.

"But I ain't sign up for it," Noah shot back.

"Take it up with someone else. On your feet. Let's go!"

Noah sighed and then tossed his hand down, revealing it to Bookie. "I was going to beat you anyway, old man," he said.

"God damn it," Bookie said, flicking his own cards as Noah waltzed out of the cell, one guard in front of him, one behind him. He had gotten used to feeling cornered.

"This some bullshit," he muttered as he stepped into the group room where tables and chairs were set up like a class-room.

It wasn't until he saw her did Noah change his mind. She took his breath away. Skin the color of mocha, dark eyes to match, and slim from head to toe. She was model thin, but from the rear she gave a man much to appreciate. Her hair was shaven down on one side with the Chanel logo lined into it, while the other side hung long in loose waves. She was fly, the look in her eyes vicious, and the sway of her hips hypnotizing. She stood next to an older black woman, mid fifties, as the two introduced themselves to the group. He took a seat.

"My name is Jenna Thompson and this is my assistant, Naomi Porter. We're here to help you better your lives. All of you are here less than five years. It's time to start making plans for when you get out. A college degree will . . ."

The woman's words became background noise as Noah focused in on the girl beside her. *Naomi Porter. Khadafi sent her,* he thought. Suddenly it made sense how he had gotten on the list and how this new program had suddenly started at the prison. As he looked at Naomi he appreciated every inch of her. She hadn't been what he was expecting at all. He wouldn't mind doing business with her; she was easy on the eyes. After seeing nothing but overweight CO's and being around nothing but testosterone day in and day out, she was easy on the eyes.

"Gentlemen, please sign in and come get your assigned reading materials from Naomi," the woman instructed.

Noah stood and joined the line, sauntering toward the front until finally it was his turn.

"Noah Langston," he said.

"Hello, Noah," Naomi replied. She handed him a small canvas tote bag. "Everything you need is inside," she said with a wink of her doe-shaped eyes.

He nodded as he bit his lip. "Thanks," he replied before returning to his seat.

He noticed that he had two textbooks. He opened one discreetly, turning his head to eye the guard before focusing on the pages. It was hollowed out; small Baggies of heroin lay inside, along with a burner phone. He quickly closed it, and as he pulled out the real textbook a smile crossed his face. Khadafi had just put him on, and it was time to get paid.

Bleu was taken aback by the luxury of the private estate. As she stood on the doorstep of the opulent oceanside villa her mind spun. She didn't know what to expect.

The doors opened and one of the most beautiful women she had ever seen stood before her. She was average height, with short pixie-cut hair and coal black eyes. Her dark skin was flawless and her perfect figure enviable. She was exotic, clearly rich, and a bit snarky as she stood there in her perfection.

"You must be?"

Bleu almost forgot that she went by an assumed name, and she was so mesmerized by the presence of the woman in front of her that she just stood there, gawking. She seemed so familiar, as if they had met before. *Where do I know her from?*

Bleu thought distractedly as she immediately felt small compared to the likes of the goddess before her.

"Do you speak?" the woman asked frankly.

"Oh, umm, yes, I'm sorry, yeah, I'm Blake," Bleu replied.

"I'm Tristan. My husband will be pleased to meet you. From what I hear, you've become very good for business. Cinco will be here shortly," she responded. "Come in. Our chef has prepared dinner."

As soon as Bleu stepped inside, a Mexican man with a scar that ran down the length of his face stepped up. He had the menacing glare of a stone-cold killer. One eye was closed permanently, and over his eyelid was a tattoo of a bleeding skull. The sight of him sent chills down her spine.

"Bruno will search you. Can't be too careful, you know?" Tristan said. Bleu held out her arms as Bruno ran his hands over her body thoroughly. He made sure to linger over her breasts, causing Bleu to cringe.

"That's enough, Bruno," Tristan intervened. She smirked. "Bruno gets a little overzealous sometimes. Please come in. We'll break bread together and then get down to business."

Bleu followed her inside, where a dinner party seemed to be taking place. "I didn't realize so many people would be here," Bleu said as she followed Tristan through the villa and out to the back, where at least a dozen other people congregated on the beach. The ocean was the backdrop and the moon lit up the night sky. A long rectangular dinner table had been elaborately set with crystal and linens on the sand, while tiki torches were lit around it.

"This is an organization built around family. We take care

of our own, Blake. Depending on what you decide tonight, these people may become your family too. Come, there are many people to meet," Tristan said. "Starting with the king himself."

Bleu and Tristan walked up on her husband as he stood overlooking the calm water, his hands tucked in a pair of Ferragamo slacks. Bleu almost felt rude for interrupting such a peaceful moment. His back was to the commotion as he stood alone. He had obviously separated himself purposefully, but Tristan insisted on an introduction.

"Our final guest has arrived," Tristan said as she grabbed his hand.

He turned around and Blake's stomach went hollow as she looked into Iman's eyes. Bitch slapped by his presence, she was speechless as her mouth fell open, but no words slipped out.

"Blake, this is my husband, Iman. Iman, this is the infamous Blake," Tristan introduced them. "This is the girl who has made Cinco's profits double in just a few weeks. Apparently she has a knack for getting weight across the border."

Blake noticed a hint of surprise as her presence stunned Iman, but he quickly recovered, not giving away the fact that they already knew each other.

She could feel tears burning her eyes as the urge to throw up overwhelmed her. *He's married. He's fucking married,* she thought. She was sick. He had played her. Mr. "tell me no lies" had told her the biggest one of them all. He was married. Never mind the fact that he was the head of one of the most dangerous drug cartels in Mexico. Suddenly the pieces were all falling back into place. *I don't even know who he is,* she thought.

"It's nice to meet you," Iman said, extending his hand. She felt insulted. Betrayed. *So this nigga is just going to play dumb?* she thought. She was seeing red at his audacity. Just days ago he had made love to her. He had put his mouth on her most private of places. Now he was greeting her with a handshake. For lack of a better response she shook his hand. He rubbed her hand briefly with his thumb before letting it go. Tristan was none the wiser.

"Tan, baby, I could use a drink," Iman said.

Tan?! Bleu thought. Suddenly she realized why Tristan looked so familiar. She was the woman who constantly called Iman whenever he and Bleu were together. *Tan is his pet name for her!* Bleu sulked. Tristan was one of those pretty girls who made her feel so inferior. She was his wife, which made Bleu—

His fucking mistress! she screamed in her mind. *This no-good, lying-ass, cheating mu' fucka, has me playing the role of his side chick!*

Suddenly all the things he had told her she doubted. He had her standing there, feeling stupid, heart in her stomach, as she watched his beauty queen wife lovingly kiss his cheek.

"Sure, love. I'll find one of the waiters and have them bring you something over. I need to find Cinco and find out why he's late as usual," she said. It was clear that Iman was trying to get rid of her, but Bleu had no conversation for him. She just wanted to get out of there before the levies on her emotions gave way. "Could you excuse me? Do you have a bathroom I can use?" she asked, her voice wavering as she willed herself to keep her composure.

Iman's eyes pleaded with her. They were saying so much, but his lips weren't moving. She could practically read his thoughts. She avoided his gaze as Tristan pointed up toward the house.

"Sure, you can follow me back up to the house. I'll show you where it is," Tristan said.

Iman watched Bleu walk away, and with each step she took he felt a stabbing ache in his heart. He knew her. The revelation of his marriage had caused her shoulders to sag, and the devastation that he had seen in her face had crushed her. He had wanted to tell her. This was certainly not the way that he had wanted her to discover it. *The fuck is she doing here anyway? Working with Cinco? Moving weight across the border? Is this why she so hard to keep up with?* Iman thought. His mind was fried from trying to figure it all out. Little Bleu from Flint, Michigan, was a scholar by day and a drug mule by night. He had to admit that he found her hustle a little bit sexy, but he was angry with her for keeping it from him. She was taking penitentiary chances with her life. He knew the game, he had come up in it, and Bleu wasn't built for it. She was too smart to be associated with the likes of Cinco, and now that Iman knew that she was in business with his brother-in-law he wondered about the nature of their relationship. Were they fucking? Did Cinco push up on her? It was known that Cinco was a ladies' man. Had Bleu fallen for Cinco's lavish playboy ways? Jealousy spread through Iman like a disease as it infected his heart. The thought of her with another man wounded him. The fact that she was here troubled him. Bleu was supposed to be his good girl . . . his college girl . . . his simple chick. She was the only thing in his world that made him feel like normalcy was something he could attain. The fact that she hadn't known about his kingpin status pleased him because he was certain that she loved him for him, not for what he represented. Apparently they both had been keeping secrets, but he knew that the ones that he had withheld from her were unforgivable. The shattered look on her gorgeous face had been like daggers to his heart. He needed to speak to her. He had to make her understand that things weren't what they seemed to be. Iman would do whatever he needed to do in order to make things right. He hadn't realized how much she truly meant to him until the moment when he thought he might lose her. He had to make this right, and despite the fact that she had some explaining to do as well, he knew that he had committed the greater of the two wrongs.

Bleu entered the kitchen, trying to keep her head low so that no one could see the anguish that was now falling down her cheeks. She ran face-first into the chef, knocking a tray of hor d'oeuvres out of his hands. She looked up. "I'm so sorry," she cried, distraught. She was shocked and also grateful to see Big Les looking down at her sympathetically.

It wasn't until that moment did she interpret the words he had spoken back in L.A. "I guess there's a new queen in the castle," he had said. Now she knew exactly what he had meant.

"He's married," she whispered as she shook her head.

Big Les grabbed her by the elbow and gently pulled her toward the hall. Fortunately for her, no one else had ventured into the kitchen. He opened the bathroom door.

"You can get yourself together in here," he said with a re-assuring nod. She nodded as he closed the door, leaving her to cry in solitude.

As soon as Bleu was protected by the solace of the bathroom a sob escaped her that she just couldn't stop. She gripped the sink as she lowered her head and cried. She was devastated. It was her first heartbreak. The thing with love was it had the power to make her feel so good, but now she was experiencing the flip side . . . love also had the power to make her feel so low. It was gut-wrenching and cruel. What she had thought to be so real now felt fake. She had been duped and it was her own fault. Trusting Iman so easily had been the wrong move. *He's married*, she thought as she shook her head in disgrace. She hadn't realized how vastly different they were until now. They were on two different planes in life. While she was thinking about childish things like school tests he was living a grown man's life. He had a wife and he had made a mistress out of Bleu. *I'm probably not even the only chick on the side. Oh my God, do they have kids?* she wondered. A knock at the door interrupted her thoughts.

"Open the door, ma."

It was him. The liar. The man with whom she had trusted her heart. She unlocked the door and then watched him as he entered. He closed the door behind him and locked it. He kept his back turned to her as he rested a fist against the door and placed his head on top of it.

"You're married," she whispered. She kept saying it because she still couldn't believe that it was real. Each time she said it, she destroyed herself.

He turned and rushed her, pressing her against the wall as he kissed her passionately. She fought him, he fought her, and through it all their lips never parted. She loved and hated him at the same damn time. She pulled away from him, furious, as she pushed his chest forcefully. "You lied!" she whispered harshly. "You lied to me!"

He let her take her aggressions out as he withstood her assault. The pain etched on her face made him sick. He was disgusted with himself for hurting her, no matter how unintentional it may have been. "Let me explain, Bleu," he whispered.

"There isn't anything to explain. It's a simple yes or no. Are you married?" she asked. She already knew the answer, but she wanted to hear him admit it.

Iman swallowed the lump in his throat and squared his shoulders. He wanted to lie to her just to keep her in his life, but he knew that she deserved better than that. He knew what it looked like . . . what it felt like for her, and his soul burned with regret as he stared into her eyes. Remorsefully he replied, "Yes."

She scoffed and covered her face with her hands as she cried. Seeing her this distraught tore him up as he pulled her into his embrace.

"Why would you make me love you? Why would you do this to me?" she sobbed. She had never felt like a bigger fool. She felt like the butt of Iman's joke. He had played with her heart and now she was left nursing emotional wounds. Nothing he had ever said to her felt true. Liar. That's what he instantly became . . . one big liar. Embarrassment filled her and her cheeks burned in shame as she recoiled from his touch.

"I'll leave her, ma. Just give me a chance to make it right," he said as he pressed his forehead against Bleu's. "I never meant to lie to you. I was going to tell you."

She slapped his hands away. "Just stay the fuck away from me," she sneered. She pushed past him as he tried to grab her, but before he could get a good grip she was out the door. She ran face-first into Cinco, who stepped back in confusion as he raised his hands in defense.

"Whoa, shorty, you in a hurry," he commented as he gave Iman a look of amusement. Bleu raced out, mortified.

"Fuck," Iman muttered as he swiped his hand over the top of his head.

"What was that all about, bro? You smashing that?" Cinco asked, wondering how Iman had even gotten mixed up with the pretty, young college girl.

"Lower your voice and go after her. Make sure she's a'ight," Iman stated seriously.

Iman wanted to go himself, but he couldn't. Chasing after her would cause a scene. He couldn't do that . . . not here . . . not now, with Tristan lurking nearby. His wife played nice, but if she found out that Bleu was the girl he was entertaining and that his affair had come knocking at their front door, she would wage war against his pretty young thing, a war that Bleu would lose. He didn't want her in harm's way and a public blowup with Tristan wasn't good for business, especially since all of his head lieutenants were present. Right now his hands were tied, but as soon as he made it back to L.A. he vowed to make things right.

21

Bleu raced out of the house, head lowered as she tried to conceal her tear-streaked face.

"Damn it!" she whispered as she realized that her driver had left. She couldn't sit still—she didn't want to give Iman the chance to catch up to her—so as she pulled out her cell phone she began walking down the long driveway that led to the main road. She half-walked, half-ran, as she tried to put distance between her and Iman. Crushed by the weight of a love that was never really real, she felt as if she would suffocate on her own grief. Why had she fallen for him? How had she missed the signs that he was not only taken but also married! *His wife is everything. The bitch is gorgeous and powerful and wealthy. So what was I to him? Nothing? Was he slumming it with me?* Her heart beat to the rhythm of a song called "Devastation" as she made her escape. Thinking about it was making her ill. Lovesick . . . that's what she was. The sound of a car behind her caused her to pick up her pace, but she had no wins against the six-inch Giuseppe pumps she wore. She stumbled, barely stopping herself from falling as she dropped her clutch and its contents all over the ground.

The car pulled up on her and she turned to find Cinco peering at her from the driver's seat.

"He didn't even come after me," she scoffed as she bent down to pick up her scattered belongings.

Cinco looked and saw the stash of meth that lay on the ground. She quickly scooped it up and placed it in her purse before getting to her feet.

He looked at her, mischief dancing in his eyes. "You smoke?" he asked.

"No," she replied, but as soon as she thought about the drugs that were in her bag she felt a knot form in her stomach. They were an instant pick-me-up, something that could turn her night right around.

"No judgment," Cinco said. "But that shit there will fuck you up, kid. Have you out here with your teeth crumbling and shit. That's trash. You making all that money and catching a poor man's high?"

She shifted on her feet to relieve the pain of her designer shoes. "What's a rich man's high?"

"Get in," Cinco stated. He noticed her hesitation. "Come on, you gon' hold that shit at the beach against a nigga forever? That wasn't nothing; I was drunk. My bad, kid. Shit was foul. I promise I'll be a perfect gentleman."

Bleu didn't know what she was thinking. In fact, she wasn't. Cinco had raped her. He had forced himself on her, the same way that her mother's boyfriend had done so many years ago. But she had learned at an early age to just live with it, to just accept it. Right now she would have taken a ride with the devil in order to get away from Iman. She stepped out of her shoes and walked around the car, hopping into the passenger side of Cinco's Lamborghini.

As soon as her butt melted into the leather seat, Cinco grabbed her clutch.

"Hey, what are you doing?!" she protested. He pulled out the meth and rolled down his window, tossing the meth into the street.

"You want to smoke something, smoke this," he said. He pulled out a blunt. He lit the blunt and pulled on it hard, causing the end to spark with amber flames. He held the smoke in his lungs, coughing slightly and inhaling through his nose before blowing it out.

Her head was spinning and heart pounding. The night's events had taken a toll on her. As she reached for the blunt she said, "Fuck it."

As she hit it Cinco watched in fascination and then smiled as he pulled away from the curb.

The car filled with the haze from the purple Kush as Bleu's entire body began to tingle and a slight ringing filled her ears. Her body was abuzz. This high was mellow and seemed to relax her brain while stimulating her entire body. Everything felt numb; her fingertips, her toes, her nipples, even her clitoris, tingled.

"You feeling it?" Cinco asked.

"I feel nothing and that's even better," she responded.

They were silent as they passed the blunt back and forth. Too much talking always killed the vibe, and she was thankful that he didn't ask her any questions. When they pulled up to a home that sat on the edge of a seaside cliff she sat up in alarm.

"I thought you were taking me back to the motel," she said.

"I thought we could kick it. There's a lot more where that came from," Cinco stated as he pointed to the blunt that she was pinching between her fingers. It was now the size of a cigarette butt. "You don't seem like you wanna fuck with anybody right now and I can guarantee you as soon as that little shindig is over Iman is coming right to your room."

She shook her head. Hearing his name almost blew her high. "Good thing I won't be there then."

She popped open her door and both she and Cinco exited the car.

His home was like a fortress. It sat atop of a hill and there were so many locks on his doors that she wondered who he was trying to keep out. Two full-grown Rottweilers met him at the door, immediately sneering at her.

"Whoa, down, girls," Cinco said as he walked past them. She slowly made her way by them, keeping close to the wall. They were eyeing her as if she were lunch.

"They're not going to eat you, girl. Get over here," he said. She followed him to his lavish living room. "Have a seat."

A wave of nausea floated over her as she accepted, sitting down on the white leather as she closed her eyes. "Hmm," she moaned. "Is it hot?"

He came over to her with a bag of weed and another small Baggie filled with dirty white rocks.

"What are you doing?" she asked. She immediately recognized the drug. She had seen it so many times growing up. It was crack cocaine. He was lacing rocks into the blunt. Her mother would make Bleu scour the carpet for hours, searching for even a morsel of it so that she could get high. "I don't fuck with that shit."

"Yeah, okay," he replied sarcastically as he rolled up, bobbing his head eagerly to a silent beat.

She watched him intently as her heart raced. Instinctively she licked her lips.

"You sholl looking for somebody who don't fuck with it," he said with a chuckle.

"I . . . I'm not—"

"You're jonesin', kid; relax," he stated. "This the same shit you smoked in the car. You had a little taste; now you want the full meal," he said with a sadistic grin.

The realization hit her like a ton of bricks. He had laced her blunt. She burned with embarrassment as fear spread through her like a virus, but still her eyes never left the work in his hands. She swept her hair out of her face. "You off this with me?" he asked. She clenched her buttocks together, her body tense and pleading as he lit the second blunt. That's why everything felt so good. Weed didn't do that to you. It was the effect of the rocks that had her rubbing her thighs together in anticipation of her next hit. Her body was stimulated in every single way. Even the hairs on the back of her neck stood up in attention. A light sweat formed on her forehead and her heart raced. He seemed to be moving in slow motion on purpose, teasing her as she eyed the blunt hungrily. She was high and it felt good . . . too good . . . so good that even upon the discovery that she had smoked crack she still wanted to hit the second blunt. She remembered Sienna telling her that she would never understand why her mother smoked. "You don't know how good it makes Mama feel," Sienna had said. But Bleu did . . . in that moment, when her heart was broken and the world seemed as if it were crashing in on her, she understood. Getting high took all the pain away and replaced it with a rush of pleasure. It was better than money, more orgasmic than sex. Not even Iman had caused her body to pour wetness like the comforting euphoria of this high did. Cinco hit the blunt long and hard, then held it out to her. Her eyes were dilated, widened, as adrenaline pushed her body forward. Bleu really didn't want to, but she really did want to, both at the same time. She leaned across the glass coffee table that separated them and then wrapped her lips around the blunt. She inhaled, this time long and deep. A rush tickled her insides and she closed her eyes in appreciation. *It's just a little weed. The rocks were mixed with Kush, so this ain't the same as smoking crack. It's not like I'm a crackhead,* she thought.

"That shit is sexier than a mu'fucka," Cinco said. "For real."

She breathed a sigh of contentment as she sank back against the couch.

"How long has he been married?" she finally asked.

"He been with Tan since high school. They go back. Without her he wouldn't have shit . . . hell, neither would I. We built this shit from the ground up off her connections," Cinco said. "The nigga think he a king, but without his bitch he would be nothing." Cinco was loose at the lips due to the weed smoke.

His words made Bleu feel like shit, and to stop the tears from welling in her eyes she hit the blunt again. Her eyes leaned dangerously low as she let her head fall back against the pillows.

Her entire body was at ease. "Fuck Iman," she said nonchalantly.

"I'll smoke to that," Cinco said with a smirk. He leaned in, resting his elbows on his knees as he steepled his fingers in front of him. "You're smarter than you look and apparently more interesting."

"I don't want to talk about Iman," she replied as she licked her dry lips and pulled on the blunt once more.

"Fuck talking about him, you should be plotting some get back on that nigga," Cinco replied.

"I prefer to let karma do my dirty work," she replied.

"Or you can let a real nigga like me help you with that dirty work," Cinco said. "He trusts you. Iman don't trust nobody, not even me. The nigga married my sister and my pops put him. He thinks he's big shit, but he wouldn't have any of this if it wasn't for my family. My pops got me working under Iman like I'm not blood. I'm blood. It's supposed to be blood over everything," Cinco stated, venom dripping from his tone. "He sitting back keeping the bricks to himself, spoon-feeding me. He don't let nobody know where the warehouse is. I saw the way he looked at you tonight. You don't even know when you got a nigga eating out of the palms of your hands. I'll bet if you stick around long enough he'll eventually show you where it is. He trusts you. We can take that shit, split it fifty-fifty, and leave Iman with one to the head. It's time this empire saw a real king."

The room got eerily quiet as Cinco stared intently at Bleu, gauging her reaction. Suddenly she remembered why she didn't trust him. He was a snake and getting too close to him was asking to be bitten. He had just laid out an entire plan to murder his own brother-in-law, all for the sake of power. The number two spot wasn't good enough for Cinco; he had to gun for number one. He wanted to be the boss and he wanted her to help him take Iman's throne. Bleu tried to play it cool, but as she passed Cinco the blunt he noticed the shaking of her hands. There was danger in the air and he could smell her fear. *If he would do his own family like that imagine what he would do to you,* she told herself. She was hot, sweating bullets from the pressure of it all. If she reacted the wrong way there was no telling what he would do.

"I don't think I'm as valuable to Iman as you think. Before tonight I had no idea who he even was. He was just another get-money nigga to me. I had no clue he was this large. He didn't let me in like that. You've got the wrong girl," she replied.

"Nah, I've think I've got the right girl," Cinco said, his tone turning menacing and his eyes turning dark.

She stood, feeling cornered as Cinco sat across from her, arms stretched over the back of his couch, legs cocked open arrogantly. "Sit down," he ordered, his voice stern. Fear crept into her. She was high and he was higher. He wasn't in his right frame of mind. He was talking reckless. She just wanted to get out of there, but the only way she was leaving his house was with his permission. Her eyes darted around the room for an exit. She was scared. Distraught. She had to hold her hands in front of her body to stop them from shaking. She felt like a mouse in a maze and she didn't know which way to go in order to get out.

"I'm k-k-ind of tired," she stuttered. "Can you just take me back?"

"You leave when I say you leave. Sit down," he stated. He reached under the couch and pulled out a short glass pipe. The same type of pipe that her mother used to get high. Bleu was terrified. Seeing the crack pipe in his hands made what she had just done so real. It didn't matter how she had done it, what method she had used . . . it was all the same. She was no better than her mother. Bleu went for the door until she heard a loud whistle over her shoulder and then turned to find the two guard dogs blocking her path, growling menacingly.

"Sit down." It wasn't a request and this time she slowly walked back to her seat obediently.

"You're gonna help me rob Iman," Cinco stated. He placed the pipe on the table along with a lighter. "Smoke it."

Her lip quivered as pictures of her mother flashed through her head. She had seen her mother do the worst for this drug. She had seen her suck dick in alleys, bring random dope boys into her bed while Bleu's father was at work. She had even watched men beat her mother and control her because of the monkey she had on her back. Bleu had witnessed the devil's work as a result of her mother's addiction, and now that it was in front of her, in its rawest form, she recognized it for what it was. Trouble. Tears welled up in her eyes. She had smoked crack. She was becoming the woman she had vowed never to be. "I can't," she replied.

"Pssk pssk." As soon as Cinco made the noise his dogs were at alert, snarling at her, waiting for the command to attack.

She wished that her will was stronger, but the truth was, her insides were screaming for a taste. The fact that he was threatening her into submission only gave her an excuse to do what she wanted to do anyway. The blunt was enough to make her crave more. She wanted that potent high, and as she reached for the pipe a tear slid down her face.

"Therrre you go," he said, fascinated at the fact that he was turning her out.

The pressure he put on her head to smoke it, to set up Iman . . . the aching split she felt in her chest from finding out about the marriage . . . the thoughts of her mother rushing through her mind, it all made her hit the pipe, again and again. Life had suddenly overwhelmed her and the sudden blast of "feel good" that this high provided had her chasing it repeatedly just to keep her sadness at bay. She creamed in her panties almost instantly as the rush flooded her brain. The high was ten times better. Sliding her lips around that glass dick and feeling her body explode had her eyes rolling in the back of her head as she closed them slowly, savoring the moment. She was smoking crack. Even worse, she liked it.

"Shit," she moaned. "Oh shit."

Neither sex nor money ever felt this good. *This is fucking amazing,* she thought.

"Feel that shit," Cinco coached as he moved next to her. He took the pipe from her hands and set up another hit before sparking and hitting the pipe himself. She melted backward into the leather, not caring that her legs were wide open as she sighed.

Cinco got on the floor between her legs and planted his hands on her thighs. She was so high that she was compliant as she slid down so that he was directly near her crotch. He reached beneath her dress, sliding his fingers underneath the thin fabric of her panties. Her love button was completely engorged. Endorphins were rushing her brain, making her hot, horny; she needed to be touched. It didn't matter that it was Cinco doing it. It could have been anyone at that moment. She was in the clouds and her mental was subdued, so she offered no protests. Her body was begging for the stimulation. He placed his thumb on her clitoris, rubbing it in a circular motion slowly. Cinco looked at her with a malice-laced stare. She was the only person who had ever denied him anything. She was too comfortable telling him no. No, he couldn't fuck her; no, she wouldn't help him with the setup. No. No. No.

"You think you're too good for a nigga like me. You're too good to get your pretty little hands dirty. You operating off loyalty to Iman, but Iman ain't operating off loyalty to you. A little smoke levels the playing field . . . it dirties you up. Brings you down to my level. Might make you reconsider some things. Giving the wrong answer wouldn't be good for you right now, so I'ma ask you again," Cinco stated. Now that he had exposed his hand, he couldn't let her leave. She knew too much. If she wasn't in on his plot to take over then she would be a liability.

"Help me help you," Cinco said. "You moving kilos across the border. Do you know how much time you will get if you're ever caught? As a matter of fact, you might not make it back to Cali this time. How easy do you think it would be to get you pinched? Put a quarter ki' in your luggage, you wouldn't even know it was there until it was too late."

She knocked his hands away, suddenly sitting up so that she could look him in the eyes. Fear shone in; she felt transparent as she replied, "I think it's time you took me back. China and Bree are probably wondering where I am by now."

Cinco stood to his feet and nodded his head. "Okay," he replied as he walked around her to the mini-bar. He pinched the bridge of his nose and then chuckled slyly as he poured himself a shot of cognac. He approached her from behind as she leaned over to pick up the pipe. She discreetly scooped a couple rocks for herself for later. This was a high she wanted to experience again, but before she could even stand back up, Cinco attacked from behind.

"You should have said 'yeah,' mama," he stated as he quickly wrapped a wire tightly around her neck and pulled on it with all his might. Her oxygen flow immediately stopped and her eyes bulged out of her head as her hands clawed at the wire. "I can't let you leave up out of here. You think I'ma let you run back and tell Iman?" Cinco asked through gritted teeth. She flung her body backward as she struggled against him. She couldn't breathe and her lungs pleaded for air. She clawed at her neck so viciously that she drew blood. The pain was blinding, suffocating, unbearable. The high was not enough to dull her senses through this. He was killing her, squeezing the life out of her, and she felt every second of it. Her heart pounded, desperately beating out its last few beats, each thump growing less intense as the room became a blur.

If I close my eyes I'll never see this world again, she thought. Her moments were fleeting. Each time she blinked her eyes she saw a different face. Iman's. Noah's. Sienna's. Wayne's. She still gripped the glass pipe in her hands, wishing that she could just hit it once to take this pain of dying away. Noah's face popped into her mind once more and she could hear him whispering to her, *FIGHT!*

She grasped the crack pipe and then stabbed behind her, sticking it directly into Cinco's eye. His grip loosened slightly and she brought her head back full force, head butting him square in the nose and causing him to let go of her completely. "Aghh! You bitch!" he growled as he flailed wildly, afraid to pull the glass out of his eye.

She choked uncontrollably, gulping in air as she scrambled away from him. She grabbed the first thing that she saw, a porcelain vase that sat in the middle of the table. She swung it hard, crashing it over his head.

The dogs attacked. She felt teeth pierce her leg as the dogs attacked, and she swung her body frantically as she tried to shake them off. They were ripping her apart, biting into her as she tried her hardest to defend herself. "Aghh!" she screamed, her cries mixing with those of Cinco, who was bent over in pain, blood filling his hands as he cupped his face.

"I'm gonna kill you, bitch!" he shouted as he scrambled for the couch. She saw him lifting the couch cushions as the glint of a silver .45 caught her eye. *He's going to shoot me,* she thought. Fear seized her. With all of her might she swung her feet repeatedly, striking the dogs with her six-inch heels until one of them ran away whimpering. Bleu scrambled across the floor, picking up the lamp once again.

"Aghh!" she screamed as she hit Cinco over the back of the head. This time she didn't stop. She just kept swinging. Again and again. Fear and crack cocaine fueled her until she was standing over him, heaving as sweat poured into her eyes.

When she noticed that he was barely breathing she stopped, holding the lamp above her head as she panted heavily, winded from the struggle. He lay a bloodied mess at her feet.

"Call . . ."—he spat blood out of his mouth as his one good eye rolled into the back of his head—"for help." He barely managed to get the words out of his mouth. They were a whisper. The desperate plea of a dying man. She thought to call Iman. She even went as far as to grab her cell out of her clutch. Her hands were so shaky that she could barely dial the numbers. She stopped before she pressed the green call button on her phone. *This is Tan's brother. Iman can't save me. They'll kill me,* she thought. Part of her paranoia was truth, some of it was the crack fucking up her reasoning and all of it scared her. There would be hell to pay for what she had done. Cinco was Mexican Cartel. He was a part of the most feared criminal enterprise in the world. All she could do was run. She looked down at Cinco. She didn't know if he was alive or dead. He was still, and there was so much blood that she couldn't tell if he was even breathing anymore. The dogs returned and began barking her way. Her back rigid, she backpedaled toward the front door. They jumped and she bolted, barely making it out without being bitten.

She ran full speed, hopping into Cinco's car. Her hands fumbled as she pulled down the visor. "Please, please, be in here," she cried. She hit the steering wheel in despair. She gripped it at the top and leaned her head against her hands as she sobbed. She picked up her phone and dialed China's number.

"Hello?" she answered.

"I . . . I . . . I think I . . . He's not breathing, China! I think . . . oh my God, I killed . . . I think I killed him."

"What? Killed who?" China responded in confusion, slightly panicked. Bleu was distraught. She wasn't even speaking in complete sentences.

"*Cinco!*" Bleu screamed. Her eyes danced around the exterior of the dark house. She half-expected Cinco's henchmen to show up at any minute. She was frantic. She could leave, but she had no idea exactly where she was. Her mind wasn't even in its right state, which made it harder to figure out an escape. She needed help.

"Where are you?" China responded.

"I don't know," Bleu replied as she sniffed loudly while wiping the mixture of snot and tears from her face. She was bugging out. Completely high. "He brought me to his house. Just get me out of here. Please, please, you have to come get me. Tell Bree to come get me."

The phone went silent as China muted the call.

"Hello?! Hello?!" Bleu whispered urgently.

Finally China came back on the line. "Okay, Bleu, calm down. You need to look at the location on your phone and text me the address, Bleu. Do it now. Don't move and don't call nobody else. We're on our way."

CLICK.

22

The hour that it took for China to arrive was the longest hour of Bleu's life. As she emerged out of the crack-induced fog, terror crippled her. She sat cowering in the front seat of the car, hugging her knees to her chest as her tears caused black streaks of mascara to slide down her face. Her bloodied body hurt all over. Her legs had gashes down to the white meat from where the dogs had bitten her. A red mark marred the circumference of her throat. Cinco had applied so much pressure to her neck that the capillaries in her eyes had burst, making them bloodred. She was restless. Her high had died off over an hour ago and now she wished she had more to keep her sane while she waited for China to come. The ticklish feeling of apprehension in Bleu's gut had her looking over her shoulders every few minutes. She wanted more . . . she was craving it. When the headlights of an approaching car shone through the rear window she sat up eagerly. Popping open the door, she practically fell out of the car and began to run toward the lights.

The car stopped in front of her and she placed her hands on the hood, heaving, frantic, as Bree and China got out of the car.

"Please get me out of here; hurry up. Get in the car; let's go," she panted.

"What happened to you?" China said, voice elevated in fear.

"He tried to kill me," she stated. "Please . . . please . . . I can explain once we're far away from here; just get in and drive." Bleu was so hysterical that she was shaking her hands and bouncing up and down as she begged them. Bree walked up to her, frowning slightly as he looked at her in concern. "Shh," he said as he pulled her in for a hug, consoling her. "I need you to relax, Bleu. What are you on?" he asked. Her eyes were completely dilated, so he knew she wasn't sober. "You on meth?" he asked, completely oblivious to the fact that her taste in highs had escalated.

"We just smoked, we smoked, and then he asked me to help him with a setup . . . please let's just go," Bleu said. "I'll explain it all after we leave."

"We aren't going anywhere until we hit this nigga safe," China said, interrupting.

"What? No, no . . . I just want to go," Bleu cried.

"We will," Bree said. "After we hit the safe." He walked her over to the car and opened the back door. "You can stay inside. You don't even have to come back in. Just stay put. We'll be right back. If you see anybody coming, blow the horn."

The fact that she didn't have to go back inside the house

made her feel slightly better. Bree tucked her inside and closed the door, then started toward the house. "You're so fucking soft on her," China spat as she followed him.

"And you're so hard on her," Bree returned. "Just ease up on her. He fucked her really bad. Anyway, don't worry about Bleu. Get your head right. If this nigga laying like I think he laying, we're about to get filthy rich."

"Yeah, whatever, nigga. Don't let me find out you got a thing for Bleu. Cuz it won't be nice for you or her," China said slyly.

"Shut the fuck up. You talk too fucking much," Bree said sternly as he pulled a pistol out of his waistline and reached for the door. As soon as he opened it the dogs were on him. He quickly snapped the door back shut.

Bree cracked the door and stuck his pistol through it.

BOOM! BOOM!

The sounds of whimpers let him know he hit his targets. He opened the door and China clung to his jacket as they entered slowly. "Damn, Bree," China said.

He ignored her and they eased into the house. Blood trailed from the kitchen to the living room. The room looked like a hurricane had torn through it. Overturned furniture, blood, and glass pieces were everywhere.

"I thought she said she killed him. Where is he?" China whispered.

"Right here, muthafuckas!"

BOOM!

A gunshot erupted as Cinco fired in their direction. He was seated on the floor in the hallway, clinging to life. He was badly injured, the back of his skull was bashed in, and his aim was off due to the pipe that still protruded from his eye. He had been trying to make it to his bedroom for his phone when he had heard them enter.

Bree pushed China to the floor and she cowered behind the coffee table as Bree popped back.

BOOM! BOOM! BOOM! BOOM!

He fired relentlessly, tearing away the plaster from the walls, barely missing Cinco. Bree pulled China to her feet and shoved her out into the open. Cinco fell for the bait and rounded the corner with his gun locked and loaded.

Before Cinco's finger could even curl around the trigger, Bree fired.

BOOM!

He caught Cinco in the abdomen, folding him like a lawn chair.

"What the fuck?!" China screamed. "He could have killed me!"

"But he didn't," Bree said.

Cinco clutched his gunshot wound as he slumped against the wall, trying his hardest just to breathe. "You're fucking dead. All of you are dead." He struggled to speak as he spat blood from his mouth.

"Shut your bitch ass up. Get the fuck up," Bree said as he grabbed Cinco under the arms and forced him to his feet.

"Aghh!" Cinco hollered.

"Damn, she really fucked you up," Bree said with a chuckle as he observed Cinco's condition. "Where's the safe?" Bree wasted no time getting down to business.

"Fuck you, motherfucker," Cinco said boldly. "I'm cartel! Does it look like I'm going to get on my knees and beg for my life? Huh, *puta*? You might as well kill me, because the longer you stay trying to get me to open my safe the less time you have to run away from the men that my family is going to send after you."

"Oh yeah?" Bree asked. He turned around as if he flicked his nose, then suddenly spun back and socked the shit out of Cinco. Cinco was too weak to stay on his feet. The blow sent him to his knees. "I've wanted to do that for years, my nigga. Next move I make is going to end you, so just come up off the location of the safe so I can clean you out and go about my business."

Cinco had to laugh. The irony of it all was hilarious. He had just plotted to rob and kill Iman, only to have someone suddenly do it to him. "Suck my dick," Cinco said.

Tired of the gangster bravado, Bree aimed his gun. Just as he was about to curl his finger around the trigger he heard a voice behind him.

"Don't," Bleu said as she snuck back into the room.

Cinco looked up at her as he groaned while adjusting his back against the wall. He squinted at her through his one good eye, blood leaking down his face, his head bludgeoned from her beating. "Better listen to her," he grunted.

BANG!

Bree pulled the trigger.

"Agh!" Cinco screamed in pure agony.

"That's one hand," Bree stated. China and Bleu stood back, fear filled. They weren't killers. They didn't know how far Bree was going to take it. Bleu closed her eyes, crying silently as she regretted ever getting in the game. She had only seen the good side. The lifestyle. The money. The clothes. The status. This was the flip side. This was the grit. With money came murder and mayhem. This part terrified her. She had gotten lost in the game, and now that she stood in a situation that she no longer controlled she realized things had gone too far.

"Okay! Okay!" Cinco shouted as he struggled to stand.

Bree pulled him up and pushed him down the hall. "Where's the safe?"

Cinco held on to the wall as he limped toward the back of the house.

Bree followed, persistently threatening him the entire way with a gun to the back of the head. They all knew that Cinco wouldn't make it out of there alive. There was no way they could let him live. He was too powerful, too connected. They would have to look over their shoulders for the rest of their lives if they didn't finish this tonight. This evening had to be one that they never mentioned again.

Cinco went to his closet and knelt down on the floor. As he heaved, his breath erratic, he lowered his head in despair. He felt weak and could barely focus as he pulled up the four floorboards that covered his safe. There wasn't much in it. He didn't shit where he ate. His real stash was nowhere in the house, but what lay inside the safe was his last chance. A black .45 was inside, safety off, ready to be fired. If he could just get to it and draw on Bree fast enough, Cinco just might make it through the night with his life.

"Hurry up, homeboy," Bree ordered impatiently.

Cinco put the combination in and reached inside, gripping the pistol in his palm. He gripped the rosary that he wore faithfully around his neck and said a brief prayer to Mary. In one swift motion he turned around, finger curled around the trigger, but he wasn't fast enough.

Boom!

Bree caught him in the back, causing Cinco to shoot wildly into the air before hitting the floor face-first.

Bree rushed over to the safe and his face twisted in rage. "The fuck? This muthafucka is empty!" he shouted.

"Let's go; let's just go now. Please!" Bleu shouted. Terror gripped her so tightly that it felt like a fist was clenching her heart. She was in over her head. Never in a million years did she think that things would take such a deadly turn for the worst.

"Shut up with all that crying! You're freaking me the fuck out!" China shot back. "We didn't do all this for nothing. We can't leave empty-handed."

Bree grimaced as he said, "We don't have a choice."

They rushed out of Cinco's home and drove away into the night. "This didn't happen tonight. Y'all hear me? We were never here," Bree coached. Neither China nor Bleu responded. They were too consumed with their own thoughts . . . their own fears of the repercussions of their actions. Each of them had contributed to the downfall of a boss, and although they didn't know how yet, they both knew that they would pay.

23

The hustle was simple. Noah had turned his stay behind bars into a lucrative opportunity. With Naomi on the outside, accepting payments from the loved ones of his fellow inmates, his system was flawless. He got paid in cash—fuck cigarettes and toiletries—Noah wanted real paper, and in return he kept heroin flowing through the prison effortlessly. With a prison guard on Noah's payroll, he never worried about his bunk getting tossed and his stash getting discovered. He had all his bases covered, and since no one wanted their connection to a good high at risk, everyone protected him. He was king inside. He was the only one with a secure link to the outside and his peers respected him for that. Everyone had their vices . . . their needs . . . their wants. Prison stripped people of these wants and Noah had found a way to give them back. He was the king and he couldn't wait to convert his newfound respect to the streets. When he touched down he had a plan to take the city over . . . all he had to do was bide his time. Until then he had a good thing going with Naomi.

As he sat in the class he found it hard to stay focused. His eyes kept diverting to the beauty at the front. They never spoke, but each time his eyes met hers they shared a silent connection. She was one of those slick chicks. Fancy, with quick wit and street smarts to match. She was arrogant in her thinking. She knew she was the shit. He did too, and he smirked as she sashayed by his desk, passing out the reading assignment that the teacher was announcing. As Naomi walked behind him she leaned down and whispered, "Stop staring, papa. If you see something you like just say something." She moved on from him without looking back, but he was definitely looking at her. She was the type of chick who held her own so well that, when paired with a king, she made the perfect accessory. She was different from Bleu. She wasn't fragile or square. Naomi was cut from a cloth that was no longer made. She was a thoroughbred, and he told himself that when he got out he would step to her. He couldn't do anything for her at the moment, but when he was free and on his feet he would check for her. He had a feeling that she wouldn't say no.

Noah heard the burner cell come to life. He was wide awake, watching the roaches as they crawled on the ceiling. He never slept. He couldn't, not peacefully at least. He only allowed his eyes to close when he could no longer take it. He didn't trust these niggas. Bookie was the only person on the inside Noah was sure of; everyone else was suspect. They only had love for him because of what he could do for them. He served a purpose and his customers served theirs. He didn't confuse that for friendship or loyalty; it was business . . . supply and demand. He reached beneath the flimsy mattress and retrieved the phone. He knew who it was. Naomi was the only person who even had the number. His antennae went up, however, because she never called him. It was he who did the communicating. He reached out to her every time. Now that she had suddenly initiated it alarmed him. He sat up and opened up the text message.

His eyes widened when an image of her chocolate skin appeared on his screen. She was flawless in her nakedness. The pinkness of her center was wet and plump, enticing him as he felt his pulse speed up. The look of mischief in her eyes was appealing, naughty. She was good at being bad and he loved it. The message read: *Maybe now that you've seen it, you can stop acting like you got a schoolboy crush and stay focused. Good night.*

He smirked as he typed back: *The crush just got bigger.*

She replied: *I've been known to break hearts. Be warned. . . .*

He smirked as he climbed out of his bunk and positioned himself on the floor. He began his nightly routine as he lowered his body to the floor, performing push-ups. He would double his count tonight. Thanks to Naomi, he had a lot of pent-up energy that needed to be worked out. He was feeling Naomi and he was putting a plan in his mind to step to her the next time he saw her.

"That young girl got you going, huh, youngblood?" Bookie asked with a chuckle, his face buried in *Moby-Dick*.

"Nah, I'm good, just putting in some light work O.G.," Noah replied vaguely.

"Yeah, whatever you say, playboy. You got one running product up in here for you, another one writing you every chance she get," Bookie said, referring to Bleu. "It's easy to manage two while you in here. Just make sure you ain't baking two cakes. You can only eat one when you get out, you hear me?"

Noah tried to keep Bleu in the back of his mind, but she filled his thoughts often. He didn't want to be the one to pull her back to Flint, so he kept his distance, remaining silent and never responding to her letters. She was too good for him, or so he thought. *She's worth more than this street shit,* he thought. He had no idea how drastically Bleu had changed or the dangerous downward spiral that she was on. Naomi was attainable. She fit him and he was about to lock away any sentiments he had for Bleu in order to pursue a new chick . . . a bad chick. The thought of Naomi was a perfect distraction to keep his mind off the best friend he wished could be more.

Bleu awoke to an ominous feeling . . . a dark cloud hung over her head, raining down misery over her as she slowly pulled herself out of the bed. Flashes of the night before invaded her mind like a bad dream. *That's what that was . . . a dream. It couldn't have been real,* she thought groggily as she shook her head. She felt heavy, weighed down by the overwhelming emotions that filled her, but in the pit of her stomach there was that tickle . . . that wanting . . . that urge. She closed her eyes and visions of her pulling on the crack pipe attacked her mind. She gasped. That's when it hit her. Everything that she wished was one horrible dream was actually reality. It had happened. She had let Cinco coax her into sucking on the glass dick. He had attacked her. She had called her friends to help her and they ended up killing him. It had all happened and there was no taking it back. She placed a hand over her mouth in horror. She hopped out of the bed, suddenly feeling pain as she looked down at the deep wounds that covered her legs. She ignored them as she ran out of the motel room and rushed to China and Bree's room. Knots filled her stomach and a lump of regret clogged her throat as she banged incessantly on their door. "Open up!" she shouted. When they didn't answer she rushed to the window, framing her face with her hands as she peered inside. The room was empty, bedsheets messy, and no bags were in sight.

They left me. They can't leave me here!!! Did they leave me?

She panicked as she hit the glass with a flat hand in frustration. She ran to the parking lot, her bare feet hitting the pavement hard as her mind slowly came to the realization that her friends had left her on stuck. She hoped that they had gone for a morning swim or that they had gone to get food, but intuition told her that they had deserted her. Bree and China weren't coming back for her. She was on her own. When she saw that the car was nowhere to be found she fell to her knees right in the middle of the road. She didn't know what to do. She had no one and, as fear and loneliness crept into her soul, she felt a pang of need in her gut. She had gotten a taste of the most devastating drug in the world and it was calling for her. It was telling her that it would soothe her worried heart. It would make her brave. It would help her plot her next move. It would make her feel so good. It would just. . . .

She sighed. Bleu wanted it so badly that her nipples hardened at the thought. She climbed to her feet and ran back to her room to gather her belongings. There was no doubt in her mind that someone had found Cinco's body by now. Would Iman come after her? Would Cinco's family? The cartel? Paranoia nipped at her until she found herself throwing clothes frantically into her bag. She had to get back across the border. If she could just make it to her stash she would be okay. Her hands shook uncontrollably as she threw on a leather jogging suit and wedge sneakers. She didn't even take the time to wash the trails of mascara off of her face before she crossed her duffel bag over her body and left the room. She was scatterbrained and afraid. She couldn't focus. She was already hooked to the high and she didn't even know it. She was running for her life, but even if she escaped the wrath that would come behind Cinco's murder she couldn't escape herself.

"All this week we're going to learn about the benefits of healthy financial credit. . . ."

The degree program would have actually held some weight if Noah could focus, but the things that Naomi did to entice him were a blatant distraction. She was beautiful, not in a girl-next-door type of way either. She was downright sexy and now that he was in her presence again he couldn't get the picture of her out of his mind. Noah wanted her in the worst way. In the way that said she was his bitch. He wanted to stake his claim, but there wasn't much that a jailbird could do with a girl like Naomi. She was the type of woman who would leave a nigga lovesick.

"A guard is going to escort you to the library one by one so that you can work with Naomi on pulling your credit report. At the end of the week we will go over each of them in class. Noah Langston . . . you're up first."

Noah stood and headed in the direction of the guard. Luckily for Noah, it was one he had on his payroll. He walked ahead of the guard while Naomi walked behind him. No one spoke. Noah knew that the eye in the sky was always on, so he played his position as the model inmate as he made his way to the library. When they entered the library Noah turned to the guard. Keeping his voice low, he said, "A little distance would be appreciated."

The guard's eyes moved around the empty room.

"Of course I'm a man that remembers favors," Noah stated. "A small package under your car seat this week would suffice?"

"I'll be outside the door. You've got thirty minutes before you have to be back," the guard stated.

Noah nodded and the guard turned to leave the room. It was literally the first time in months that Noah didn't have eyes on him. The privacy felt awkward as he instinctively looked up toward the camera. He walked toward Naomi, who was browsing through the books. The height of the wooden shelves obstructed the view of anyone who might be watching.

She felt like prey as Noah walked on one side of the shelf while gazing through the gaps in the books, trying to get a glimpse of her on the other side. Finally they met at the end and he grabbed her hand, roughly pulling her into him, his body on brick as she gasped in shock. When their lips met it was electric and his hand hungrily roamed her body, with him appreciating the feel of a woman. His hands slipped skillfully up her thighs as he slipped her panties to the side. At any minute they could be caught, but neither of them cared. It added to the intensity of it all. She wanted this. He wanted this. A thick fog of lust hung in the air as he slid into her wetness. Sheer ecstasy. That's what her tightness felt like. It was slick with her natural honey as her strong thighs worked slightly as he held her up. They found their rhythm. It was fast, guttural, animalistic. Noah didn't mean to be rough with her, but it had been too long since he had been inside of a woman. He was chasing the orgasm. His girth parted the delicate folds of her, causing her face to contort in pleasure. She bit her lip to stop herself from calling his name.

He buried his head in the nook of her neck as her perfume infused his senses. They were on a race to the finish line and he hoped she made it first, because he couldn't hold out much longer. When she felt her body tense and a flood of her warmth he dug deeper, and deeper, and harder, until—

"Shit, ma," he whispered as he placed his forehead against hers as he spilled his seed inside of her. They both panted, out of breath, as they adjusted their clothes.

"Don't fall in love," she said. She pecked him on the lips and gave him a flirtatious smile before sashaying out of the room.

"We're done here," she told the guard as she disappeared into the hall.

Noah wiped his goatee as he smirked to himself. She was so hard, so real. He had to have it. She wasn't the type of chick you could take score on. He had smashed, but you couldn't count that as a win. She was too seasoned, too unattached, too thorough to see it as anything more than what it was . . . sex. The only way to conquer her was to capture her heart. He saw through the tough visage. He knew that if he was wise he would heed her warning, but he wanted her and he would have her. It was only a matter of time.

24

The only time Bleu could calm the craving was when she was unconscious, so she slept as the bus drove her back to L.A. The nightmares of what had occurred plagued her sleep, but still she didn't want to open her eyes. The entire way she told herself that she would never smoke again, but her bubbling gut told her otherwise. It was only a matter of time before she indulged again. Even if it was only to take the sting of reality away . . . she wanted it. Filled with nervous energy, she climbed off the bus, looking over her shoulder as she made her way to her parked car. The darkness enveloped the parking structure as she made her way up the ramp. She stopped walking briefly, rummaging through her bag to find her keys, but when she heard footsteps behind her she froze. She spun on her heels as a sudden fear seized her. With one hand in her bag, clutching the small vial of pepper spray, her heart pounded. The echoes of footsteps stopped. She looked around frantically, wondering how many of Cinco's goons had come to avenge him. She sped up, half-running, half-walking, as she tried to get to her car.

"Hey!" The voice behind her was a harsh whisper, and when she looked back a hooded figure was walking toward her in haste. She took off at a full sprint, popping her locks repeatedly. Her heart had never beaten so fast as she opened the door and hopped inside, trying to pull the door closed.

"Hey! Hey! Chill the fuck out; it's me!" The man appeared at her side, pulling the door open violently before she got a chance to lock it.

"Bree!" she shouted, half-pissed, half-relieved, as she got out of the car and pushed him in frustration. "What the fuck?! Why did y'all leave me there?! Where the fuck is China?" Bleu couldn't control her volume as her emotions took over. Her fear dissipated into anger.

Bree gripped her by both arms, shaking her. "Chill the fuck out!" he barked.

"Don't tell me to fucking chill," she spat as she snatched herself away from him. "Y'all left me in Mexico after we—"

"I said we don't talk about that," Bree interrupted, fire dancing in his eyes, threatening to slap the shit out of her if she dared to speak of the dirty deeds they had committed. "That bitch beat me for my bread, hid my passport, and left me in Mexico. I need to hold something."

"You leave me on stuck and now you want to hold something? You got me really fucked up, Bree. Kick rocks," she said as she got back in her car and attempted to close the door.

"What if I get you some of that shit you was on?" Bree

asked, stopping her in her tracks. The glint in her eyes gave her away and Bree knew he had her. "That wasn't no meth you was on, Detroit. What was it? Heroin or crack?" he asked.

Her lip quivered as embarrassment filled her. "I don't know what you talking about; move," she said, attempting to pull her door shut.

He forced it open. "Don't front, Bleu. You're edgy, jumpy. I can see that you want it. Your eyes got big as golf balls from the thought," he said. "I move dope; you think I don't know that look?"

"How much do you need?" she asked, willing to sell her soul to the devil for just another little taste.

"Just a few thousand to get out of town," Bree stated.

She could have easily spent $20 to buy a hit, but she didn't know where to go or who to see and, more important, she was too embarrassed to walk up to someone and buy it herself. So she would give Bree what he asked for, just to save face.

"I want my shit first," she snapped.

When Bleu pulled up to skid row she gripped the steering wheel as her anxiety caused her chest to tighten. Bree looked over at her, feeling slightly guilty, but he still popped open the car door and sauntered down the block in search of someone to cop from.

Bleu shook, she was so terrified. The fact that she wanted a fix so badly made tears come to her eyes. She looked down the alley. There were hundreds of people, huddled sadly along the city street. Most of them were drunks or addicts, some just down on their luck, all of them thrown away by society. She jumped when a woman tapped on her window. Bleu looked out but didn't roll down the window. The woman's bloodshot eyes stared into Bleu's, her clothes filthy, her hair stringy and greasy, her lips so dry they were bleeding and cracked. Bleu was staring into the eyes of a fiend, and she couldn't help but wonder if her mother looked anything like this woman by now. She was witnessing what crack would do to her. It was right there staring her in the face, warning her not to ever take another hit, and still she had the urge. It was like an irritating itch that she just had to scratch. A tear fell down her face because she just wanted not to feel. She didn't want to feel the disappointment from failing at UCLA or the heartbreak from trusting Iman. She didn't want to miss Noah's presence in her life. She didn't want to feel . . . period. Crack was like a happy pill. It filled her to the brim with an orgasmic rush. The only problem was, it didn't last long enough. She had to constantly feed her high in order to maintain her vibe. *Damn, I hope he gets enough,* she thought. She rolled down her window.

"Do you have any spare change?" the woman asked.

The old Bleu would have said no. She would have been quick to judge the woman and turn up her nose. In her current state, Bleu empathized with her. Bleu was saddened for her because she knew that the woman was at the beginning of the long road named addiction. Bleu pulled out a ten-dollar bill and passed it to the woman, who snatched it up quickly before scurrying away into the chaos of the night.

Bree crossed in front of Bleu's car and then slid into the passenger seat. "I got it; let's go," he said.

Bleu pulled off as she held out her hand. Bree passed her a

stem. "You'll get the dope when you keep up your end of the bargain."

"Bree, just give it to me! Damn!" she protested, irritable.

Bree leaned against the passenger-side door and peered at Bleu. He was taken aback by her persistence. This wasn't the same sharp girl he had met months ago. "You know what, Bleu? I'm good on the cash; just pull over. You can let me out right here. You're fucked up right now. You need to get a grip. This shit will kill you, and if it don't, you're gonna wish it does. It'll have you walking around here like the walking dead," he said. "I'll take my chances out here. I'm not contributing to this bullshit. This ain't gon' be on my conscience."

She pulled over abruptly, causing cars behind her to swerve, to barely miss rear-ending her. "Now you want to develop a conscience? You ain't have no problem leaving me on stuck in Mexico. Get the fuck out then!" she shouted, feeling judged as tears came to her eyes. "Leave it on the seat."

Bree shook his head as he tossed the dope across the car, hitting her in the face before slamming the door. "Do yourself a favor and get out of town before Cinco's people find you. The way you're headed, you'll kill yourself before they even get to you."

"Fuck you, Bree," she sneered as she sped out into traffic, burning rubber as she left him in her rearview mirror. *He acts like I'm a crackhead or something. I can handle myself,* she thought. She sped through the city streets, headed toward the school. She needed to grab the money she had stashed and a few of her belongings. She had no idea where she was going to run to. It felt like she had spent her entire life running away. She had run from Flint to L.A., and all of her dreams were supposed to come true. Instead of dreams she had found nightmares, and now she was on the run again . . . headed to nowhere . . . fast.

"No, no, no, no, no!" Bleu shouted as she tossed expensive shoes from her closet while rifling through the boxes, looking for her stash. She had hidden $20,000 in her closet, but it was nowhere to be found.

"Bitch," she muttered, knowing that China had beaten her to it. Bleu slumped to the floor and planted her face in her hands, distressed. It was her rainy day fund, and life had brought about a sudden downpour. She had nothing and no one. She needed that money to get by until she could figure out what her next move would be. She had never anticipated her hustle would end so suddenly. Dough had been pouring in by the boatloads for months, but now she was right back where she had started . . . broke. She couldn't even get lost without money to help her hide. She stood up and walked through the bathroom that connected her room to Aysha's. *Maybe she will let me borrow some money until I land on my feet,* she thought. She was desperate. She didn't have a choice but to ask for help. She knocked on the door.

"Aysha, you in there?" Bleu called out anxiously. "I need a favor. I'm in trouble." The light shining under the door told her Aysha was inside her room. "Aysha, open up!" Bleu called. She frowned when she didn't get a response and she twisted the knob before pushing the door open slightly. "Aysha?" Bleu crept into the room and when she saw her friend a scream erupted from her. She stumbled backward, back into the bathroom, falling hard onto the tiled floor. Aysha was hog-tied and gagged, her body hanging from a steel bar in her room, her lifeless eyes still wide open in horror. Her throat had been slit from ear to ear. Utter fear paralyzed Bleu as she sat there, staring at her friend. This was the work of the Mexican Cartel. Aysha hadn't even been involved with Cinco's death and she had still been dealt a brutal hand. Bleu hated to see what they were going to do to her if they ever caught her. She couldn't help but wonder if Iman was behind this. He was the boss, right? It was his empire? Or had it been Cinco's father? Whoever had tortured Aysha would come back for her; Bleu was sure of it. Cinco had been too powerful. There would be repercussions for what she had done. The Mexican Cartel would make her pay with her life. Her phone vibrated in her hand and Iman's name appeared on the screen. Everything in her wanted to slide the bar across and answer for him, but she couldn't trust him. His hands could very well be the ones that had slid the knife across Aysha's throat. Bleu wouldn't bet her life on a love that was obviously untrue. Iman was now the enemy. She had to push her feelings for him out of her mind in order to survive.

25

Bleu sat on the edge of Aysha's bed, staring straight ahead, playing nervously with her fingers as the coroner rolled Aysha out of the room on a stretcher. The body was covered with a white sheet, but Bleu would never get the image of her friend out of her mind. Bleu's nerves were shot. She just wanted to smoke. The pack of dope Bree had gotten her was burning a hole in her pocket. That was the escape she needed. Reality was too much for her right now. She wanted to zone out. Her mental needed some relief . . . some feel good . . . some get right. She hoped that the police didn't search her. She was barely able to sit still as they questioned her, and her antsy nature made them suspicious.

"Did Aysha have any enemies? Was she involved in anything dangerous or illegal?" they asked.

Bleu's leg bounced rapidly as she brushed her hair out of her face. "I don't know. I don't think so," she replied, vague in her answer. She didn't want to give any concrete responses, for fear that they would catch her in a lie. Not only had Aysha been involved in some hot shit, but Bleu was in it right with her also. She had to keep her mouth closed. She was already in enough trouble; she didn't need the law gunning for her as well.

"According to our medical examiner she was killed about three hours ago. Where were you around the time of the murder?"

Bleu's mind wanted to come up with a lie, but she couldn't think fast enough. The police were flustering her. "I . . . umm . . . I was at the b-b-beach," she stammered.

"At night?" the detective asked skeptically.

"I've had a stressful week. I failed a few finals and needed to clear my head," she said, finally sounding believable.

"What happened to your eyes? Your neck?" The detective motioned to the marks on her body and her bloodred eyes. She had forgotten about her appearance. She looked as if she had been to hell and back.

"I had a fight with my boyfriend," she lied.

The detective sighed, fed up with her lies. He removed his card, passing it to her. "If I could I would take you in until you gave me some answers. I think you know more than you're saying. If you feel the need to be more cooperative give me a call."

She nodded. "Can I go now?" she asked.

"Yeah, unfortunately, you're free to go," the detective said.

Bleu rushed out of the room and back into her own, closing the door behind her in relief. She rested her back against it and closed her eyes briefly as she took a deep breath. *I have to get out of here,* she thought. She hurried over to her closet and began stuffing her belongings into one large suitcase. She didn't know where she was going. All she had was the money in her handbag. A few hundred bucks would only get her so far. She had nothing to show for the risks that she had taken. If she had been smart, she would have been stacking her dough and making it amount to something. More cash had gone through her hands than some people made in an entire year and she had recklessly blown it. The only things she had to even prove it existed were the clothes she was stuffing inside the bag. Even her car wasn't truly hers—it was leased—and as soon as she stopped making those payments the bank would take that back as well. She was back at square one. Out on the streets in a city that wasn't her own with only one bag to her name. That's the one thing about those tables; they always turned, and she had come full circle.

She was about to walk out of the room when she halted at the door. A tingle traveled down her spine just as she crossed the threshold and she paused, her head whipping back to look at China's side of the room. Bleu rushed over to China's desk and opened the drawers, frantically searching through her belongings.

Bleu moved from the desk to the bureau, pulling out clothes and dumping drawers until finally a bag of crystal meth fell to the floor among the contents. She scooped it up and then grabbed one of China's smoke pipes, tucking the paraphernalia inside her bag. It was no longer her drug of choice, but a high was a high, and she knew that the dub that Bree had scored for her wouldn't last long. Life was turning her out.

Looking around the small space one more time, she felt a pit form in her stomach. This had been her dream for so long, and once she had achieved it she had sabotaged it. When other people were the cause of your life being thrown off track it was easier to swallow, but when it was no one's fault but your own, it ate away at you. Bleu had done everything wrong; from the day she set foot in L.A. her choices had been self-destructive. It was too late for regrets, however. What was done was done. There was no turning back.

With only $500 in her pocket, a motel room wasn't in her budget. The inside of her car would have to do until she figured out where to go next. Going back home would mean failure. She couldn't admit to her fuckups and tuck her tail between her legs. Not too many people made it out of Flint. There was an entire team of people waiting for her to fall on her face. She couldn't give them the satisfaction. She would rather struggle to survive than book a ticket back home. Besides, there was nothing waiting for her there. She had no family and her only friend was locked away. There was no point in returning. The loneliness and struggle would be the same there as it was in L.A. She might as well stay.

She sat inside the car, silent tears streaming down her face as she gripped the stem in her palms. She was at the lowest of lows. Nothing was stopping her from jumping off of the cliff. At first she had school to consider; she couldn't let herself become addicted to drugs, but now, what was she depriving herself for? Why was she denying herself the right to feel so good when life had beaten her miserably, causing her nothing but pain? Her very body was begging her to just smoke the drug in her hand. She wanted it so badly that her hands trembled. Snot ran down her nose. She was a mess. Fear and sadness wrecked her as she sat idly parked in the lot in front of her dorm.

This was that moment. She was at the point before the darkness when she should ask for help, but she didn't want it. She could handle everything; at least that's what she told herself. She reached for the Baggie filled with rocks and emptied a portion into her hand. This was it. This was the hit that would send her life on a downward spiral. She prepped the stem, placing the crack rock inside, and applied the flame. Her eyes popped out of her head like golf balls as she anticipated the smoke filling her lungs. The smell of it alone, burning, bubbling inside the glass, made her stomach groan in anticipation.

Sssss

She pulled on the pipe, long and hard . . . desperately awaiting the moment when her problems would disappear into thin air. She was sucking on the devil's dick unabashedly, waiting for that moment . . . for that ecstasy . . . for the climax. She wasn't disappointed. As she released the smoke she exhaled her emotions right along with it.

That shit was like a miracle drug. It felt so good she wondered how it could possibly be bad. She smoked it all without a care in the world. It numbed her broken heart. Her phone rang and Iman's name flashed on the screen. She wanted to demand an explanation, to curse his ass out, to beg him for forgiveness, to tell him what had happened with Cinco, but instead she gave him the fuck you button, sending him to voice mail. Things were too far gone between her and Iman to look back. "You married, lying motherfucka," she said to herself. She put the car in drive and headed back across town. Now that she had gotten her tongue wet, she wanted to feed her appetite. The meth in her purse she would save for a rainy day; she had a taste for another type of blast, and crack was surely becoming her preference.

26

Bleu climbed out of her car and immediately locked the doors as she frowned at the men and women around her. They were disgusting, pathetic . . . the lowest members of society. Skid row was home to junkies of all kinds, but while she was looking down at them she neglected to realize that she was out there for the same reason they were . . . to score. Her drug use was hidden by her expensive clothes, her shiny car, her pretty-girl looks, but many of them had once been shiny too. Years of living the street life had grimed them up, turning them into the walking dead. This was an entirely new world. These were the types of places her mother used to take Bleu when it was time to cop. She couldn't believe that she was the one walking down this path now. How far she had fallen. Her hatred for her mother lowered slightly now that she fully understood the demons that Sienna battled. If Bleu had a monkey on her back, Sienna carried a gorilla. Bleu had seen her mother do things that no woman should ever have to do and felt herself sliding down that slippery slope, but still she didn't care. Bleu was beyond the point of turning around and going back to her car. She wanted a blast and she had money to spend.

"Hey, you," she said, noticing the woman she had given money to just hours before. "Hey—"

The woman hurriedly walked in the opposite direction of Bleu, tucking her head as she stuffed her hands in her pockets.

"Hey!" Bleu said, going after her.

"If you want your money back, I ain't got it," she said.

"I don't want it back," Bleu said. She pulled the woman's arm and the woman turned on her, whipping out a switchblade before Bleu could even blink.

"Whoa! Whoa!" Bleu said as she backed up slightly. She went in her purse and pulled out five hundred-dollar bills. "I'm just trying to spend," she explained. She looked around nervously and then back at the woman. "I've never bought any myself. I just . . . I wanted you to . . ."

The woman's eyes sparkled in the moonlight as she eyed the money in Bleu's hand. "What's your poison?" she asked.

Bleu hesitated. It was the first time that she would have to say it aloud. She fidgeted from foot to foot, growing anxious. She just needed one hit to calm her nerves. "Crack." Her face burned with embarrassment as she added, "Just a little. It's nothing serious."

Her inexperience oozed off of her. She was too shifty, too nervous, too worried that everybody was looking at her. "Yeah, nothing serious," the woman replied sympathetically. She knew that vice all too well. "Look, sweetheart, I'll go cop for you and you can stay here, a'ight?" the woman asked.

Bleu knew that crackheads were fast talking. She had seen her mother beat plenty of suckers for their dough, and Bleu's skepticism was written all over her face. "You think I'm going to run off with your money?"

Bleu didn't want to offend the woman, but that's exactly what she thought. "I can come with you," she said.

"Well, come on then," the woman replied. "Shit. But don't be all on my ass when I'm buying. You stand back."

Bleu nodded and then followed the woman as she started up the block. "I'm Lady," the woman said.

"I'm . . ." Bleu paused because she didn't want to give her real name. She didn't want anyone, not even this woman no one would ever know she met, to know that Bleu Montclair was on crack. "I'm Blake," she said, giving her alias. She had once used the name to move bricks; now she was using it to smoke rocks. She couldn't fall any further from grace.

"You be careful out here. A pretty girl like you . . . these streets can be dangerous," Lady said. "A lot of people looking to come up off a young girl like you." She stopped abruptly, causing Bleu to bump into the back of her. "Get off my ass, nah," she chastised harshly.

Bleu put up her hands. "Sorry."

"My guy is right over there. Give me sixty dollars," Lady said.

Bleu gave her a hundred-dollar bill and Lady walked up to the guy who was posted by the liquor store. "You working?" Bleu heard her ask.

Bleu watched, shuffling from foot to foot as she rubbed the

goose bumps that had formed on her arms. The transaction was quick and Lady was back at her side in no time.

"Here," Lady said, handing her a dub.

"Where's my change?" Bleu asked.

"Do it look like the dope man give change? Lesson number one, have correct change or they keeping your shit," Lady schooled Bleu, lying through her teeth. She had already overcharged Bleu. Lady had only purchased a $20 rock but had told Bleu it was $60 and on top of that she kept the $40 that the dope boy had given her back. So not only did she cop herself her own smoke, but she also pocketed some paper for later. She turned to Bleu. "You sharing?" It was just like a fiend to be greedy. Lady was going to smoke up Bleu's little high before she started in on her own. Bleu was too green to the scene. It was inevitable that she be taken advantage of.

"This ain't nothing to share," Bleu replied. She pulled out more money and started to walk over to the guy who had just served Lady.

Lady stopped her. "Un-uh! What you doing? He don't know you like that," Lady said.

Bleu sighed in exasperation as she handed Lady $200 more. She played the back while Lady copped and then followed her back down the alley. "We can go back to my car," Bleu suggested.

"Nah, not out here. You fire that shit up in your car and the police gone break up the party. I've got a little room," Lady stated, leading the way.

Bleu followed her, a little jittery and ready to re-up on her high. A queasiness settled into her stomach as she followed

Lady into the Motel 6. When they were finally inside, Lady sat down at the wooden table and laid their spread out in front of them. It was like a crack buffet; they were set up for a good time.

Bleu watched as Lady tore off a piece of Brillo and stuck it into the end of the stem before adding the rock. The flick of the lighter was like music to Bleu's ears. Her nipples hardened as she watched the flame do tricks under the glass. The clouds that billowed as Lady took her hit excited Bleu. It was all about the clouds. That's where the high lived. Once the clouds were gone, the rock was smoked. She wanted to run away, but her feet were planted firmly as she waited for her turn. She was ready to make her own crack clouds. Lady passed her the pipe and Bleu sat down and set her own blast up. Tiny beads of sweat formed on her forehead as she let the smoke fill her lungs. She sighed in relief.

"So, where you from? You out here in your fancy clothes with your fancy car and hundred-dollar bills. You must be one of them spoiled rich girls with daddy issues. You out here slummin' it for the night," Lady said.

Bleu wished that were the case. She would take those rich-girl problems any day over her own. Her demons were much more complex. The things that haunted her, the emotions that pushed her to suck the devil's dick, were far worse than anything Lady could imagine. Bleu had the murder of a drug lord hanging over her head. Part of her wanted to disappear in the slums because she knew that no one would come looking for here there. Among the crack clouds was the perfect place to hide. It was far removed from the glamorous culture of L.A.

that she had once belonged to. *If Lady only knew*, Bleu thought. "It's not like that," she responded. "Frankly, I don't feel like talking about it. I just want to ride this ride to the top," she said as she sucked in more of the poison, her lips cupping the stem as she closed her eyes. She exhaled the smoke and then let the pleasurable waves ripple through her body. Crack did things to her clit that she had never felt before. It swelled and she clenched her thighs. "I'll be back," she said as she stood up and walked over to the bathroom, crack pipe and lighter in hand. She locked the door and then sat on the toilet as she slipped her hand into her panties. Crack was an aphrodisiac for her. It made her horny and she couldn't help but touch herself as she let her thighs part in bliss. Her mind was out of it as images of Iman, then Noah, then Iman, flashed as she rubbed circles on her love button. She just needed to get off, to release this tension. Her face wrinkled in pleasure as she bit into her bottom lip. Her breaths were rapid as she panted as she applied more pressure. A moan escaped her lips as her mouth fell open and she gave her swollen bud one last squeeze. "Aghh," she groaned as she exploded. She reached for the crack pipe and lighter, then leaned forward, balancing her elbows on her knees. She lit it and this time without thinking twice she inhaled.

Twelve hours later

Bleu awoke to the sound of incessant banging. She wiped the crust out of her eyes and frowned as she looked around the dirty motel room. Glass pipes, liquor bottles, and empty Baggies lay around. The bathroom door was closed. "Lady, somebody's at your door!" Bleu groaned as she sat up and brushed her messy hair out of her face. She was dragging, exhausted, feeling the lowest of the low as she stood to her feet.

KNOCK! KNOCK! KNOCK!

"Lady?" Bleu called as she went to the bathroom door. She knocked once and when she got no response she pushed the door all the way open. The room was empty.

KNOCK! KNOCK!

"Open up this door!" a man's voice called. "Checkout was hours ago. It's time to go!"

Bleu turned around in confusion, searching for anything that said that Lady would be coming back, but all of her things were gone. Bleu rushed over to the nightstand where her purse lay and she quickly unzipped it. "No, no!" she shouted as tears flooded her eyes. Lady had gotten her. The rest of her money and her car keys were gone. Bleu heard the lock on the door as someone slid a key card in the slot and she turned around to find the manager glaring at her.

"I'm leaving; I'm leaving!" she shouted as she snatched up her bag and darted for the door. Sheer panic ran through her as she rushed down the block, headed back to the place where she had parked her Benz. She hoped to God it was still there, but sure enough, when she arrived the space was empty. She had gotten got. After smoking nonstop with Lady for over six hours Bleu had thought she had made a friend on the streets, but she had learned a tough lesson. There were no friends among addicts. Everyone was looking for a way to get high, use or be used, and Bleu had just gotten played. Better yet, she had played herself by trusting a fiend. Bleu felt like crying, which made her feel like smoking. That was becoming her answer to everything nowadays. Every problem, every disappointment, every heartbreak, could be solved with the flick of a lighter. Smoke it all up into the air . . . fuck it.

27

Six months later

"Langston, you got a legal visit!" the CO called as he came to the cell and slid the rectangular slit on the reinforced door to the side. Noah stood and sauntered over to the door.

"Legal visit from who?" Noah asked. He had no lawyer representing him. His public defender had disappeared as soon as he entered his plea deal. Noah had no idea who was visiting him now. He frowned. "You sure it's for me?" he asked.

"Guess you'll see. Hands through the door," the CO instructed. Noah placed his wrists through the hole and the officer placed handcuffs around them before opening the cell. Noah wasn't sure what this was about, but when he stepped into the private room and saw the white woman sitting in a thousand-dollar designer suit he knew she was about her business. He stood, hands bound in front of him, waiting for her to greet him.

"Hello, Noah," she said with a smile. "I'm Sarah Bosworth. I've been retained to represent you."

"Retained by who?" he asked curiously. He knew that his mother couldn't afford to hire a hotshot defense attorney.

"By Naomi Porter," she replied.

Noah smirked. Naomi was proving to be nothing but loyal, and the more he was around her, the more invested he became. He took the college courses simply to be around her. Seeing her twice a week for an hour was his respite. Her face kept him sane, and she didn't even know it. They were making money with the prison hustle, but Naomi was using her cut to pay for his legal fees. It didn't get any realer than that. "Due to over-population in this jail, I was able to pull some strings. You're getting out."

Noah took a seat on the chair across from her. "When?" he asked.

"I don't charge one thousand dollars per hour for nothing, Mr. Langston. You're getting out now," she said. "The only condition is that you must serve the remainder of your sentence on probation. So you can't leave the state for the next four years."

He gave her a charming smile as he nodded his head. He held up his wrists. "Can you talk that big lawyer talk and get these mu'fuckas to remove these tight-ass cuffs?" he asked.

She smiled as she snapped her fingers toward the glass mirror that acted as a two-way window. A guard came in. "While you're processing my client out, I'd like these removed," Sarah said.

The bracelets came off and Noah massaged his wrists as he said, "You're worth every penny."

As soon as he walked through the gates, Naomi stood there leaning against a pearl-white Jaguar. A huge smile graced her face as she gripped the collar of her leather jacket. He crossed the distance between them with a confident stride. He had transformed in prison. He was no longer the petty hustler who had gone in. He had emerged a boss, and it was evident in the way he carried himself.

"Remember how I told you not to fall in love?" she asked as he scooped her up, spinning her around as he kissed her lips.

"Yeah, I remember," he said.

"Well, I broke my own rule," she answered. "I'm feeling the shit out of you, mister."

"Good to know, cuz I'ma need a queen," Noah stated as he opened the passenger door for her and nodded his head, indicating for her to get inside.

"A queen, huh? That's what probably what you call all the pretty girls!" Naomi shot back.

"Nah, just the one that I'ma place beside me. I'm about to take this bitch over. Flint need a new king," he said.

She squeezed her body past him, rubbing her ample behind against his crotch as she slid into the car. He closed her door and then made his way to the driver's side. When he was sitting beside her she said, "And every king needs his chariot. It's yours. The cell on the charger is yours too. There are clothes in the back, Cole Haan shoes, Ralph Lauren slacks, all that fly shit."

Naomi blew his mind with the gifts. She was far from average. She was giving away big-boy toys and welcoming him home as if she were his personal concierge. He silently wondered how she had afforded it. They were getting money, but not that type of money. The prison thing was a small hustle. Whatever she was into, it was major. "I'ma give you the keys to the city, ma. Thanks for holding me down."

"Always," she replied. "I've got a surprise for you. It's from Khadafi."

Noah's back stiffened at the name of his father. He had mixed emotions about the man. He had never been a part of Noah's life coming up. He didn't need Khadafi then and wasn't going to start opening up the doors now. "You can keep that. I don't want it."

"What's the deal with you and him?" Naomi asked.

Noah grimaced as he maneuvered the car. "No deal. I just don't fuck with him," he replied.

"Well, he fucks with you heavy. Just wait and see," she said with a smirk.

The three-hour drive back to Flint was filled with laughter as Naomi's big presence filled the tiny space. She was a fun girl. She seemed so serious with the world, but when it came to Noah, she let herself be soft. She trusted him, and he appreciated her for showing him the vulnerability that made up a woman. She made him feel free. After she did a quick bid, her personality was infectious. He could see himself keeping her around for a while.

She guided him into the city, and when they pulled into a storage unit facility he frowned. "Where you taking me, girl?"

"You'll see," she replied with a sneaky grin. "It's that one right over there." She reached in her handbag and pulled out the key, handing it over to him.

He parked and walked over to the unit. When he opened it he frowned. "What, we opening a coffee shop?" he asked as he looked at the barrels of coffee beans that lay inside. The aroma was so strong that as soon as he lifted the unit it hit him.

"We're definitely opening shop," she said. She opened one of the lids and scattered some of the beans aside. She pulled out a brick of cocaine and a fish scale and tossed it to him. "Told you. This was a gift you want to accept."

Noah saw gold, but he didn't want any handouts. There had to be at least one hundred kilos of cocaine hidden in those barrels. *This shit don't make up for me coming up without a father,* he thought. "Send them shits back," he replied. "I don't want shit for free."

Naomi walked up to Noah and placed her hands on the sides of his face. "He said that you might say that. So he's fronting them on consignment. He says when you make your money you go pay your mother. Apparently, he owes her a debt," she said with a wink. She walked out of the unit and headed back to the car as Noah stood, baffled, conflicted, and excited all at the same time. He was the son of a drug king-pin, and the keys to the kingdom had just been passed down to him. He couldn't help but wonder if he could handle it . . . this was no small-time prison hustle. It was the big leagues, which meant big adversaries . . . he would need to build his team from the bottom up. He looked back at Naomi and suddenly Bleu crossed his mind. He hadn't heard from her. Her letters had slowly stopped and he couldn't help but be disappointed that she had forgotten about him while he was locked up. It was supposed to be her who picked him up from prison. She was supposed to be the beauty by his side as he took over the city. Time, distance, and unusual circumstances had caused them to grow apart. There was a dull ache in his chest that accompanied her memory. He looked over his shoulder to make sure that Naomi was tucked inside of the car, out of earshot. He picked up his phone and dialed Bleu's number, hoping that it hadn't changed.

"You playing, shorty? You gon' suck this dick or nah? Cuz a nigga don't got time to be holed up with your ass all day."

Bleu's fingers no longer shook as she set up her blast. She knew the routine like the back of her hand as she stuffed the stem with Brillo and then placed a crack rock behind it. There was no shame in her game—she loved this shit—and dope boys like the one talking shit over her shoulder fed her habit willingly in exchange for sexual favors.

"Shut your ass up. I said I got you. Just let me get a little smoke in," she replied, irritated. It had been days since she had wrapped her lips around a crack pipe. For months she had tried to kick the habit, but after a few days she always ventured back to the dark side. She was jittery and long overdue for a hit, but the dealer in front of her had little patience.

He walked up behind her and fisted her hair tightly, applying pressure to her scalp as he forced her down onto her knees. "You pay before you fire up. Wrap your pretty-ass lips around a real dick. Fuck that glass dick over there for a minute," he said.

Bleu was dirty. She lived on the streets, sleeping in twenty-four-hour Laundromats and women's shelters, and to support her habit she made runs for the dope boys. The only reason she even still had a working cell phone was because one of the d-boys in particular had a soft spot for her head game. She had become quite skilled at the art of fellatio and he wanted to reach her anytime for her services, so he paid her bill monthly. She maintained by the skin of her teeth. She lived, slept, ate, smoked, on the same blocks. This had been her routine for months, but at least she was alive. At least Cinco's people hadn't found her. Life was hard, but she was still living. Life was bullshit, but she had fared better than Aysha. Or had she? Sometimes she wondered if death was easier than the existence she led. Life had beaten her down so low that to stop herself from thinking about the things she had done she smoked more. It was a cycle and she was stuck in it. There was no glamour about this part of the L.A. lifestyle. This was the struggle . . . hell on earth.

She grimaced as he pulled her hair, forcing her face toward his exposed member. He reeked of musk as tears flooded her eyes. If she didn't give him what he wanted, she wouldn't get what she needed. It was a business transaction, nothing more, nothing less. Fair exchange. As she closed her eyes and took him into her mouth her heart broke. She remembered when she had valued her body. Her temple, Iman had called it. Now she sold it for $20 rocks and temporary highs. She was lost and she knew it. Her tears slid down her cheeks, landing in pools of regret at her feet. *This wasn't supposed to be me,* she thought.

But what she didn't realize was that it wasn't supposed to be anybody. Crack was a monster and all it took was one hit to trap her in its clutches forever. As she sucked the stinking lowlife in front of her she grew enraged. After she was done, she would smoke, but she would need more, which meant more hustling, more fast talking, or more dick sucking. She was tired of that routine. The highs seemed to get shorter and shorter every time she fired up. So she found herself being degraded more often just to keep up. She was chasing that first-time feeling, that blast, that mental orgasm, but it would never be that potent again. She had killed the pleasure sensors in her mind. Crack had mind-fucked her and now she smoked it trying to achieve a sensation that she would never feel again. It was like her virginity; she would never get that first-time crack high back. So now she was fucked and was at the mercy of the streets. The thought of it all overwhelmed her. *I'm not doing this again tonight. I can't,* she thought as she tried to stop herself from gagging. She looked down at the jeans that were bundled around the man's feet and eyed the plastic Ziplocs full of rocks that lay inside. A gun lay in a holster on the belt loop. Desperate times called for desperate measures.

CRUNCH!

She bit down on his manhood as hard as she could.

"AGHHH!" he hollered as he pushed her off of him and cupped himself in agony. She scrambled for his pants, picking

up his gun first and pointing it at him. She didn't even know how to use it, but he didn't know that. She had no idea that the safety was on, so even if she pulled the trigger she would have no wins.

"Bitch, I'ma kill you," he groaned as he doubled over in pain.

Her hand wasn't even steady, but her resolve was. She needed his stash. "Kick your pants off all the way!" she said, full of jitters. Her eyes darted around the room as she jabbed the gun at the air as she spoke.

"Okay, okay, bitch . . . I'ma remember this," he spat as he kicked off his pants. She inched toward them and didn't even bother picking the pockets. She just scooped the pants up.

"Get in the bathroom," she ordered.

"Bitch, your crackhead ass got my stash; just take it. You better run though cuz—"

"Shut up and get in the bathroom!" she shouted, frantic. He was showing too much resistance. She kept her distance to make sure that he didn't lunge for the gun, because she knew if he did he would kill her. Her urge had made her take things too far. She seemed to forever be on the run. From Flint, from Cinco's goons, now from this random dealer. She was beginning to think that she attracted trouble. The man held his privates as he walked to the bathroom with a grim look on his face. If looks could kill . . .

"When I find you, you're done. Better believe that," he threatened. She pushed him inside the bathroom and then used all her might to push the dresser in front of the door, barricading him inside. She then wrapped the gun up in his jeans and rushed out of the room. She ran full speed, without looking back, and she didn't stop for blocks, bumping people out of her way as she made her escape. She couldn't do this anymore. The street life was too much for her. She needed at least a place to rest her head at night. Going back to skid row wasn't an option. The dealer she had robbed owned those corners. She wouldn't even be able to go back around there to cop, but, thanks to the caper she had just pulled off, she had a few days' worth of drugs to keep her good and high. She would worry about the rest later. Right now she just wanted to find a place where she could smoke in peace.

She found herself roaming to the other side of town. It took her two hours to get there, and when she finally did arrive she was shocked to see that there was a sign that read: FOR SALE BY OWNER plastered in the window. Picante had closed. She didn't know why she had come here. Perhaps because Eddie and Marta were the only people in L.A. she knew who would see her and help her. She didn't know, but it no longer mattered, because they were nowhere to be found. Thunder rolled through the sky as rain began to accompany her disastrous mood. It was fitting. God was crying over the life that he had given her, because she had wasted it. She was a disgrace. Bleu looked up at the building to the vacant apartment that sat on top of the restaurant. Looking left, then right, she started up the fire escape. The apartment was empty except for an old cot that had been left behind. She tried the window.

Thank God, she thought when she discovered it wasn't locked. She climbed inside, finding shelter from the downpour. There were no lights or air-conditioning to add to her comfort, but she couldn't complain. Just a place to sleep peace-fully and a roof over her head were enough. In fact, it was the most comfortable place she had slept in in months. Beggars couldn't be choosers. She was just glad to be off the streets and away from skid row. She peeled off her clothes and settled onto the cot. She had an eight-ball of crack in front of her. It was better than hitting the lottery . . . hell, it was just like hit-ting the lottery. She set up her next blast, desperately needing to unwind. She was so used to this routine that it no longer aroused her. It was more habit than excitement, more need than want. Crack was now who she was, not just what she did. Crack was her life. It had consumed her. She sparked the flame of her lighter, and just as she was about to bubble the rock in-side the stem her phone buzzed in her pocket, startling her. Bleu fumbled to answer it, dropping her pipe on the floor.

"Damn it!" she shouted in frustration as she got on her hands and knees to find the rock that had scattered. Using the lighter as a flashlight she searched on hands and knees until she located them. She hurriedly put the rock back in the Bag-gie as the vibration of her phone urged her to answer. She won-dered if word had spread on the block about what she had done. No one called her anymore. Iman had stopped using the number months ago after she had refused to answer for him. The last memory she had of him was a voice mail telling her how much he loved her and how sorry he was. She had never returned the call, because sorry didn't make him single. He was still married and he had still lied and, worst of all, he was related to Cinco. She missed Iman and she used to listen to the voice mail all the time, just to hear his voice, but even she had moved on. She had a new soul mate . . . crack. Since falling in love with the drug she hadn't even pressed "play" on Iman's voice mail. So who was this calling her now? She looked at the screen and her heart dropped into her stomach when she saw the area code 810. "Flint?" she said aloud.

"Hello?" she answered, voice unsure.

"What's up, B?"

His voice caused butterflies to form in her stomach and she sat her butt on the floor.

Tears accumulated in her eyes as she whispered, "Noah? Hey . . . hey, how are you?" She cleared her throat, suddenly embarrassed, as if he could see her through the phone. "How are you calling me right now? Did you get my letters?"

"I got them, B," he replied. "I'm out."

She gasped as a smile crossed her face. "You're out? It's only been a year. How?"

"That don't matter," he replied. "How's school? When them letters stopped I figured you forgot about a nigga."

She hesitated. She wanted to tell him that she needed help. She wanted to beg him to come get her. He was the one person she knew who could rescue her from herself. He could love her enough to make her quit and would stick with her through the inevitable downs that accompanied recovery. Noah was her friend, her best friend, and she loved him so much that she didn't want to break his heart. She didn't want him to see her like this. She wanted his thoughts of her to be good ones. So even though she was standing on the edge of death and was in desperate need of his type of love, she didn't pull him into her drama.

She simply replied, "School is good. L.A. is everything I imagined, Noah. I'm doing so good out here." She cried the most sorrowful tears and she had to cup her mouth to keep herself from whimpering too loudly. Her silent anguish was torture, because she wanted nothing more than for him to come for her.

"That's good, B. I'm glad that you moved on with your life and that you're safe and happy," Noah replied.

"I am," she confirmed as she sniffed while wiping her nose.

A silence filled the line as they both withheld things that they really wanted to say. "I'll have to make my way out there to visit you one day, B," he said.

She closed her eyes, because she knew that the day would never come. It was just Hollywood talk. Their year apart had turned them both into different people. A lot had happened during that time. A lot of bad things, none of which were revocable. Bleu would never let him visit her as long as she was strung out. She wasn't the same girl he remembered.

"One day," she responded. "I'm glad you're out, Noah."

"If I asked you to come home, would you?" he asked. "Remember that conversation we had when I went in? The things you said. Do you still feel that?" he asked.

This was it. This was her moment to tell him she needed him. She grimaced and lowered her head. They say if you love something you should let it go. She loved Noah enough to do that. "I met somebody here, Noah." She knew once she said it he would never broach the subject again. She covered her mouth as she sobbed.

"Take care of yourself, Bleu," he said.

"I love you, Noah. You too," she replied.

She ended the call and then let her emotions spill from her soul. This pain, this emptiness, was heavier than anything she had ever felt before. She wanted to call him back, but she didn't. Instead she reached for the crack pipe. She couldn't handle this loss alone. She needed something to cope.

Bleu stayed holed up there for two days straight, smoking through the entire eight-ball in record speed. As she lay on the cot, completely crashing after her binge, she was completely oblivious to the land of the living. She never heard the Realtor as she walked into the space. Bleu hadn't meant to squat for so long. She only wanted the apartment during the night so that she wouldn't have to sleep on the streets. To avoid being caught she had planned to leave during the days, but she was coming down from her high, and the effects left her dragging with depression.

"Excuse me! You're not supposed to be here! I'm calling the police! You're trespassing."

When Bleu heard the voice behind her she sprang up, out of it, eyes widened in fear. She felt like a cornered animal as she held up her hands. "Please no! No! I'm not trespassing. I know the people who own this restaurant. Please . . . I'll just leave. You don't have to call the police."

"Oh? You know the owners?" the woman asked skeptically as she frowned at Bleu's appearance. "We'll see. They're right downstairs. They're on their way up."

Bleu looked around for an escape, but there wasn't one. She would have to face Eddie and Marta looking like . . . *a crack-*

head, she thought sadly. She shifted nervously as Eddie and Marta came walking through the door.

"Do you know this young lady? Because I'm two seconds from calling the police!" the realtor said, distraught.

Eddie put up his hand to silence the irate woman, and Marta hurriedly came to Bleu's side, her hand over her mouth in shock as she stared at her. Bleu could only imagine how she looked. Her hair was unkempt and matted, her clothes dirty, her lips cracking and ashy. Her skin always had this sheen as if her body was trying to sweat the toxic out. She looked disgusting, and in that moment, as they gawked at her, she was humiliated.

"Hey . . . hey, Marta. I'm sorry. I didn't mean to—"

Marta grabbed Bleu's hand, tears shining in her eyes as she fought back her emotions. "Pobrecita," she said sympathetically. "It's okay," she said, turning to the real estate agent. "We know her. The *policia* are not necessary." She patted Bleu's hand lovingly and nodded in determination. "It's okay. Everything will be okay."

When he saw her, his heart broke into a million pieces. She lay in front of him destroyed, looking nothing like the girl he had met a year before. Iman was a strong man. He had seen many things. He supplied the streets with the very drug Bleu craved. He had murdered, robbed, and seen the ills of the game without flinching, but when he saw Bleu . . . when he saw his beloved Bleu, his pretty young thing with the sharp wit, ambitious goals, and beautiful smile, laid before him strung out, it broke him. He had to turn around and face the door for a brief moment to stop the tears from leaking out of his eyes. She didn't deserve this. L.A. had chewed her up and spat her out. Somehow he felt responsible. It had started with her cravings for the life. She had wanted to indulge in all things luxurious. Clothes, cars, hair, diamonds, the night scene. It had been fun for her, but he had seen that path destroy many. He should have spoken up. *I could have stopped this before it happened,* he thought guiltily. His heart no longer beat the same. The moment he saw her, its rhythm had been forever altered. He looked at Eddie and then at Marta, who both stood solemnly to the side.

"How did you find her?" Iman asked. He had searched high and low for her to no avail. He would have much rather never found her than discovered her like this. It hurt him too badly to witness this.

"She was in the apartment above the restaurant. The real estate agent found her first," Eddie said.

Iman walked over to Bleu and got down on his knees at her bedside. He rubbed her hair, stroking it softly as he whispered, "Hey, beautiful."

Her eyes fluttered open, but instead of welcoming his image, she sat up in alarm and scrambled out of the bed in fear as her eyes darted around the room.

"Please, please, don't hurt me!" she shouted as she held her hands up in defense. She was paranoid and completely afraid as she looked at him with pleading eyes. The fact that she thought he would bring her harm wounded him as he slowly approached. It was as if he were running up on a wounded animal.

"Nobody's gonna hurt you, Bleu. I just want to help you," he said, voice cracking with emotion.

He walked up on her and she started swinging, fists and feet flying, thinking that she had to defend herself. She did fear Iman. She remembered what had happened to Aysha. Bleu didn't know if he had done the deed personally, but he ordered the hits. *Same thing,* she thought. As she fought him, Iman wrapped her up in his arms, tightly pulling her to his chest so that she couldn't move. When she could no longer defend herself she simply cried. She let her head fall on his chest as her legs gave out. He scooped her up into his arms. "It's okay, Bleu. It's okay. Everything is okay now . . . I promise you."

He carried her out to his car and tucked her safely inside. His uncle and aunt came rushing out after them. "Where are you taking her, Iman? She needs help," Eddie said.

"I'm taking her home," Iman said, determined.

"You can't just tuck her away in Calabasas by herself, *mijo,*" Marta said. "She's strung out. She needs rehab."

"I'll be her rehab. She won't be in Calabasas by herself. I'll be there with her. Every minute, until she's clean," he said, emotional as he gritted his teeth. He hit the top of his car with a closed fist as he leaned over it, angry with himself for allowing this to happen to her. He couldn't help but feel like he was the cause. Like once she had found out he was married she had jumped off the edge of the cliff.

"Tan will never allow it," Marta said. "Don't get that girl into any more trouble. She has enough problems."

He nodded and then kissed Marta's cheek before he

rounded the car and got into the driver's side. He no longer cared about severing ties with Tan. His reluctance and hesitance to divorce her were what had made Bleu run away from him in the first place. Fuck it, if he had to stay married to Tristan in order to keep his connection to the Mexican Cartel he would give it up. He had enough money, enough power, enough love from the streets. He could find a new supplier, or better yet, he could retire altogether. That was every hustler's dream, right? His mind raced as he sped out into traffic. He looked over at Bleu. He could get her clean and start a life with her. All of these things could happen if he played his hand correctly.

"Are you going to hurt me?" she asked.

"I'll never hurt you again. That's my word," he assured her. She frowned because they were clearly having two different conversations. She was talking about punishment for Cinco's death. Did Iman not know that she was involved? She studied his face, and the amount of love he had for her shone brightly, oozing out of him as if he couldn't contain it any longer. It was then that she knew that Iman had no clue what she had done.

"I'm sorry," she whispered.

"Don't be sorry, Bleu. I just want you to be better. I'm going to help you. You're going to hate me for a while and it's going to hurt. Your body will hurt, you'll go through emotions that will make you feel like you can't do it, but I'll be right here with you every step. I just want you back . . . the real you. The smart, pretty, plain girl from Flint, Michigan. You have to promise me that you'll get clean, Bleu. Do you trust me?"

Bleu hesitated, because she wasn't sure if she did. "It's okay to tell me you don't. I know I fucked that up. I'll earn it back. I'll earn you back, but for now I just want you to focus on kicking this shit."

He reached over and held her hand. It was so bony. Her scrawny fingers felt like they would break if he handled her too harshly. The drugs had eaten away at her. In months she had lost so much weight that she looked sick . . . almost breakable. He brought her hand up to his lips and kissed her wrist while keeping his eye on the road. She could see his love for her. She could feel his energy as it emanated from his hand to hers. The pain in his face at the discovery of her condition plagued him and he couldn't hide. She teared up just witnessing how much he cared, because she knew that she didn't deserve it. *I don't want to stop,* she thought. *It feels too good in a world that's so bad. I'm going to disappoint him.*

"I'll try," she whispered. "It's hard." Her voice cracked. "But I'll try."

"That's all I ask," he replied.

28

"Open this door! Iman, please just let me out!" Bleu's pleas fell on deaf ears as she banged on the wooden door. Iman heard her—in fact, he was sure the entire neighborhood heard her—but he couldn't let her out. She had already tried to take money out of his wallet and steal his keys while he was asleep. He had to keep her confined in order to wait out her withdrawal. Listening to her cries tore at his soul, but he kept a hard resolve and didn't respond. "Open this shit up now!" Bleu shouted, getting angry as she hit her flat hands against the door in frustration. Her moods were high and low. One moment she was weak and sulking; the next she was animated and livid. She was out of control and he couldn't believe that it had gotten that bad in six months. What he didn't know was that it had been six months of bingeing. She had smoked day and night as often as possible to stop herself from feeling. "Iman!!!" she screamed before giving up and sitting in a heap on the floor as she planted her face in her hands. Her entire body was wet with sweat and she felt as if she would die if she didn't get out of that room. Iman had made a comfortable stay for in her the west wing of his home. She had every luxury available to her, but with a monkey on her back it felt like a prison. "Ughhh!!" she screamed. She just wanted a hit. One deep pull on a crack pipe would do her so much justice. She missed it so much that she even missed the coolness of the pipe when she placed it between her lips. It had only been three days. The first two had been a daze. She slept, depressed and out of it, as the world seemed to crash down around her. She had no energy to get up and protest, and the cold sweats that soaked her clothes kept her tucked into a shivering ball, bedridden. Her entire body itched and she scratched so hard that Iman had given her socks to put over her hands so that it she wouldn't scar herself. It felt like something was crawling on her all the time.

"At least bring me some water!" she shouted. Her mouth was dry, her tongue stale. She hadn't eaten in days. She refused to. The only thing that she was truly hungry for was a blast of a crack pipe. Nothing else would nourish her the way that it could. It fed her soul and she felt like she was experiencing a slow death without it.

Her mind was playing tricks on her. She had relied on the drugs to make her feel good for so long that without them she felt nothing but sorrow. The physical ailments were minimal, but the mental and emotional ones were unbearable. Crack had a hold on her that was so strong she just wanted to give in and get high. Every time she thought about it she would get aroused by the idea. Her mind was trapped. When she looked in the mirror she saw her mother, literally saw her mother's face. Bleu felt like she was losing it and if she didn't score soon she would go insane. What she wouldn't do for just one little hit. The thought alone made her tremble. She heard the lock on the door as Iman entered and she turned to look at him. Sympathy filled his eyes.

"Everything just hurts so bad, Iman. You can't do this to me . . . not like this. I'm not strong enough," she cried.

He knelt down on the floor. "You are," he said. "It's mental, Bleu, so if it's hurting to think about shit then get it out. Talk to me. I won't judge you."

"What about rehab? What if I promise to go to rehab?" she asked. She knew that she couldn't fully disclose the things that haunted her. The regrets she had, the things that she had done, being a part of Cinco's murder. She couldn't admit those things to Iman.

"You just want to go there because you think it'll be easier to run away. I'll bring rehab to you. Whatever therapy you need to get better," he said.

"I never wanted it to be like this," she whispered, her voice full of angst.

"Neither did I," he replied. He got to his feet and walked over to the bed, pulling back the covers. He didn't say anything, but she took the hint and slowly climbed to her feet.

Another knock at the door caused her to look up to find Big Les standing in the doorway. She smiled at his presence.

"It's good to see a real queen back in the castle," he said with a wink. "Hello, Ms. Bleu."

"Hi, Big Les," she replied. He pushed a small circular table on wheels into the room. It was covered in a white cloth and set beautifully for one.

Bleu looked up at Iman. "I can't eat. I'm not hungry."

"You've got to get your weight back up. You being this small scares the shit out of me. Just eat a little, a'ight?" he responded.

She nodded. She was too focused on being deprived of drugs to realize that she was deprived of food. Her body needed all the nourishment it could get. Not leaving it up to her, Iman walked over to the table and snagged the plate.

He dipped a fork into the meal as he sat at her bedside. She opened her mouth, accepting the food. It wasn't until she tasted it did she remember how long it had been since her last real meal. Shelter meals and scraps, bags of chips from the liquor store weren't enough to live on. She closed her eyes, savoring it as she moaned in satisfaction. She damn near snatched the plate from his hands as she began digging into the meal. He had to stop himself from chuckling as she annihilated the food. He looked up at Big Les and nodded his appreciation. Big Les nodded back.

"Glad you like it," Big Les stated jovially. "Feel better, Ms. Bleu."

He left them alone so that she could finish her meal in peace.

"I need to leave for a few hours. Big Les will be here. I need to know that you will be here when I get back," he said seriously. He wanted to stay, but he needed to make a run. He didn't want to play games anymore. Juggling his marriage and his relationship with Bleu was what had caused him to lose her in the first place. He didn't want Bleu on the side. He wanted her in the forefront, and in order to make that happen he had to end things with Tristan.

"I will be," Bleu said.

"I got something. It'll help you sleep. I contacted a detox-ification counselor and she recommended sleeping pills. I want you to take it. It'll help," he said.

"You don't have to put me to sleep, Iman. I won't run," she said.

He wanted to extend his trust, but he wasn't a fool. He knew how addicts got down. They made promises they couldn't keep. He wasn't setting himself up for the disappointment. If he were in a smaller city he could have put word out on the town to cut her off, anyone who served her would face deadly repercussions, but this was L.A. It was too large to put an advisory over every corner, so instead he would have to keep a close eye on Bleu until the poison was out of her system.

She could see the worry in his gaze and she sighed as she nodded. "Okay."

Iman went into the pocket of his slacks and pulled out a pill bottle. She held her mouth open and he placed a pill on her tongue before handing her the water glass from the table.

"Feel better?" she asked.

"I do," he confirmed. "I won't be long. If you need anything, ask Big Les."

Iman pulled the key to the bedroom out of his pocket and her face fell. "Please don't lock me in here, Iman. I won't go anywhere," she said, eyes misting. "It makes me feel like I'm in a cage or something. Like I'm an animal or something."

Iman nodded and leaned in to kiss her on the top of her head. He didn't mean any malice. He had none when it came to Bleu. He simply wanted to keep her safe, but perhaps his reins were too tight. "Okay," he said simply before getting up to leave.

Bleu waited for him to exit the room, and as soon as he was gone she spat the pill out of her mouth.

There was no way she was staying put. Her gut rumbled and she made a dash to the bathroom as suddenly it felt like she would erupt. She hadn't eaten that much food at once in months and her stomach was betraying her. She rushed to the toilet, barely making it before she released. As she sat on the toilet, miserable and sweating bullets, another urge hit her. She reached for the trash pail that sat beside the toilet and brought it to her chest as she vomited simultaneously. Withdrawal was rough on her. Doing the right things to her body after doing so many things wrong to it threw her system into a frenzy. It was easier to stay on drugs than to quit and she was desperately feigning for a hit. She flushed the toilet and then weakly turned on the shower to clean herself. She was so damn exhausted. It felt as if she weighed a thousand pounds. The misery that had her in chains was pulling her down . . . drowning her. She stripped and then stepped into the stream of water, turning it cold, hoping to shock her body out of the funk she was caught in. Leaning against the tiled wall, she sobbed. Nothing in life had ever been so hard. *I just want to smoke*, she thought in despair.

She let the water rain down on her until her skin started to prune. When she was done she wrapped a towel around her body and climbed out. She knew that there was no getting out of the house. Iman surely had Big Les on guard, and even if she got past him she had no car, no money. Calabasas was too far away from any hood to score. No dealers were working this far out in the suburbs. She was stuck, but she was resourceful and determined to get any kind of high she could get her hands on. She made her way to the hall, looking left, then right, to make sure that Big Les wasn't lurking before she proceeded to the master bedroom. She hurried on tiptoes and walked into the master bath, pulling open the medicine cabinet in such haste that some of the contents fell out, clanging on the sink. She cringed at the noise as she put the items back inside while searching for something . . . anything . . . to take the edge off of being sober.

Her heart skipped a beat in excitement when she came across a bottle of Vicodin. She opened the top, anxiety filling her chest, but when she turned she found Big Les standing in the doorway, silently brooding.

Like a kid with his hand in the cookie jar she froze.

"I . . . um . . . I have a headache," she lied.

"Hmm-hmm," Big Les huffed. "I'm not going to tell you not to do it, because from what I know 'bout this drug thing is if you want to do it you're going to. But I do know that the pretty young girl that walked in here months ago was too smart for this. That girl had the world at her feet and she's still in there somewhere, but if you swallow those pills you're going to lose her forever. You got to want to do better . . . for your-self, not for anybody else. It's on you."

His words made her fall apart as tears rolled down her cheeks and she plopped down right there on the bathroom floor. "I don't want to be this person."

"Then you know what to do," Big Les responded. He went to turn around and Bleu stopped him from leaving.

"Can you just stay please?" she sniffed. "To make sure."

He nodded and folded his arms across his broad chest as he watched her intently. Bleu's insides screamed at her to just swallow a few of the pills, but instead she shook them out into the toilet, closing her eyes so that she couldn't see the high that she was flushing away.

"Good girl," Big Les said as he helped her to her feet. "Now let's get you back to bed. The thing to kicking this habit is dis-traction. You've got to learn to keep busy. Anybody ever teach you how to cook?" he asked.

Iman stepped into the condo that he shared with his wife. The atomosphere was ice-cold. White walls, white furniture, a si-lence so heavy that it clung in the air, intimidating him as soon as he stepped inside. It fit her personality to a T. There was no warmth left in Tristan. It had disappeared long ago, and as she approached him with a glass of red wine in her hand, wearing a silk floor-length kimono and stiletto heels, she smirked. "You remember that you have a home?" she asked.

He rubbed the side of his face, preparing himself for the inevitable fallout to come. "Tan, I need to talk to you," he said.

"So talk!" she shot back as she sipped. The glassy look in her eyes told him that she was already halfway into the bottle. His absence made her cling to the nightly ritual. She was miserable. He was miserable. So what was the point?

"I want a divorce, Tan," he said softly.

She chuckled condescendingly and sipped from her glass. "I'll pretend like I didn't hear that," she replied.

"I'm serious, Tan. You can have the houses, the cars; I'll always take care of you. I'll hit you off with whatever you need as far as money, but my heart, you can't have that. It's with someone else now," he said.

Tan's face turned red as her eyes glowed with rage. She threw the red wine in his face and then glared at him, daring him to do something. A part of him wanted to slap the taste from her mouth for the disrespect. She knew better. She was testing him. She wanted an emotional reaction from him. A reaction, it was something that she hadn't received from him in years, but he gave her nothing. He clenched his strong jaw and stepped away from her as he grabbed a paper towel from the kitchen countertop. He wiped his face calmly and said, "I'm done."

He walked out as her screams began to fill the air. "I made you, you *puta*! You don't walk out on me! My father will kill you! He will kill you for breaking my heart!"

Iman knew that it was probably true. Lisbon Sandoza would definitely bring beef to Iman's door, but he was fully prepared for it. To him, Bleu was worth it.

29

Iman smiled as he watched Bleu move around the kitchen. She was slowly but surely getting her weight back up, and the color had come back to her cheeks. The way the sun shone through the kitchen window, illuminating her features, made her look almost angelic. This was the girl he had remembered. She was finally getting back to the old her. There were so many things that he wanted to tell her, but he knew that she couldn't handle much right now. It had taken a full two weeks just to get her body off of the drugs, but her mind still was in a delicate place. He did his all to keep her busy, stepping out of his comfort zone to fill her days with positivity. He was from the streets, a hood fella with money; there were certain things that he just hadn't done to spoil a woman. Women gave in to him easily, giving him what he wanted before he actually had to put in any effort, so the courting part of a rela-tionship he often missed. With Tan he had been too young

ASHLEY ANTOINETTE

to know exactly what to do, but with Bleu he was going all out. They frequented museums, he took her on hot-air balloon rides, and they went to corny paint-and-sip classes just to keep her moving. That was the life of a crackhead . . . always busy . . . always moving . . . he knew that during her stint on the streets she had gotten used to that pace. He tried to accommodate that. She placed a plate of food in front of him and the aroma of homemade French toast filled the air. He pulled her arm, drawing her near. "You're getting good at this cooking thing, ma. I won't need Big Les in a minute," he said with a wink.

She laughed and then tensed when she noticed how closely he held her. They hadn't taken their relationship there yet. It hadn't been rekindled. They were working on building a friendship, because Bleu was fragile. They slept in separate rooms, because he knew that she wasn't ready to take it there with him. They hadn't even spoken about his marriage or the fact that he had broken her heart before, because he didn't want to overwhelm her. When emotions ran high so did her urge to smoke, and he was trying to avoid any setbacks.

She recoiled, slightly uncomfortable with their intimacy. There were too many loose ends left regarding their past. Too many questions unanswered. Uncertainty shone in her eyes.

"I know you have questions . . . I'ma answer them for you one day. In fact, I have questions of my own, but you're not ready. Let's just focus on you making it through another day . . . clean . . . happy. Are you happy?" he asked.

She thought about it, but before she could respond the sound of gunshots rang out into the air.

"Go upstairs," Iman said as he reached under the table he was sitting at and suddenly pulled out a strap of his own. He stayed ready. There were guns placed strategically in every room of his house. Bleu's eyes widened in fear. "Go!" he said as he moved to the front of his home. He walked out of the house, enraged at the fact that someone would bring beef to his home. He didn't give a fuck who was busting at him, he was ready to clap back, but when he saw Tristan standing outside, gun at her side, he lowered his gun. He approached her and grabbed her by the face sternly. "Have you lost your fucking mind?!" he said through gritted teeth. He snatched the gun from her hands, tucking it in his back waistline, and then mushed her hard. He could smell the liquor coming out of her pores, she was so drunk. "Get your ass in the car before I hurt you, Tan. How the fuck did you even drive out here? You're fucking faded."

She pushed him hard in the chest. "I should fucking kill you!" she screamed, causing a scene in his affluent neighborhood.

He pointed his finger at her in warning. "I should slap the fuck out of you right now. You could have killed somebody! You know I don't need this type of attention. What were you thinking?"

"Fuck you!" she said, snatching herself away from him. "My name is on this house. As a matter of fact, my name is on everything," she said as she stormed past him. The realization that Iman had found someone new had hit Tristan hard and she refused to lose to another woman. It wasn't about love. It was about control. Iman was hers. She wasn't giving him up.

"Is she here?" Tristan asked as she stormed through the front door.

He followed her, trying to stop her, but she was too persistent. "Is the bitch in my house?" she shouted, loud enough for Bleu to hear. Bleu came down the steps, and when Tristan saw her she scoffed in disbelief, recognizing her instantly. "Her? You're fucking with her? You brought this bitch into my house! You had her moving my father's cocaine, putting money in her pocket, and all along you were fucking her?!"

Tan lunged at Bleu, but before she could reach her Iman intervened, grabbing Tan up.

"I'm going to kill you! You fucking whore! You're fucking my husband? In my house? In my bed?"

"You're out of fucking control," Iman said as he hemmed her up against a wall as Bleu stood back, distraught. She felt cheap. She instantly remembered how badly loving Iman felt. He wasn't hers. No matter how nice he was, no matter how much he helped, no matter how much she wanted him to be. He was married.

Big Les walked in with two grocery bags and halted when he saw the scene unfolding. Iman let go of Tan and pushed her toward Big Les. "Take her home," Iman said.

"I *am* home. I'm not going anywhere. Take her home," Tan sneered. "Everything in here belongs to me . . . including you."

Bleu nodded. "She's right," she whispered. "I have no place here. . . . I'll leave."

"You're not leaving," Iman said sternly, but Bleu was already headed for the door. "Bleu!" His tone was more like a bark as his frustrations mounted, halting her midstep. He cleared his throat as he took a deep breath. "Please, ma."

"I hope you know you're a dead woman," Tan said, becoming emotional at the sight of Iman's connection with Bleu. Tan had put up with side chicks and groupies, because it came with the territory—powerful men needed playthings—but there was clearly love between Bleu and Iman. Tan could feel it and it made her sick. She wasn't making idle threats. She had so much power at the tips of her pretty little fingers and she was a jealous woman. If she gave the order, Bleu would be nothing more than a memory. He had to de-escalate the situation before it got out of hand.

He grabbed Tan by the upper arm and forced her out of the house. He turned to Big Les. "Don't let her leave," he said. "I need to handle this."

Big Les nodded and Iman shot one last look at Bleu before disappearing.

The overwhelming urge to smoke planted itself in Bleu's subconscious, but she fought it. She refused to let Iman be the one to drive her down the road to disaster ever again. Hours had passed and Iman hadn't returned. She was left feeling stupid all over again. *Of course, she's his first priority. That's his wife,* Bleu thought, realizing that she was just living in a dreamworld if she thought that he would ever leave Tan. *I deserve to be somebody's number one,* she thought.

She picked up her phone as her mind drifted to Noah. She just wanted to get out of there. She wanted to go back home where she belonged. Iman was her crutch in L.A. He was the only thing keeping her off the streets, and landing back in them would only sabotage her recovery. She needed to go back to Flint. She had clearly overstayed her welcome in L.A. Noah would come to her rescue. She was sure of it. All she had to do was ask.

She put her pride to the side and dialed his number.

"Hello?" he answered, voice groggy as she realized that he was asleep. She had forgotten the time difference between Michigan and California.

"I'm sorry, Noah. I really need you right now. Can you come get me?" she asked as she began to cry softly.

"Come get you? B, where are you?" he asked, suddenly alert. He had known her long enough to realize when she was really in distress. She had been on his mind ever since they last spoke. She hadn't sounded like herself then and she didn't sound like herself now. He couldn't help but wonder what had happened to the Bleu he used to know. He could ask those questions later, however. He turned over to make sure that Naomi was still asleep and then hopped out of their king-size bed to make his way into the hallway.

"I'm in L.A. at a friend's house, but I just need you. I just want to come home," she whispered truthfully. "Please just come. The address is Seven Five Eight One Lions Estate," she whispered. "It's in Calabasas."

"I can just send for you, B. I'll buy a plane ticket in the morning," he said.

She closed her eyes, because he didn't understand her plight. She was a recovering addict. If she left Iman's on her own, she might never make it to the airport. The urges would flood her, and she would find herself back on skid row, searching for something to satisfy her cravings.

"I need you to come get me, Noah. I promise I will explain later. Just please. I've gotten myself into some things I can't handle. I need you."

Iman walked in and she ended the call abruptly. The sight of her crying tore him to pieces.

"I'm leaving," she said.

Iman crossed the room and placed both hands on the sides of her face. He rested his forehead against hers and kissed her lips. "Don't leave me, Bleu. I'm not whole without you, ma," he answered.

"You're married," she whispered. "You're married. She shot at this house today, Iman. You're hers."

"I'm yours," he replied.

"But you're not," she cried.

"I'm leaving her, Bleu. I told her when you first got here that I wanted a divorce. My attorney delivered the papers to her today. That's why she came here. I've still got some business to work out with her family, street shit, but that has nothing to do with her. I just want you. I would have said something sooner, but I was holding my cards, focusing on getting you healthy. You can't leave me, Bleu. I've got everything—cars, money, power—but all this shit is shallow without you. It's worthless," he said. His words were melting her. Her heart urged her to do one thing, while her mind told her to answer the phone that was vibrating in her pocket. She knew it was Noah, but she ignored it because Iman was saying all the right things. She loved this man and yes, he was complicated and he came with baggage, but she was too. She was a recovering crack addict and yet he still loved her. Her baggage was a lot heavier than his. Who was she to walk out on him?

She kissed him back passionately as she pulled at his clothes. They were in love, they were in lust, and nothing, not Tan, not Bleu's fears, not her addiction, was going to keep her and Iman apart. He picked her up, carrying her up the stairs as they kissed, and then laid her gently on the bed. She felt different in his arms, less timid, as if many men on the streets had put her on her back. He closed his eyes to dismiss the thought from his head because he knew it would haunt him forever if he dwelled on it. He was just grateful for her presence, and as he slid into her love he knew he was never letting her go. He rocked. They rocked as their bodies moved to the beats of their hearts. Their lovemaking was epic. The hardness of him, inside of her, her wetness, it was the perfect combination, as if he were designed to fit inside of her. He was the key to her lock. He growled in her ear as he sped up, feeling his tensions rise and rise. She moaned, clawing his strong back until she reached bliss and he exploded inside of her.

It was imperfect, but at the same time it was just right and neither of them wanted it to end.

"Are you sure I should be here for this? This is Tristan's father you're meeting with. Maybe I should—"

"This is your home now," Iman said. "You don't have to go anywhere."

"Do you mind if I just skip dinner? I don't really have it in me to sit in front of them. You're divorcing her because of me. I don't think it'll be friendly if I'm there," she said skeptically.

"It's just business, ma. You can play the back if you prefer. Sandoza might cut me off because of the shit between me and Tan, but I doubt it. Perhaps you *should* sit this one out," he replied.

The doorbell rang and Bleu nodded. "I'll be upstairs."

She started up the stairs as Iman answered the door, but when she heard the voice of his guest she froze in fear.

"You're looking good, bro. Looks like you're doing better. Come in," Iman said.

"Thanks, fam."

It only took two words for her to recognize his voice, and when she turned around Cinco stood in the doorway, shaking hands with Iman. Cinco looked up with one good eye; a patch covered the other. A large bubble scar was visible on one side of his shaven head. She had done a number on him. When he saw her his face turned to stone. Tension filled the air.

He's supposed to be dead. How is he not dead? I saw him lying in his own blood, she thought frantically. Iman looked up at her.

"I see why shit between you and Tan is rocky," Cinco said as his eyes never left Bleu. "A pretty little piece like this—"

"Where is your manners?" an older gentleman said as he stepped into the house behind Cinco. "That's your sister's business. I don't care who you're fucking. I'm not wearing a skirt."

"Sandoza," Iman greeted the old man, pulling him in for a hug. It was evident that there was no love lost.

Iman turned to her. "You might as well come down, ma. Let me introduce you," he said.

"Please," Cinco said as she sucked her teeth as he stared at her with vengeance on the brain. She could see his malice . . . feel the energy coming off of him, and she trembled as she descended the steps cautiously.

"Bleu, this is Cinco, and this is the man that taught me everything I know . . . Lisbon Sandoza," Iman introduced them.

"So this is serious?" Sandoza asked. Bleu kept her eyes on the floor as tears pooled in them. She was panicking. She could barely breathe as Cinco stared a hole through her. Why he hadn't busted her out she didn't know, but she could feel his hatred for her.

"It is," Iman confirmed. "Tan and I have been unhappy for a long time, Sandoza. I loved her once. I still love her. I'm just not in love with her. Once the anger goes away she will admit that she doesn't love me anymore either."

"You will do right by her in the split," Sandoza said sternly.

"I wouldn't play it any other way," Iman replied. "I hope this doesn't stop our business."

"You make me too much money for it to stop anything, but I need Cinco to be pulled closer. You need a right hand," Sandoza stated.

Bleu stepped back. "Excuse me," she said. "It was nice meeting you."

She damn near ran up the stairs, her legs were barely stable enough to carry her. She went into her bedroom and closed the door behind her. Leaning her back against the wall, she placed both hands over her mouth in horror.

Her tongue started to tingle as the back of her throat closed up. She was getting the urge. She wanted to smoke so badly. She had to get out of there. She needed some fresh air. She needed to run. Cinco was alive and he knew her whereabouts. It was only a matter of time before he reached out and touched her. Aysha's brutal murder popped into Bleu's mind. *He's going to kill me,* she thought. She grabbed the keys to one of Iman's cars and her bag. *I have to get out of here.*

She snatched open the door, but when she did the devil was on the other side.

"Remember me, bitch?" Cinco snarled as he put his hand around her neck, choking the life out of her. Bleu wanted to scream, but she couldn't find her voice. He pinned her up against the wall. "Thought I was dead? I should watch you die right here, you dirty bitch."

She clawed at his hand desperately as urine streamed down her leg. She was terrified.

"If you want to live you're gonna do exactly what I say, whenever the fuck I say. That little plot to kill Iman? It's back on, bitch, and you're going to help me do it," he said. He pulled out a $20 pack and her eyes sparkled. It was like she was hypnotized. She could smell the dope through the Baggie. "Yeah . . . bitch . . . you remember this shit? How it feels? How it tastes? This will make you a little more obedient." He slipped it into her purse and gave her neck one last squeeze before letting her go. "I'll be in touch."

She ran down the stairs, crying silently as she raced out of the front door. She was desperate to get away from there, but even more desperate to use the dope that Cinco had slipped her. It had been so long and she had tried so hard, but the drugs were burning a hole in her handbag. Cinco's presence was too much to deal with. It had pushed her over the edge, and as she climbed into the car she knew that she was too addicted to ever let go. She might as well drive away. She might as well never look back, because Cinco would torture her if she stayed and with him around she could no longer resist her addiction.

EPILOGUE

Three months, seven days, six hours, and twenty-two minutes. That's how long it had been. "One day at a time. Every day counts, every hour, every minute, every second," Bleu whispered as she sat in her car, surrounded by the darkness of night while gripping the steering wheel for dear life. There was urgency in her tone . . . panic . . . fear, because although she was completely alone she was afraid of herself. Her heart pounded furiously. With the power of thoroughbred horses it beat, causing her shirt to rise and fall with her distressed breaths. She could feel herself weakening as the tears slid down her face. Mascara marred her flushed cheeks. Snot rested on her trembling lip. She needed help. *Three months, seven days, six hours, and twenty-three minutes.* It was how long she had been clean. She distinctly remembered the last hit she had taken like it was yesterday, and the thought of the euphoric rush it gave her caused her to become aroused. Her nipples hardened and she clenched her thighs, because the possibility of feeling that type of high once more was seducing her. Her knuckles turned white as she held on to the steering wheel with a death grip. She wished that she could glue her hands to it, to stop herself from doing the inevitable.

"Please, God, please," she whispered, but she knew there was no use in praying. She had prayed for everything her entire life only to end up empty-handed and disappointed. The devil had ahold of her. It was like her soul had been compromised from the moment she had taken her first breath. That was the only explanation for her hard-lived existence. Nothing came easy, and anything good that came to her was quickly taken away. One blast. That was all it would take to end her misery. She had not thought about getting high in three months. In fact, a huge celebratory trip had been planned to commemorate the one-year mark. She had done it. She had kicked the vicious drug habit that had taken ahold of her. She had lasted three months seven days, six hours, and twenty-four minutes, but now it was calling her.

She reached into her bag and pulled out the package. It was eerie how the rock cocaine seemed to sparkle in the Baggie. She poured the small rock out into her palm and marveled briefly. She licked her lips, her mouth suddenly dry as her body craved the drug. She could feel the hair rising on the back of her neck. It was like a thousand bugs were crawling up her legs, starting at her toes and making their way up her thighs, to her spine. She itched, she wanted the hit so bad. With her emotions on 10 she was susceptible to sabotage. Overwhelmed by desire, she turned her purse upside down, causing all of the contents to spill over her front seat. Grabbing the water bottle from her cupholder and a ballpoint pen out of the mess, she was on a hunt for paraphernalia. She rolled down her window and poured most of the water out. She was like a surgeon as she drilled a hole into the side of the bottle. She bit the end of the pen, causing the ink vial to come out, hollowing out the shell of the pen. She had done the routine so many times she had it down to a science. Most crackheads would just hit the rock straight out of the pen, but Bleu liked to think she was above that. That desperate toke would only lead to burnt lips and fingertips and she had her looks to uphold. In the thick of it she had glass pipes, but the poor man's version would work just as well . . . she was chasing the high and it didn't matter at this point how she caught it. Her eyes searched through the mess on her passenger seat until she found a condom and a cigarette. When she had picked up the habit she told herself that nicotine was the lesser evil compared to what she could have been smoking, but in her heart of hearts she knew that a true addict always kept cigarettes handy. The ash residue from cigarettes was necessary to make a functioning crack pipe. She held the cigarette between both lips while her hands opened the condom. She threw the sticky rubber out of the window and then used the foil wrapper to top off the water bottle. She emptied the ashes onto the top of the foil and then inhaled sharply as she placed a nice-size rock on top of it all. Her eyes were as big as golf balls as she applied the flame. Her long red stiletto nails far fancier than those of any crackhead anyone had ever seen. The rings on her fingers far too expensive be on the hand that was hugging the makeshift pipe. This wasn't supposed to be her life, Bleu was supposed to be so much more, but as the tears slid down her face and the smoke accumulated inside the bottle she couldn't help but think of how this tragedy had begun . . . it all started with just a little Adderall and speed. Who would have thought it would have ever gotten this bad? Three months, seven days, six hours, and twenty-five minutes were all wasted as she wrapped her lips around the hollow pen. . . .

The approaching headlights that shone directly into her car caused her to toss the homemade pipe onto her passenger seat before she could even take a puff. When she saw Noah's face her heart stopped. She climbed from her car and looked back up toward the house. She was terrified. The devil was inside. She had thought that she had killed Cinco. How had he survived? No, here he was, back to wreak havoc on her life. It overwhelmed her, pushing her back to the dangerous edge that she had narrowly escaped from. She looked up to see someone exiting a big-body Benz, and when they locked eyes she gasped in shock.

"Noah," she whispered in disbelief as she climbed out of the car in shock. She felt like she was dreaming as she held her hand up to her eyes, frowning as the lights shone in her eyes. She ran up to him, crying, distraught, as he welcomed her with open arms.

"What's wrong? B, I missed the shit out of you. What's wrong?" he asked as he held her close, holding the back of her head so that she could cry on his shoulder. It felt so good having her in his arms. Their bond was so familiar, but everything about her was different. He pulled back and stared her in the eyes. "You're scared?" he said, knowing her, reading her like the back of his hand.

"Just get me out of here . . . you have to get me out of here." Her voice was frantic as she looked back to the house to make sure that Cinco hadn't pursued her.

Iman came out of the house and stood at the top of the steps as he looked down curiously at Noah, holding his girl. He placed a hand in the pocket of his Gucci slacks. "Bleu!" he called to her with authority.

"Who the fuck is this nigga? This who you scared of?" Noah asked defensively as he pushed her behind him, squaring his stance as he ice-grilled Iman.

"Who the fuck are you? On my property, talking to my bitch? Shit can get real ugly real quick out here, partner; I advise you to mind your business," Iman said sternly, face calm but voice cold. "Bleu, let's go—"

She went toward him, but as soon she took a few steps Noah called her. "Bleu!"

She stood in the middle . . . between them, conflicted. She loved them both. Each of them had a piece of her. Both expected her loyalty, but she didn't know whom to extend it to.

"Bleu . . ." She looked to Iman.

"Bleu . . ." She looked to Noah.

When Cinco came out of the house she stared into his eyes, his evil intentions shining through.

"I can't do this." She ran to her car full speed.

"Bleu!" She ignored Noah, distraught as she pulled away from him as he tried to grab her arm. She hopped into her car and sped off, leaving them both standing there, watching her flee. She didn't know where she was headed. She didn't know what she would do. She didn't know whom she should choose.

Bleu!

There was no one else in the car. The voice that was calling to her was her own demon's. She was too overwhelmed . . . too emotional . . . too afraid. These mixed feelings were the makings of a disaster for her recovery, and although she had escaped Iman and Noah, she was still faced with a choice, a deadly one. Crack was the one calling her name now. The question was . . . would she answer it . . . ?

TO BE CONTINUED . . . *LUXE 2:* Coming Soon